The Rosaries

A Novel

Other books by Sandra Carrington-Smith...

The Book of Obeah

While fulfilling the final request of her departed Grandmama, Melody Bennet, a young professional raised in the genteel suburbs of North Carolina, is plunged into the clandestine world of an ancient West African religion – via the Louisiana bayou. In unearthing a mysterious religious manuscript, Melody collides with those seeking powers believed to be contained within the text, from The Vatican to individuals claiming it as their legacy. She accepts the task of safeguarding the book and finds lives are threatened, including her own, sometimes from unexpected directions. As her knowledge grows and perceptions shift, Melody's path is fused with that of the sacred book. She risks body and soul to protect both and, unbeknownst to her, secures the future of an esoteric, divine prophecy.

"This book captured me from the start and would not let me go. I kept looking for a stopping point, a place I could relax and take a breath, set it down and go to sleep, but there was none. I was physically attached to the characters and the prose and I could not stop until it was over, at 4:30 am. The last time a book took hold of me this way was a long time ago." ~ Rebecca Cox, Reviewthebook.com

"Carrington-Smith brings all the loose ends, past and present, and binds them into a bewitching story, but also a classic story of greed. An exciting, riveting novel with many twists, this book will surely satisfy mystery fans and paranormal/mystical fans. The descriptive nature of the book brings us right into the heart of a wonderful old city and the people of the bayous. I thoroughly enjoyed it all the way through with no desire to take a break before finishing it." ~Betty Gelean, "Night reader"

"A fine choice and a highly recommended read." ~ Midwest Book Review

"A psychological thriller filled with suspense." ~Stephanie Rose Bird, author of "Stick, Stones, Roots and Bones"

Housekeeping for the Soul: A Practical Guide to Restoring Your Inner Sanctuary

The first book to combine how-to, self-help and spiritual genres to address the needs of millions of readers as they strive to detach from the Culture of Chaos and embrace a life of balance. It is through this inner harmony and balance that one may then create a meaningful, authentic reality. With a down-to-earth approach, the reader is guided through the process of emotional healing and renewal of spirit through the familiar analogy of housekeeping: cleaning, organizing, and "airing out" our lives, room by room, task by task.

"Housekeeping for the Soul carries its lovely, practical message with a lilting voice and eclectic viewpoint. The author helps us clear out some spiritual cobwebs and make our next 'spring cleaning' apply not to our homes but to the deepest part of ourselves." -- Victoria Moran, author of international bestseller *Creating a Charmed Life*

"Sandra Carrington-Smith 'brings home' the need to simplify and let go of psychological 'clutter' in order to be more fully present in our everyday lives. Housekeeping for the Soul overflows with important concepts presented in a style that is fresh and relatable. A unique, 'must read' debut from this eloquent author." -- S.T. Underdahl, Clinical Psychologist and author of *The Other Sister* and *Remember This*

"A great soul gripping and informative book to live by." ~Dr. Robert E McGinnis

Killer in Sight: A Tom Lackey Mystery

When a young woman is found murdered in a public park, it is up to RPD detective Lt. Tom Lackey to locate her killer. With the help of his longtime girlfriend and professional photographer, Kathy Spencer, Lackey unravels a mystery laden with psychosis and unexpected revelations. While Tom is busy following the multiple clues pouring in from different directions, Kathy gets to work to prove her own theory: The last image viewed by the dying person can be lifted from the eyes of the victim to identify the murderer. Using her background in photography and her passion for iridology, Kathy enlists the help of Dr. Greer, a snow-haired medical examiner who allows her to take shots of Tracey Newman's eyes. Her findings are puzzling, but they are supported by Alexis Howard, the dead girl's ten-year-old half sister who volunteers information she claims was delivered to her by her imaginary friend Lily. With multiple suspects floating up to the surface and skeletons yanked out of unlikely closets, Tom must rely on his methodical expertise and on Kathy's insight to find the killer before tragedy strikes again.

"Sandra Carrington-Smith leads off with a glimpse of the victim's thoughts and feelings before her murder. She sets the scene so vividly that as the story progresses the reader mentally returns often to the scene of the crime as Detective Lackey and his photographer girlfriend piece together clues. To add unique flavor to the mystery is a bit of paranormal suspense as Tracey's sister imaginary friend, Lily, moves the story forward. The flavor of the paranormal is just enough that every reader can picture the sequences without it "being over the top." I love that the story held my interest to the very last page and every question I had about a character was answered." ~ Jean Ferratier

"What Carrington-Smith has written instead is a first-rate thriller, with sympathetic characters and a completely believable story line."~ David Workman, author of *Absolute Authority*

Coming soon...

Shadows of a Tuscan Moon

A beautiful mother of two mysteriously disappears without leaving a trace, apparently swallowed by the darkness of a frigid winter night. The local law enforcement gets right to work, but as time goes by every lead turns into a dead end. Has the woman decided to run off and turn her back on her too-tight family life, or is her disappearance the work of a skilled killer who has left no clues behind? Many shadows lurk in the timeless beauty of a small Tuscan town; one of those shadows, maybe the darkest one of all, holds the key to a terrifying truth…

The Key (Book III of The Crossroads Series)

As the ancient prophecy continues to unfold, more lives become entangled in a web of sticky secrets and astounding revelations. Join Melody Bennet and Natalie Sanders on this new leg of the journey, as they travel to Brazil for a new adventure filled with danger and startling discoveries.

The Rosaries
A Novel

By

Sandra Carrington-Smith

This book is a work of fiction. Names, characters, places and incidents, are the product of the author's imagination and are used fictionally. Any resemblance to actual events, locales, or persons, living or dead, is purely coincidental.

First Edition

ISBN- 13:   978-0-9855558-2-5

CROSSROADS BOOKS

http://www.sandracarringtonsmith.com

*I dedicate this book to my children,
Stephen, Michael and Morgan, and to
P.L. who never fails to amaze me.*

Acknowledgements

When I wrote The Book of Obeah, my first novel, I didn't know what to expect. As all new authors, I, too, had high hopes for the future, but I must admit that the road ahead looked a bit scary at the time.

Today, I am happy to say that The Book of Obeah (book number one in The Crossroads Series) has grown its own feet and legs, and it is busy exploring new territories. Within the last few years, The Book of Obeah has won an award, has been translated in Portuguese, and it is now undergoing two new incarnations: An audio book narrated by Dave Fennoy (better known as The Hulu Guy and Lee Everett in the video game Walking Dead), produced by Cherry Hill Publishing, and a movie production scheduled to begin filming in mid-2013. Thanks to Milena Rimassa-Merrill, Melody and the gang will soon come to life on the silver screen!

Two years after The Book of Obeah was released, The Rosaries is now ready to make its debut. Will it have the same success its older sibling enjoyed? One can only hope, and the answer to that question will surely come in time.

For now, I would like to thank everyone who's been in my corner since the beginning: First in line are my children, Stephen, Michael and Morgan, my husband John and his family, my parents, my uncle and my sister, followed by all the friends who have supported my efforts, both online and in real life. A special token of gratitude must go to Mr. Ed Powers, my number one fan, and to Dena Patrick, Pam and Fred Scarboro, Mia Smith, Donna Freeman, Scott Schultz and Toni Overby. I would like to thank my agents, Natalie Kimber, Krista Goering, and Daniel Doglioli, and the Facebook group Writers and Artists Share! Tremendous gratitude certainly goes to Sherrill Suitt-

Craig, my talented cover designer and editor extraordinaire, to Shannon Choppa, the creator of the beautiful rosaries featured on the cover, and to Julie Wall (Wall2Wall Photography). Julie's superb photographic skills allow me to show my face on websites and magazines without being embarrassed. And of course, many thanks to my readers for the continued support. I would have never made it without you.

Preface

"There will come a time when powerful signs herald a crossroads for Humanity. Events affecting one part of the Earth will instantly be known to the rest of the world and shall be recognized by a chosen few as the prophesied signs. Consequences of action and inaction will be apparent, cause and effect manifesting faster as this cycle draws toward conclusion. Inequities and imbalance will be painfully evident on individual, regional and global levels. Feelings of isolation, disconnection, and confusion will be widespread. Few will express these feelings, most choosing to mindlessly walk through their daily tasks, numbing themselves in countless ways. Hardships will flood the vast majority of people from every direction, creating a rising sea of anxiety. This will be reflected in Mother Earth being out of balance, with cataclysmic events taking place more regularly and more. A long-ago gathering of elders who revered and held sacred our connection to Mother Earth foresaw the time of this crossroads. A divinely inspired plan was conceived to counteract this state of imbalance, to be put into place at this crucial time. Over a preordained period, four distinct, devastating conflicts among societies throughout history will be confronted—one at a time—so as to heal suffering at the core, bringing about a state of wellness and balance. The elders' descendants became protectors of this ancient wisdom tradition, with their lives intrinsically entwined in guardianship of the sacred prophecy. The painful disparities of the past and present must be exhumed to be honored and healed. Accountability will be imperative once a shift toward stability is initiated. The fate of all rests with a universal awakening…"

Translation of Choctaw tribal shaman proclamation; Bayou-Lacombe, LA; Circa 1878

Prologue

Raleigh, NC. Late 1970's.

When the nurse knocked on his door, Dr. Huey Anderson was scanning entries on the bank statements from the last few months. He shoved them quickly into one of the desk drawers and ran a manicured hand over his thinning, gray hair, while his tall, slim body shifted anxiously as the nurse walked in and spoke.

"The patient arrived shortly ago, Doctor. I helped her get settled into her room and I already administered the sedative."

"Wonderful, Ms. Roberts, thank you."

Dr. Anderson smiled and locked eyes with the nurse, who lightly blushed and smiled back. Huey Anderson was a natural born charmer; thanks to his charisma and the extra money he paid his staff under the table, he was able to sustain a very profitable side business. Fifty-five years old now, he figured he would be able to retire before the respectable age of sixty.

Dr. Anderson leaned back against the soft black leather chair and stared at the Monet print on the wall directly across from his desk. *La Promenade* depicts a lovely scene in which a young woman takes a walk in the company of a small child; the woman looks happy and very dainty, in her flowing white gown and dark umbrella. Childless women aren't as happy as women who get to experience the gift of motherhood – of that he was absolutely certain. He was doing a good deed, and each time he turned a frustrated woman into a happy mother he contributed a great gift to the world. The fact that he was amply rewarded for his services was an added benefit to his side trade, but wasn't his only reason for continuing on his quest.

He was fortunate to have a staff that believed in his vision, ready to support and cheer his efforts, and he paid them dearly for their loyalty; each and every one of them. He ran his operation smoothly and was able to carefully build an anonymous clientele. People who knew what he did sent their close friends who had lost all hope of becoming parents -- Huey Anderson was their hero.

"Please, Ms. Roberts, let the patient know I will be there in just a minute. I only need to put away a few things and go change." He crossed his hands over his lap and smiled benignly.

"No problem, Doctor. She will probably be asleep by the time you will get there."

"That's great, thank you."

The nurse, a pretty young thing with mid-length dark hair and sparkling hazel eyes, nodded and opened the door to go back and check on the patient.

"By the way, Nurse," He asked Ms. Roberts before she left, "is the baby ready?"

"Yes, Doctor, everything is ready for the procedure." The nurse's voice was cold and methodical as usual, but Dr. Anderson detected a light in her eyes that he didn't like much. She seemed troubled, as if something tugged at her soul.

He didn't have time to explore her mind right now, so he dismissed the nurse with a nod and went to replace his white coat with surgical attire. One of the orderlies, a young man in his late twenties, with big dreams and little education to back them up, was mopping the sanitized white floor, and nodded in Huey's direction as the doctor walked by.

"Good evening, Ralph; I hope your day is going well." Dr. Anderson said.

Ralph nodded once and smiled. "My day is super, Doctor. I hope yours is too."

"Oh, it is, Ralph; another lady is going to celebrate her baby going home. That fact alone makes my day a wonderful one."

"That's great, Doctor. I hope my wife and I will experience the same joy soon. We have been trying to have a baby, but we've had no luck so far. It always amazes me to think that a woman can only conceive twenty-four hours out of each month and the world is filled with unwanted children. We would love to have a little boy or girl of our own."

Dr. Anderson lowered his head in contrite expression; "It is sad, isn't it? And that's why we are here – to bring a smile to those who aren't successful with the traditional methods of conception. Keep me posted, Ralph, and if all else fails, I would like to examine your wife. Free of charge, of course."

Ralph was stunned by the offer. "I will keep that in mind, Doctor, thank you."

He walked past Ralph and strolled slowly past the cluster of patients' rooms, before he reached the operating room.

The patient was sleeping peacefully, the sedative having gloriously done its job. The baby was going to be premature, but that was not a big concern, thanks to modern technology.

He went to the sink and washed his hands, making sure to scrub under his nails and up to his elbows. The surgical table was already set up and placed near the patient's bed, and the shiny surgical instruments glistened under the bright light of the room. Nurse Roberts had already prepped the patient, so he picked up the scalpel from the instrument tray with confidence, ready to make the first incision.

It was a hell of a night, with heavy rain pouring down and banging against the glass of the window, but Dr. Anderson found the rhythmic sound of the rain quite relaxing. His long hands were firm and ready – each cut, each baby, marked one step forward toward the completion of his plan. Less than ten minutes later he delivered a healthy baby girl. She was small but appeared strong and determined to live. He handed her to nurse Roberts, who immediately whisked her away to get her cleaned up.

Everything was proceeding smoothly, and he felt a deep sense of excitement rush through his electrified body. He only hoped nurse Roberts would not begin to experience any unnecessary pokes from her conscience. If she did, he would have to deal with her before she caused any trouble.

Chapter One

Wilmington, NC. Late spring 2009.

There were two things Natalie Sanders hated above all – shoes and hateful people, especially if the latter happened to be members of her own family. Last night she had endured both -- especially Aunt Catherine, that old spinster, God bless her cold heart -- and could still feel a twinge of tension in her neck muscles. She couldn't help feeling that way any time she was summoned to a family function, and sometimes hoped that, as she sat alone on the shore as she did tonight, a wave could swallow her in its voracious black bite and make everything go away. Natalie was not the philosophical type, but often wondered what the meaning of life is, if pain and frustration are all one is allowed to experience on this earthly journey. There were times in her life when she had felt exhilarated, but after the initial high she always felt emptier than before. Something was missing – something had always been missing, since before Natalie could remember.

She wasn't going to think of that tonight, though. As she looked far into the horizon, she focused on the line that separated the ocean from the moonless sky and became lost in the vastness of the display spreading out in front of her. She loved the feeling of the cool sand under her feet, and wondered how she could transfer this very same sensation to one of her yet-to-be-discovered paintings. The wind picked up about a half hour before and was now blowing sand into her face and hair, which she had cut shorter just the other day. She still surprised herself every time she walked in front of a mirror, and couldn't help smiling at the sassier woman staring back at her. The deep rusty highlights complemented her hazel-green eyes and softened her face only slightly, still allowing her spunky personality to shine through. She stood up, brushed the sand off her turquoise sundress, and picked up her leather sandals. She could hear sounds from the boardwalk in the distance, and smiled when she distinctly heard a little boy fighting with his brother. How lucky he was! Natalie always wished for a sibling, someone she could share secrets and dreams with, but her parents could not have any children and had only adopted one. *They were disappointed enough with me...*

She pushed that thought away – she couldn't change history, but she would be damned if she was going to allow her family's twisted views of a perfect child to spoil her present and future. She instinctively ran a hand through her hair and quickened her step. She had plenty of reasons to be excited about her future, and hoped that her life would change after the upcoming art show in Wilmington. Wilmington NC, population 95,476, was certainly not as glimmering and pretentious as New York City, but it was a start. Mrs. Wilson, the owner of the gallery in town was impressed with her work, and Natalie had a chance to show the world her hidden potential.

The show was still a month away, but preparations were already underway and her level of excitement was growing by the minute. She had to send out invitations, shop for a new outfit, and go by Mr. Allen's shop to get some fliers printed out. Good old Mr. Allen opened the shop after retiring as a school teacher, and he put as much pride into his present job as he did, for many years, instilling knowledge into the minds of his sleepy pupils. Natalie loved Mr. Allen, and looked forward to telling him all about her recent success. She was fairly sure that both he and his wife Belinda, the owner of the antique store on Princess Street, were going to be thrilled for her, and would be first in line to attend the event.

As her mind processed all these thoughts, Natalie walked in a daze until she was in front of Briggs', the old donut shop proudly dating back to 1939. No matter what thoughts were running through her mind, the heavenly aroma of fried dough and fresh coffee always brought her back to reality. She decided to stop in and treat herself to a donut and a cup of Java – in fact, why not two donuts? She grinned at the thought that Aunt Catherine would certainly disapprove. She could hear her now…*A lady must always watch what she eats, Dear. And how could you enjoy anything that is so bad for your health?*

When she walked into the store, the place was still full of tourists and she had to wait in line for a few moments, in spite of the fact that it was already nine o'clock at night. Natalie loved the Mom and Pop feel of the place, and used the waiting time to scan the walls for old pictures of happy moments gone by. She didn't see anything from local artists, so she made a mental note to ask Mrs. Payne if she would be amenable to displaying at least one of her prints.

When it was her turn to order, Natalie looked up at the young cashier in front of her – she had long blond hair tied in a pony tail and a deep tan, and wore low-cut shorts and a T-shirt bearing the logo of the store. She looked vaguely familiar but no name came to mind, so Natalie ordered two donuts and a large cup of coffee, paid what she owed and left the store to find herself once again on the crowded boardwalk. She walked in front of the arcade packed with acne-ridden teenagers too busy cutting up or making out to notice anyone looking in their direction.

Her place wasn't too far from the boardwalk, only a couple of blocks. She walked slowly down Carolina Beach Avenue and turned left on Atlanta heading toward Hamlet. She loved the night air -- pregnant with the salty embrace of an ancient mother reaching out to caress her skin. Without the moon illuminating the streets, the houses looked indistinguishable from one another, and the area appeared more austere; during the day, the bright colors of the homes stood out against the Carolina blue of the maritime sky. Lost in the details of the surrounding scene, she reached Hamlet Street and quickened her step toward her house, a green two-story rental with a white front porch she quite accidentally found two years ago. She remembered that day clearly. She had driven down from Wilmington one Sunday morning, hoping to find a quiet place to sit, think and paint, and as she cruised the streets toward the waterfront, she had seen the for-rent sign in front of the house. It was a decision dictated by impulse, and she knew, even as she parked her yellow VW, that she was going to catch hell for it from her family. After all, her parents already arranged for her to have a place of her own near their house, yet not too close for fear she would embarrass them with her bohemian lifestyle. And hell she got, but Natalie didn't really care. Grandma Elsie left her a small inheritance when she passed, and although it wasn't a sum that allowed her to be rich and travel, it was certainly enough to live on without worrying about her next meal.

She walked up the three steps to the front door and suddenly heard a meow. Leave it to Billy, her cat, she thought, to play host and welcome her at the door. She walked in, fed Billy, and dropped the bag of donuts on the kitchen counter, just a moment before the phone rang.

Who could be calling at nine-thirty at night? "Hello?"

"Natalie? This is Ryan Wheeler. We met last night at your parents' house. I hope you don't mind me calling so late."

Natalie rolled her eyes, but she successfully stifled the annoyed sensation she felt and blocked it from creeping into her voice. Her family had struck again – the son of one of the few tobacco dynasties left in the south, and the sole heir to their fortune, Ryan was in their eyes a perfect candidate for marriage. Too bad Natalie didn't believe in arranged matrimony.

"I remember you perfectly well, Ryan. How are you?"

"I'm doing great. I was wondering if you would like to get together sometimes. Your Aunt Catherine took the liberty of giving me your phone number, and said that the two of us have quite a bit in common. She's so sweet, isn't she?"

"I would really like to, Ryan, but I am working around the clock to finalize the details of my upcoming art show, and I doubt I will have any time to socialize."

"Art show? Wow, Natalie, I didn't know you are an artist!"

Just one more of my bohemian downfalls, didn't sweet Aunt Catherine tell you about that? Natalie thought, and quietly snickered at the sad private joke.

"But I won't take no for an answer," Ryan said, "in fact, I can come down there where you are and help you. Managing time is my hidden talent."

"Really, Ryan, I wouldn't want to inconvenience you…"

"No bother, Natalie. I would love to help, and it would be really great to see you again. I will be down the day after tomorrow and I will call you to get exact directions to your place."

Natalie was too busy silently cursing Aunt Catherine in her head to think of a quick reply to avoid what she knew would be a boring encounter, and Ryan took her lack of a prompt response as an affirmative sign.

"Awesome! I will see you on Wednesday, then."

Before Natalie could reply, Ryan had already hung up. The sound of the communication being cut off brought her string of silent litanies to an end.

"Wonderful. Now I even have Mr. Perfect coming down to stick his nose into my business!" She realized she was thinking out loud, and smiled when she noticed Billy had curled up against her feet and was purring madly. Too tired and annoyed to eat her donuts, she started toward her bedroom when the phone rang again.

"Miss Sanders? This is Ms. Nettie, your neighbor. I am just watching the news and heard there is a terrible fire in downtown Wilmington. I remember you telling me that your family lives near there and I called to make sure everybody is okay."

"Downtown Wilmington? Where, Ms. Nettie? Wait, let me turn on my TV – are they showing it right now?" Natalie asked nonchalantly.

"Yes, it's breaking news, Ms. Sanders. Your family is okay, right?"

Natalie could no longer hear Ms. Nettie, as blood thundered in her ears and made her head spin. The phone dropped beside her and she nearly collapsed on her bed when she turned on the TV set and saw flames engulfing a building that looked quite familiar. It took a moment to process what she was seeing; in front of her eyes, the art gallery was turning into toast, and with it, Natalie's paintings. She shook her head in disbelief, and closed her eyes for a moment to shut out her shock at the horrifying sight. It couldn't be! Her work of this whole past year was in that gallery; her dream of becoming a well-known painter was screaming in agony from its prison of hungry flames. She stared at the TV screen as if hypnotized, unable to move or catch a liberating breath. It was all gone - her passion, the proof that she could do something right, her chance to accomplish something on her own merit. Once again, Natalie wished to be swallowed by a wave.

Chapter Two

Catherine Bouvier sighed as she tried to motivate her old bones to cooperate with her wish to get out of bed. Time had surely taken its toll on her, and she couldn't help but feel a little melancholy when she thought of times when she could spring as agile as a doe in a field. Those days were long past, and gone with them was Catherine's opportunity to create a real life for herself. She had received the best education money could buy, and had attended all the right socials a young lady could dream of, but when it came to relationships she was always a day late and a dollar short. She never crossed paths with the right man, or more precisely, her timid demeanor was never a match to her sister Angela's southern belle charm, and every possible suitor Catherine found attractive always ended up falling in love with her prettier and giddier sibling.

In her mid-thirties, when the ghost of spinsterhood had first begun to flash its ugly face, Catherine knew she was battling time. She embarked on a relationship with a gentleman who was already married, but assured her of his undying love. When she became pregnant and unwanted, her family sent her away to have the baby, using the excuse that she was gone to further her studies and indulge her passion for the fine arts in Europe. By the time she came back, Catherine's heart was broken from having given away her child, and she was angry for allowing herself to be so vulnerable.

Losing her daughter shifted something inside of her. Suddenly she hated children, despised women who were as loose as she had been, and vowed that never again she would allow herself to be that open with her feelings. She became a model of etiquette and committed her life to taking care of her aging parents. Of course, the constant demands of elder care forced her to forfeit any type of social life, but by then Catherine had made her choice – a sheltered and boring life was far better than the heartache she had suffered, and if she was to spend her life alone to save herself any more pain, then she was happy to accept the consequences of her choice. Everything worked smoothly and efficiently in her life for a while, until she met Phillip…

"Ms. Bouvier?" Lakeisha's voice echoed softly in the grand hallway behind Catherine's bedroom door. Lakeisha was the nurse her sister Angela insisted to hire to help Catherine in her daily affairs.

"Yes, Lakeisha, come in. I'm just getting up."

"Would you like some breakfast, Miss?"

Catherine was not hungry, but worried that if she didn't make an effort to swallow at least a few bites, Lakeisha would immediately report to Angela. The last thing she wanted to do today was to once again explain to her sister that she didn't need a baby-sitter.

"Just some toast and coffee will be fine, Lakeisha. Thank you."

Lakeisha lifted her right eyebrow as she always did when she wanted to say something that was really none of her business. The tiny gold stud on the side of her nose caught a ray of sunlight coming through the cream colored curtains and sparkled against the smooth caramel tone of her skin. Her hair was cropped short enough to highlight the fullness of her face and she had a pleasant smile that made her whole bulky, five-foot-ten frame appear less imposing. Catherine liked Lakeisha, and although she didn't feel she needed a nurse, nor a housekeeper, Lakeisha was quite discreet and allowed her to maintain some dignity by not intruding in Catherine's personal space unless she was called.

When Lakeisha disappeared again through the big mahogany door and closed it quietly as she exited, Catherine got out of bed and began her morning rituals. She opened the window to let in a little morning breeze. Although summer hadn't officially started, the days were already warm and humid; if she hoped to get any fresh air into her room, this was the time to do it. She always considered the early morning breeze to be a messenger of sorts, and loved to listen to the sounds of the town as it woke up each day. Her gaze rested for a few seconds on all the things she was familiar with -- the antique poster bed, the ornate vanity, the Victorian chest, the creamy lace curtains which gave the room a soft, dreamy feel, complemented by the lilac flowers embroidered in the hand-sewn bed spread. By the time she sat at the vanity table and began to brush her hair, Lakeisha came back in with a tray, which she sat on the desk near the window before gently taking the brush from Catherine to stroke the old lady's long, gray hair.

"I couldn't believe how many fire trucks went by last night. It was a real mess out there." Lakeisha said.

"Fire trucks? Was there a fire?" Catherine was genuinely surprised and locked eyes with Lakeisha through her reflection in the mirror.

"Goodness, Miss, you didn't hear the engines going through? There was a fire at the art gallery on Main. The whole building is reduced to a charred skeleton. The owner, Mrs. Wilson, is beside herself, I hear. She was preparing for an art show next month, and was very excited about a local artist who, according to her, is a new impressive talent. Nobody knows who that is; Mrs. Wilson was determined to keep her new pet a secret until the show."

Catherine shook her head. "A promising artist discovered in Wilmington? Mrs. Wilson is quite the dreamer." She said, a hint of disdain only slightly lacing her perfectly trained and controlled tone of voice.

"Isn't that niece of yours a painter too, Miss Bouvier? You don't think…"

Catherine sighed deeply, as the awareness that the artist *could* be her niece rose to her mind for the first time. "I must admit that I have never seen her paintings, but unfortunately, my niece and I don't always see things eye to eye. That girl has been an embarrassment and a cross to bear for my family the whole time she has lived with us. The good Lord must have really been angry with my sister for giving her such an untamed brat."

Lakeisha was unsure if she should even respond. While she didn't know Natalie Sanders well, she remembered the girl as being well mannered and pleasant. She still remembered how her senses were jarred when she first saw Natalie upon her arrival at Ms. Catherine's house. The girl had an uncanny resemblance to someone she met long before, someone from her past, but after carefully asking Ms. Catherine, she learned that

Natalie was an only child, so there was no chance they had met before. Something about her nagged at her soul, but she quickly dismissed the feeling and focused on her new job in the Bouvier household.

"Now, now, Miss Catherine, gold can be found in a river full of common pebbles. I'm sure this young lady has some good qualities."

Catherine yanked the brush away from Lakeisha's hand and slammed it on the vanity table. "There is nothing in her but bad blood, Lakeisha. You don't know her, so I would appreciate it if you could keep your thoughts to yourself. I will call you when I am done with the tray."

Lakeisha was stunned into silence by the old lady's heated reaction. What was the matter with her? Why did she hate that child so much? Catherine Bouvier was a bitter old lady, and Lakeisha was sure the old bat was fighting incipient dementia. How could Catherine Bouvier not have heard all those sirens last night? They came blaring right past the house at a time when it was too early for her to be sound asleep, and were loud enough to break the barrier of numbness from the two Ambien Catherine took every night to shut out the demons that ate her up during her waking hours. There was something deeper and more disturbing in the old woman's venomous feelings against the Sanders family -- Lakeisha could feel it in her bones. She was no psychiatrist, merely a common nurse, but her spiritual training had given her an extra edge into the human psyche. Regardless, it was really none of Lakeisha's business, so she headed for the stairs and had only gone a few steps when she heard a muffled sound come from Miss Bouvier's door. The old lady was crying...no, she was downright sobbing, and all Lakeisha could hear was one phrase repeated over and over...*Why, Phillip? Why?*

Belinda Allen got busy polishing some of the items in the store while she kept a watchful eye on the activity on the street. The acrid stench of smoke and burnt dreams still hung heavily in the air, and sneaked in every time a customer opened the door to inquire about the price of one of the antiques on display.

Buying the store had been a late life business decision when she and her husband both refused to retire to a couch. They started two small businesses doing something they enjoyed, and they were both quite happy to meet at lunch and dinner to discuss daily events. Today, she could not wait to meet her husband, and find out if he heard any more details about the fire at the art gallery the night before. All she knew was that an electrical problem was the likely cause of the initial spark, and in a place filled with canvas and flammable paints, it didn't take long for the flames to spread. Within fifteen minutes the building was almost completely charred, and Mrs. Wilson was devastated. Belinda made a mental note to go by her place this evening, after closing the shop, to comfort her old friend.

The small chime on the front door announced someone entering, so she glanced once more at her image in the antique mirror and smiled -- she was fairly satisfied with the pretty lady looking back at her. Her light make-up accentuated the impish light perpetually dancing in her bright blue eyes, and her blond hair was elegantly coiffed in a soft bun pinned right above her neck line. She wasn't too tall – something she always wished she could change about herself – but was quite proportioned and in decent shape. If anything, being petite, she could always find good deals at the Sears bargain basement. She loved pretty clothes, and took great pride in matching her outfits. Today's ensemble was a baby powder cotton suit, which she had accessorized with a delicate strand of fresh water pearls and matching earrings, aside from the usual silver spider brooch she wore every day. She wasn't sure why she liked spiders so much, but she suspected her fascination with them came from an old tale her mother told her many years before. According to the tale, spiders were magical creatures that took care of the souls of the dead, and if someone died a violent death, the spiders would lend them their bodies, so they could come back to punish the person responsible and restore balance. She knew it was only an old tale, but in her heart she liked to think that victims were at least allowed the dignity to take final justice into their own hands. She turned away from the mirror and greeted the new customer.

"Hello, and welcome to Hidden Treasures. Let me know if I can help you find anything."

The man looked around for a while, then approached the counter as Belinda was busy organizing sales receipts from the previous day.

"Actually, I am looking for something specific," he said, a charming smile quickly spreading over the handsome face. "My mother is passionate about prayer beads, and I thought of finding some for her upcoming birthday."

Mrs. Allen arched her brow. "Prayer beads? Do you mean rosaries?"

The stranger's eyes opened a bit wider and he leaned closer across the counter. "Yes, exactly."

Belinda Allen shrugged her shoulders and shook her head. "I'm afraid I don't have anything like that at the moment, I'm sorry. I've had some in the store before, but I sold them already."

"Would you know of any other antique dealers in the area that might possibly carry something like that?"

"There are several antique shops around, but I haven't visited them in quite a while, so I wouldn't know for sure."

The stranger smiled and turned toward the door. He had broad shoulders and hair as black as the wings of a crow, and Belinda estimated his height at maybe six feet one or two. He was casually attired in a pair of corduroy slacks and a white collared shirt, and wore a thick gold chain around his neck. He hesitated before exiting and walked back to the counter. He wrote down a phone number on a small card with a golden pen he pulled out of his shirt pocket.

"Should you by any chance have a rosary coming in, would you please call me?"

Belinda Allen took the card and placed it inside her cash register, a little surprised at the stranger's insistence. "I certainly will. Meanwhile, would you like to look around to see if you might see something else your mother would like?"

"No, it's okay. My mother has a very selective taste. Thank you anyway." With those last polite words, he was gone, the chime on the door announcing his departure.

Belinda took the card out of the register and looked at it. It only bore a first name – Chris - and a phone number, which appeared to be local. When her husband walked in, she placed the card back into the drawer and went through the familiar motions of closing up for a few minutes to enjoy mid-morning coffee, before stepping out together, hand in hand like newlyweds. And it was probably because of her interest in what her husband was telling her that Belinda didn't notice the same man who had just visited her store hiding behind the corner, when they passed him by. He watched the couple walk away and smiled. He was sure she knew where the rosary was, and he was going to find it, one way or another.

Melody Bennet stood in front of Applebee's and took another quick glance at her watch - two o'clock. Her husband's delay was beginning to worry her. Mario was seldom late for a date, and was usually the one waiting; he rationalized once that his obsessive punctuality was likely the result of having a father who had no routines – in Mario's mind, randomness was synonymous of instability.

She tried his cell phone but got no answer, so she called the house again, in the event he forgot something and went back home. No answer there either. Where could he be?

She was just beginning to dial his cell number again when she saw him walking across the parking lot toward her. He raised his hands in apology, and smiled that smile of his that could turn water into steam. After two years of marriage she was still in awe of his good looks. His tar black hair was cut very short and it emphasized the chiseled jaw line and deep-set chocolate brown eyes. Because of his constant training, his body was a masterpiece of muscles that would have made the statue of David green with envy. In her heart of hearts, although she was often told that she was a beautiful woman, Melody still couldn't believe her good fortune. As far as she was concerned, her shiny brown hair, bright green eyes and petite figure paled in comparison to Mario's raw beauty.

"I'm sorry, I'm sorry, I know I'm late. But wait until I tell you where I was."

Melody pretended to pout and tapped her right foot on the pavement.

"It'd better be good, Mister. I'm starving."

Mario zipped his lips with his finger and smiled mischievously.

"No comment yet, but I promise it is worth the wait".

So far into their relationship, Mario never let her down, so Melody giggled and reveled in the delicious feeling of the upcoming surprise as they walked into the restaurant.

The hostess led them to a booth at the right end of the room, and Melody was pleased to see that not too many people were around. With his new job at the SBI and her around-the-clock work at the farm she had inherited from her grandmother, their chances for a romantic rendezvous were few and far between. Mario waited for the waitress to come and be gone with their orders before he said anything – watching Melody giddy with anticipation was too delicious a treat to spoil it with a quick burst of information.

"So, are you going to tell me already?!" Melody couldn't contain her curiosity much longer.

"Patience, patience, my child…."

"Mario! Spit it out!"

Mario laughed heartily and took Melody's hand into his. She loved the feeling of it, and closed her eyes to savor the moment.

"Okay, ready?"

Melody opened her eyes wide, as if ready to swallow him in her glance. "I've been ready! What is it?"

"Remember when we talked about going on a little trip for the honeymoon we never had when we got married?"

Melody held her breath, and only nodded for fear of breaking the spell.

"Well…how would you like to go on that trip now?"

"Now…? But…where? When?"

Mario pulled out something from his pocket and unfolded it for Melody to see - brochures from a travel agency. Melody's pulse quickened.

"It's almost our anniversary, Melody. Well, technically it isn't for another couple of months, but I figured it would be okay if we celebrate a little earlier, given the opportunity we have to go somewhere special."

He displayed the brochures in front of her and she saw that two of them were of London, England. She looked up at her husband, a bit confused.

"Don't get me wrong, Mario, I love the idea, but why London? I thought we were both more in tune with tropical locations."

Mario smiled mischievously, revealing that there was more to the story.

"True, true…but there is something else you don't know."

There. How did Melody know him so well?

"Paul called this morning. Your cousin Olivia is finally getting married to that guy she met while working at the hotel. Remember her telling us about that?"

How could Melody forget? The hotel in New Orleans where Olivia worked was the place where Melody's life had begun to turn upside down. She had gone down to Louisiana to honor her grandmother's wish to have her ashes sprinkled on her native land, and Melody had found herself thrust into an assortment of family secrets and oddities that belonged more into an adventure book than in real life. Discovering she had extended family there had been a shock and a blessing.

"That's wonderful, Mario! When did Paul call?"

"He called early this morning, right after you left. That's why I rushed out and went by the travel agency before I came here."

"I'm still stumped. What does London have to do with Olivia getting married?"

"Dear beloved, have you forgotten the gentleman your cousin fell in love with is from London? We are going to the wedding. I've already called Paul back and told him we will attend."

Melody was stunned. She hoped Olivia wasn't planning to move to London; her father, Paul, would be crushed if he lost her again after having been reunited with his only daughter just a few years ago. Olivia was the fruit of an extra-marital affair, and Paul wasn't even aware of her existence until the young woman set out to find her biological father; by then, she was an adult and he was an old man, and the bond they developed was strong and sincere.

"Why are they getting married there? I thought marriages customarily take place in the hometown of the bride-to-be."

"Traditionally they do, but I suppose they really wanted to do something special. Paul said that Graham is hoping to make arrangements to rent the Spencer House for the occasion. Graham told Paul that the house was built in the 1700s for Earl John Spencer, an ancestor of Lady Diana Spencer, the Princess of Wales."

"Goodness! Olivia must be ecstatic! She missed out on a lot while growing up, and tried so hard to make something of herself. She deserves such a grand wedding."

The waitress came back with their orders, and they both dug in. They ate in silence until Mario swallowed the last bite and came forth with another interesting possibility. "And you, my dear, will probably be asked to be one of the bridesmaids. Paul said that Olivia will be beside herself when she hears we'll be there."

Melody smiled and squeezed Mario's hand.

"Oh my God, I just can't believe it...Olivia is getting married, and we are going to London! Pinch me, please."

Mario burst into laughter so sensual it made Melody shiver.

"Do I get to pick the place to pinch?" He said winking at her. "Unfortunately, I'm going to have to take a rain check on the pinching until tonight. I have to head off to work. Dwayne covered for me this morning, so I have to return the favor and let him spend a little time with his newborn son tonight."

"See how you are? First you tease, and then you retreat."

Mario smiled and caressed her cheek as he stood up. He kissed her gently on the lips and took his keys from the table. He had already taken a few steps when he suddenly stopped and turned around. "I'm sure Paul will be happy to hear from you; you might want to call him back.

"I will. I'll call him as soon as I get home."

Mario left, and Melody was suddenly in deep thought. She dreamt of Paul just the night before, and in the dream he looked pale and sick. Now he was going to London, halfway across the world, to give away his only daughter in marriage. Melody felt a strange sensation of doom and shivered. She took a sip of her water and hoped this wasn't the beginning of another wild ride.

Chapter Three

Natalie Sanders was still in shock. Months of work were wiped out in less than fifteen minutes, and now she felt totally lost, empty and alone. She wanted to call her parents but knew that they didn't really approve of her artistic career, so she killed the idea before it could turn into a full thought. She had no real friends, aside from Billy, her cat, who was now lovingly curled beside her chest while she lay on the couch in a nearly-comatose state; he purred loudly as if to let her know he was there, always by her side, and Natalie stroked its ginger fur to convey that she had gotten the message and deeply appreciated it.

Someone knocked on the door, and she hoped that, if ignored, they would go away. When they didn't, she got up slowly, running a hand through her unwashed hair as she walked. She opened the door and stared at Aunt Catherine standing in the doorway, wearing self-righteousness as her usual favorite outfit. Natalie took one look at the old lady and decided she wasn't going to argue with her today. She waved her hand in dismissal and walked back to the couch, leaving Catherine standing by the open door, visibly appalled.

"Well, young lady, are you going to let me in, or are you just going to make me stand here like a delivery boy?" Catherine's voice was ripe with judgment.

Natalie was already upset, and Aunt Catherine's uppity demeanor was something she really could not stomach today. "Sorry I didn't summon the town band to announce your arrival,

Aunt Catherine, and I'm afraid I misplaced the number for the local newspaper." Natalie was sure Aunt Catherine was ready to start with her etiquette bullshit, and she also knew the old bat couldn't have picked a worse day to piss her off. To her amazement, what spilled from Catherine's lips froze her in place.

"I came by to see how you are, Dear."

Natalie arched her eyebrow – had Aunt Catherine driven twenty miles out of her way to check on the welfare of her outcast niece? Not a chance. Something was up and Natalie was going to play along and find out where the rat was hiding. "I'm fine, Aunt Catherine, thank you for asking. It's very nice of you to come by. May I get you something to drink?"

Aunt Catherine was obviously pleased with Natalie's manners, and the usually cold light in her eyes warmed up ever so slightly, melting some of the ice she normally exuded when talking to people she considered inferior. "Some tea would be wonderful, Dear, if you have any. Let me get straight to the point, Natalie, there is something I want to ask you."

Natalie led the way to the small kitchen and removed oil paints, extra canvas and a bowl of cat food from the table, before she went to the stove to boil water for tea. She saw Aunt Catherine shaking her head out of the corner of her eye, but said nothing. She was often amused when the old lady became outraged by her lack of manners and organization, but today it didn't seem so funny -- in fact, it was downright annoying. How dare she come into other people's houses and pass judgment on them, even silently?

"Tea will be ready in a few minutes, Aunt Catherine. Now, going back to what we were talking about before…what is it you want to know?"

"The gallery that caught fire last night – was your work in there?"

Natalie knew Aunt Catherine better than that, and knew the old lady wasn't just concerned about some works of art.

"A wealth of local talent was in that building, Aunt Catherine."

"I didn't ask that, Natalie. I asked if *your* paintings were there."

"Why, yes, Aunt Catherine. The work of several months is now completely gone, with nothing to show for it. I guess you've always been right – art is a flaky thing, here one day and gone the next."

"That's nonsense, child. Art is a beautiful thing and its vulnerability is what makes it priceless."

It wasn't just Aunt Catherine's words that sounded foreign – her face also looked more relaxed and human. Natalie was at a loss. Catherine seemed to have captured her niece's confusion, and smiled with sincere affection – something she had never done before.

"I've been doing a lot of thinking this morning, Natalie. If art is what drives your inner passion, then your family should support you. You are different than the rest of us, and even if your lifestyle has offended our sense of decorum at times, you are not a bad person. And as Lakeisha said, all of us have hidden qualities."

"Lakeisha? Isn't she your housekeeper?"

"Well, she is my baby-sitter, really. Not officially of course, but I think your mother is afraid I am not able to care for myself any longer."

Natalie detected both humor and sadness in Aunt Catherine's statement, and didn't know what to make of it, so she held her peace and sealed her lips.

"My paintings are gone, Aunt Catherine. I just took them down to the gallery two days ago, when I went to dinner at my parents'. Mrs. Wilson wanted them there in advance so I took most of them."

"Mrs. Wilson is surely insured, Natalie."

"She is, she already told me so, but it's not really the money I'm so heartbroken about. This was my chance to showcase my work to others, and prove that I am not all that bad after all."

As hard as she tried, Natalie couldn't control hot tears from rising up to her eyes and escaping down her cheeks. She wiped them quickly, but it was too late – Aunt Catherine had already seen them, and quickly pulled out an ironed white kerchief from her handbag which she handed to Natalie.

"There, there, Sugar. It will be alright. You are the new talent Mrs. Wilson was so proud to show off, aren't you? You can paint again."

Natalie wasn't sure whether her tears were coming from pain or from shock. What had happened to Aunt Catherine? She dried her tears and looked up at the unfamiliar kind face of a lady she didn't know, and she could barely utter a few words. "Thank you, Aunt Catherine."

Aunt Catherine smiled, and then delivered the real whopper.

"After I heard of the accident, I called my old friend Tom. He has a gallery in London, England, and said that he would be pleased to display some of your work when you are ready for it. I told him I was going to talk to you about it, and I would call him back this afternoon."

Natalie was speechless. She shook her head, hoping to release her vocal cords from the grip of utter surprise, but no sound came out. It took her a moment to process that last sentence. Finally, her voice came back around.

"London? Tom? Aunt Catherine, I didn't know you knew anyone in the world of art. Wow… Europe?! I would love to exhibit my work there!"

Catherine smiled, and her eyes slightly glazed in remembrance. "There is quite a bit you don't know about me, Child. Now go on, and make yourself presentable. We'll have tea and then I'll be on my way to call Tom."

Natalie went to shower and dress, while Aunt Catherine prepared tea for both of them. By the time she came back to the kitchen, she felt refreshed and hopeful, but more than anything she felt like she had just been united with a relative she never truly met.

He sat in the shadows and lit up a cigarette, watching the rings of smoke disperse quickly in the air-conditioned room. He was running out of time – of that he was fairly certain – but he had no earthly clue how to proceed from that moment on.

Finding the rosary had been an all-devouring obsession since he met Celeste Hudson. He felt that his meeting with Celeste, the prostitute he encountered after she left New Orleans in the aftermath of Hurricane Katrina, was a divine appointment.

Celeste's great-aunt, Sister Serene, was the keeper of the rosary, and upon her death she passed the legacy to Celeste, her only living survivor, instead of entrusting it to one of the other nuns. Before her death, Sister Serene instructed Celeste to keep the rosary safe and revealed to her that it was a vital element in the unfolding of a grand prophecy. Celeste didn't really know if she should believe her aunt's words, but she loved Aunt Serene like a mother, so she solemnly promised to look out for the rosary. When she mentioned the prophecy to him, he was electrified.

Unfortunately, Celeste had soon stumbled into the demon of addiction, and had chosen to trade the mystical beads for a handful of cold hard cash. He still remembered her face when she told him about the sale to Hidden Treasures, and the way she tortured herself for betraying Sister Serene's trust. Tears had streaked her tired and heavily made-up face, giving her the appearance of a sad clown. He almost felt sorry for Celeste that night; sorry enough, in fact, that he held her for a long time, forfeiting the fleeting pleasure he had paid for.

He was so absorbed in his thoughts that he literally jumped when Tess walked in the room with a cup of steaming coffee. Her platinum hair was pulled into a tight bun, and her deep blue eyes looked darker in the dim light. He watched her as she turned the small lamp on the side table, savored her every move, and swallowed hard when the curve of her breasts rubbed ever so slightly against his shoulder. God, she was beautiful! He thought himself a bit foolish, but he couldn't help feeling like a school boy when Tess was around, even if flirting with her was equal to playing Russian roulette. His wife and his God would never forgive him.

"These papers came in for you today. Would you like me to file them?'

He shook his head. "No, that's okay. Leave them on my desk and I will take care of them."

"Anything else I can do for you before I leave?"

"Nothing I can think of. Have a great evening."

If Tess could read his mind she would know there was plenty she could do for him, but professionally she was done for the night.

She smiled and headed toward the door. "See you in the morning then. Will you be here?"

"Of course, why wouldn't I be here?"

Tess shrugged her shoulders and smiled." Well, you weren't here this morning. Anyway, see you tomorrow."

And with that she was gone, leaving behind a barely detectable scent of citrus. He waited for her to close the door and picked up the yellow envelope Tess brought in. Inside were a fake ID, a passport, and a birth certificate, all in the name of Chris Barnum. He stood up and looked in the small mirror he kept in his office for when he needed an emergency shave. "Yes, I definitely look like a Chris Barnum."

He smiled, "The game is on."

Lakeisha Jackson waited until the tub was filled with lukewarm water before throwing in the small bag she prepared that afternoon. Taking a purifying bath before retiring was a ritual she repeated every day, since she became a nun. As the warm water soaked the bag, a light scent of lemon filled the room. She took pride grating the peel herself, every single afternoon, just for that simple olfactory pleasure. Salt and lemon - two ingredients common enough to be found in every kitchen, yet powerful enough to cut through any kind of negative thought-form or dark vibe. She stepped into the water and gently lowered herself until her whole body was soaked, and almost immediately, thoughts of Catherine Bouvier filled her head.

Something was wrong, deeply wrong. Could the old lady be somehow connected to the prophecy? Was this the reason why Lakeisha was sent to live here with her? Lakeisha doubted it highly, but also knew that appearances can often be deceiving. She was not one of the elders, but she knew enough of the prophecy, by now, to be certain that nothing was happening at random. However insignificant something might appear, things were unfolding in the manner they were supposed to, and everything was speeding up toward the fulfillment.

She said three prayers – her usual – then got out of the tub and towel-dried her short hair. After getting into her nightgown she opened a book she kept buried behind a box in her closet and pulled out a piece of parchment Sister Justine had given her to read every time she felt doubtful or impatient. It was only one sentence, a mantra to be repeated over and over, but Lakeisha felt it vibrate in her hands as she read.

"The fate of All rests with a universal awakening…"

*The fate of All rests with a Universal Awakening. W*hat was her specific role in this? The last time she asked Sister Justine, she was told it wasn't for her to know – signs would lead her to her purpose in Wilmington, NC. So far, Lakeisha hadn't seen any signs. All she had seen was a bitter old lady who cried in her room every night, who didn't seem, in any way, connected to anything sacred.

She doesn't seem, Lakeisha…that doesn't mean she isn't…things aren't always as they seem.

The words were hushed by her ear with the gentleness of a lover's kiss, and although Lakeisha was quite certain nobody had spoken, they were still vibrating in the silence of her room. She lit a candle and some incense, before she opened her laptop and prepared to update and send her daily report. She knew Sister Justine was waiting for it, and as she did every night, Lakeisha humbly complied with her task without asking unnecessary questions. She had just clicked on the send button when she heard something outside her window - an owl singing his song of mourning, an omen of death. Lakeisha crossed herself and said a silent prayer.

Ryan Wheeler stretched out on his king-size bed and stared at the ceiling. Even if he was quite tired physically, his mind was reluctant to let go of the incessant flow of thoughts rushing through his head. He was planning to go see Natalie tomorrow, but as he lay in the quiet stillness of his room, he wondered if he was making the right choice. He was still very angry with Ashton Logan, but was undeniably in love with her. However, Natalie was the sole heiress of the Sanders' fortune, and Ryan knew that his father counted on him.

Natalie Sanders was a beautiful girl; certainly he would forget about Ashton in time, wouldn't he? His family wouldn't accept Ashton, a poorly educated waitress, as his wife anyway; and Natalie's family had money, real money; the type of money that could save his family from a financial catastrophe. There was no doubt his father couldn't survive losing everything; and his mother…what would be of her? Although their hardship was well concealed, it would only be a matter of time before the devastating news leaked to the rest of Wilmington's upper crust. Ryan was the eldest of the Wheeler sons, and the only one with some business acumen, so it only made sense that he would be the one to save the reputation of his family. He turned on his side and reached for the phone on the bedside table. It rang four times before Natalie picked up.

"Hello"

"Natalie! Ryan Wheeler. How are you?"

Natalie sighed on the other end of the line. "You haven't heard? There was a fire at the art gallery and my paintings are gone. I thought Aunt Catherine, or my mother, would have passed the word."

"Oh, no, I didn't hear. I am so sorry, Natalie."

"Yeah, I'm sorry too. Six months of work gone with the wind. Or with the flames, I should say."

"What are you going to do now?"

"I guess I'm going to start back from square one and paint away. Aunt Catherine said she knows someone in London who wouldn't mind to exhibit my work."

"London? That sounds awesome! Better than Wilmington by far, that's for sure. Listen, would you still like to get together?"

"Sure, why not? Do you know how to get here? Take 421 S until you see signs for Carolina Beach. I'm at 431 Hamlet, four blocks down from the boardwalk, on Pleasure Island."

"I'm sure I can find it, I can Google the address. Would ten or so be good for you?"

"Ten is great. See you then."

"See you tomorrow, Natalie. I look forward to seeing you again."

"Yeah, me too. Bye for now."

Ryan smiled as he realized his task was going to be easier than he had originally envisioned. Natalie was upset about the paintings and he had the opportunity to be her shoulder to cry on, her comforting force. "It will be a piece of cake, Dad. Our family is going to be okay," he thought out loud, and smiled to himself.

Belinda Allen felt uneasy. Something wasn't right, but she couldn't quite figure out where the feeling was coming from. She talked to both her children and they were fine; her husband, Jim, was resting comfortably on the recliner in the family room, and she passed her yearly check-up with Dr. Thompson with flying colors. No reasons to worry about anything in particular –

so where was this feeling of foreboding coming from? Belinda had experienced strange sensations in the past – premonitions about something imminent to happen – so she had learned to pay attention, but this time the feeling was stronger than usual and she felt almost as if someone was lurking in the shadows, ready to surprise her at any moment. She found that sensation quite unnerving, and she had done her best, since yesterday, to conceal her lack of ease from her husband. She didn't want to worry Jim; with his heart condition, strong emotions could be fatal, but even a slow simmering anxiety could have long lasting negative effects.

"Belinda" Jim called to the kitchen while she finished cleaning up after their evening meal, "have you talked to Claire Wilson?"

"Not yet, unfortunately. I was planning on stopping by her house after I closed the shop, but then I remembered I had to go by Dr. Thompson to get my results."

"That's right. Was everything okay?"

Belinda smiled, turned down the kitchen lights and walked in the family room.

"Everything was fine, thankfully. The doc said that I will live to be a hundred at least. Oh yes, he also said that he would like to put you on a new medicine to control your cholesterol level. He told me to ask you to stop by tomorrow or the day after."

Jim snorted jokingly. "Did you tell him that my level of cholesterol is down to below zero since you are the family chef now?"

Belinda laughed. Jim still couldn't swallow the fact that he was no longer allowed to rule the kitchen and fix his own famous southern breakfasts. "Go on, complain if it makes you feel better…you should be happy I'm looking out for your health." She walked up to the recliner and stamped a loud kiss on Jim's forehead.

"I'm very happy. We'll both live to be a hundred. We'll be a couple of old farts and live happily ever after."

"Yep, that's my goal."

"Say, Belinda, did you hear anything about the paintings that burned down? Gossip had it, today, that most of the works belonged to Natalie Sanders."

Belinda looked at Jim in surprise.

"Angela Sanders' daughter? I didn't know she's a painter."

Jim pulled off his reading glasses and put down the crossword puzzle he was holding in his hand. "I didn't either, until Mrs. Stewart, the librarian, told me Natalie is Mrs. Wilson's protégé, but art was one of her favorite subjects even when she was a little tyke this high, so I'm not too surprised."

"That's quite amazing that Angela's daughter would be so creative and spontaneous. Angela never struck me as the artist type."

"Actually, if you ask me, I don't find it too strange. Kids always end up doing what their parents loathe, especially if they are fought tooth and nail on it. The Sanders never accepted Natalie for the person she really is and they both downright rejected her when it became apparent she didn't fit the social mold."

"Jim! You can't be serious…that bad? I've met Angela several times, but to my knowledge I have never met Mr. Sanders, although I have always heard he is a nice if slightly whipped man."

"Oh yes. He definitely fits the description - he won't do anything to displease his wife. From what I've heard he is a much different man around her than he is when she is not there. Quite a shark in the courtroom, they say, but a goldfish at home, eagerly awaiting the flakes she dispenses to him on occasion. You should have seen how they always treated that poor kid. I don't even know why they adopted her."

"Well, I think Angela Sanders believed that she could take a poor, unfortunate little girl and turn her around to become a grand southern dame. When that didn't happen, the power struggle began."

"You missed your call as a teacher or therapist, Belinda." Jim smiled affectionately.

"I went through intensive basic training as a mother."

Belinda got up to go prepare some tea. Somehow, those little rituals always made her feel better. Right now she really needed the comfort of a good cup. As she stood by the kitchen sink to fill the tea kettle with water, she noticed a shadow darting on the deck outside the kitchen window. Afraid to alarm Jim, she didn't say anything but her heart leaped. She got a bit closer to the pane and looked out but saw nothing unusual – maybe it was just nerves. She turned the burner on high and pretended to look for a book. Her hands were still shaking, and she tried to stay occupied so that Jim wouldn't notice how jumpy she was.

Natalie was running, clutching a velvet pouch in her hand. The house was large, the walls were visibly impregnated with age, yet the scenery looked strange and unfamiliar. There were paintings on display, but it didn't look like any gallery she had seen so far, and it was dark despite the light coming in through the tall windows. She couldn't see who was chasing her, but knew, somehow, that she couldn't fight that power alone. She ran outside and saw a young woman standing by one of the lights on a street she had never seen before; she silently pleaded with the woman for help, but the stranger only looked sadly in her direction without speaking. Her skin was ghostly white, and her light blond hair was dirty and matted. She touched Natalie as the two came close, and Natalie felt her bony fingers tighten on her arm.

"Please, help me, he wants to kill me!" Natalie pleaded with the stranger who just stood silent.

The stranger opened her cracked lips and softly whispered words that were almost too quiet to be heard, "It will be okay, Natalie. It's all part of the design. You already have half the power." Then the stranger hung her head low and started to cry, rubbing her abdomen; her soft sobs echoed in the empty street.

"But how? What power? Help me! He is trying to kill me!"

The sad woman said nothing, only looked at Natalie with eyes haunted by personal demons.

Natalie could feel the shadow closing in…he was only a few steps away now. She broke free of the woman, and started running again when she heard someone sing, so she stopped for a moment and turned around. The same woman was kneeling beside the street light and looked small and even younger, only a few years older than a child. She sang to herself, a soft and haunting lullaby, her skinny arms wrapped around herself, rocking back and forth. She stopped singing and extended one of her arms out toward Natalie.

"Don't be afraid, Natalie; it will end soon and you'll be safe." The woman was crying again; her wails impregnated the night air and seemed to come from all directions.

Natalie covered her ears, but the sobs became so loud that she soon felt that her head was going to explode.

"You are like me, a lost soul, but soon you will find completion." The woman said.

"Stop it! I am not like you."

"You are" The woman said between sobs, "you just don't know it yet. But, unlike me, you won't walk alone forever."

She heard another sound behind her – he was right there. She could feel his energy even if she couldn't distinguish him from the rest of the shadows.

"Who are you?" She screamed at the dark figure inching toward her, "Leave me alone! What have I done to you? What do you want from me?"

She saw another woman, walking toward her. This new figure appeared more peaceful, stronger than the first one, and she wasn't scared. Natalie rushed toward the woman, and when their eyes locked, her breath caught in her throat. Natalie was standing in front of herself.

She screamed, and suddenly the strange scene was gone. She sat up in bed and tried to control her breath, looking around the dark room to see things that were familiar to her. She turned on the lamp on the bedside table and threw off the covers. Her mouth was parched, so she got up to go get a drink of water and shivered when she looked down the dark hallway. She reached out for the light switch and felt a wave of relief as light suddenly flooded all the dark corners. She went to the kitchen and searched for her cigarettes. She normally didn't smoke inside, but the thought of venturing anywhere outside her safe haven, right now, seemed to border on the unthinkable. She lit a cigarette and went to sit at the kitchen table.

What had happened? Natalie hadn't had a nightmare in years, and certainly she had never had one quite so scary! Just thinking back about the shadow in the dream made her tremble and she quickly pushed the memory away. After crushing half the cigarette in the ashtray, she saw Billy sleeping soundly on the small love seat in the adjacent family room, so she marched right up to him and picked him up. She needed to feel a warm body, and Billy was a purring bag of melted sugar. She held him tight despite his meows of complaint at being awakened so abruptly, and walked with him toward the bedroom. She gently laid the cat on the bed and lay beside him, stroking his soft fur. Billy looked up and pushed his face into her hand, letting her know she was forgiven.

Wide awake now, she tried to relax but sleep was nowhere near. After lying there for an hour she got up, pulled out a fresh canvas from the closet in her studio and prepared her colors. She felt a yearning inside, a primal call she didn't understand. Her brush was the mouthpiece of her soul, and Natalie spoke of the anger of the shadow, the sadness of the woman on the street, and the feeling of relief she had felt when she had seen herself as a strong, fearless woman. She painted furiously, bringing to life an image of herself slightly different than what she presently looked like; the eyes were the same vibrant hazel green, but her hair was different – chestnut brown, this time, and shoulder-length.

Chapter Four

Catherine Bouvier looked outside her window. This year the weather had been exceptionally beautiful, with warm sunny days and generous overnight showers which the locals considered a blessing for the typically water-starved crops.

Last night she didn't sleep very well, as short spells of deep sleep were repeatedly broken by a strange weight on her chest and a suspicious shortness of breath she still experienced long after she woke. She vowed to keep her discomfort from Lakeisha and Angela. The last thing she needed right now was to be treated like a child. Something had shifted inside of her the past two days and although she didn't want to face it, Catherine knew it was time to face reality before it's too late. She was happy to have called Tom and her lawyer. She felt another fleeting sensation of pain in her chest, and again her breathing became labored. She stood up with effort and called Lakeisha, her previous thoughts of ignoring the symptoms quickly being replaced by a growing sense of alarm. A moment later, Lakeisha came into her room.

"Did you call, Ms. Catherine?"

The instant she laid eyes on the old woman, Lakeisha knew something was wrong. Catherine's eyes looked as if they had sunk into her face and deep dark circles stained the creamy skin around them. Her lips appeared thinner and very white.

"Are you okay, Ms. Catherine?"

"No, Lakeisha, I don't feel very well today. I need you to do something for me."

Lakeisha nodded and touched Catherine's arm to feel her body temperature – stone cold.

"Ms. Catherine, it'd be best if we get medical help…"

Catherine raised a hand and stopped Lakeisha before she could say more.

"There is something I must do first, Lakeisha, and I need your help."

"Anything, Ms. Catherine, what is it?"

Catherine turned her eyes toward the desk at the far corner of the room. "I wrote a letter to my niece, yesterday. I suppose my old body already knew something was going to happen, even if I wasn't aware of it yet. I put the letter in the top drawer of my desk. Should something happen to me, please, take it and give it to her."

Lakeisha swallowed hard. "Of course, Ms. Catherine. You know I will do as you ask, but let's get you ready now, and let's call your sister."

Catherine felt weaker by the minute, and had no strength to fight Lakeisha's decision. She nodded and watched as Lakeisha packed a few things for her, in the event she was admitted to the hospital. In a few minutes Lakeisha was done and was already dialing Angela's number. It was a brief exchange and Catherine assumed her sister had instructed the nurse to call an ambulance. She saw the paramedics arrive, but by then her breathing was so bad that her oxygen level must have dropped very low, and she barely had enough air to remain conscious. She was strapped to the stretcher and whisked away before she had the chance to say goodbye to all the things she held dear throughout her life. Somehow, Catherine knew she wasn't coming back. Maybe Natalie could make better all the wrongs she had done.

From the time Lakeisha called and told her what happened, Natalie felt as if she was moving in a surreal dimension. She rushed to the hospital in a daze, her heart screaming at the injustice at hand – she had finally broken through the barrier which separated her from Aunt Catherine, and as soon as she peered through, Catherine was now in critical condition in a hospital room.

Natalie sat gently on the bed and took her aunt's hand into hers. Catherine's fingers were cold and her skin was translucent, and a soft smile formed on her cracked, tired lips when she opened her eyes and saw her niece.

"You're here, Natalie."

"Yes, Aunt Catherine, don't worry. I'm right here."

Catherine attempted to lift her arm to touch Natalie's hair – something she had only felt compelled to do in the last two days – but she only managed to squeeze her hand a little. "Oh, I'm not worried, Sugar. You shouldn't worry either; it's just that my journey here is over."

Natalie felt tears rising up to her eyes, threatening a flood. "Don't say that, ,. You'll get better, you'll see."

Catherine smiled, amused by her niece's attempt to lift her spirits. "No, Natalie, I'm not going to be better. In fact, I'll be gone very soon. I need you to listen to me very carefully."

"Of course, what is it?"

"I arranged for you to get in touch with Tom, my friend in London. I wrote all the details in a letter I left in my desk drawer, in my room. I instructed Lakeisha to give it to you, should something happen to me. My heart is very weak and I know I'm on my way to meet my Maker, even if the doctors are trying to tell me everything will be okay."

Catherine coughed and seemed to have a hard time continuing. Natalie took her hand into hers and leaned closer when her aunt tried to whisper something else.

"I have done some wrong things, Natalie. Some of them can't be fixed, some others maybe you can make right for me. Many years ago I had an illegitimate child, a daughter, and I gave her away right after she was born. Her father was a married man, and he said goodbye the moment I found out I was expecting. My family sent me to London to have her – that's when I met Tom, the man who owns the art gallery. We became friends and we have kept in touch throughout the years. He will help you with your paintings, Natalie."

Natalie felt more tears rising up and squeezed her aunt's hand a little more. She swallowed hard and listened carefully.

"I have something I would like my daughter to have, Natalie, and I would like for you to bring it to her; it's all detailed in the letter I left you. I think she still lives in London, so maybe if you go, you can look for her and give her my gift. It's not much, but I hope she will keep it as a token of my love for her. I never forgot her sweet smile, and thought of her every minute of each day."

Catherine coughed again and, as Natalie pushed the button to call the nurse, the shrill sound of the heart monitor filled the room with the impatient call of death. Aunt Catherine was gone and Natalie was left with a herculean task to fulfill.

Natalie went back home and decided to take a walk on the beach before going to Aunt Catherine's house. She was fairly certain there was going to be a good deal of pandemonium there, as her mother was likely to be already at work to finalize the details of the funeral arrangements. She fed Billy again, though he already ate that morning, then grabbed her sandals and purse and walked the short distance to the beach.

Even if it was past noon there weren't too many people out yet, aside from a few kids looking for seashells and an old gentleman – a tourist most likely – testing his luck with a fishing rod and a handful of cut shrimp. It was a glorious day; the sun was bright and the breeze was saturated with the salty, sticky scent of the ocean.

She sat near the shore watching a sand crab poke its head out and digging furiously back in to burrow in the safety of the underground; she drank the moment of pure peace and hoped to keep it alive for the days to come. She couldn't believe Aunt Catherine was gone. Acute congestive heart failure, the doctors said, and Natalie didn't even know the old lady was that sick. She was still in shock at the way Aunt Catherine had changed the past few days, and couldn't wrap her mind around the fact that her most hated relative turned out to be a supporter of her passion for painting.

She left the beach and drove to Wilmington seemingly on automatic pilot -- the roads mapped in her mind from years of back and forth travel. When she reached downtown – only a few blocks away from Aunt Catherine's house - she was annoyed with the heavy traffic, but drew a deep breath and tried to focus on the Spanish moss dripping from the trees lining each side of the street. It only took her a few more minutes to reach the antebellum masterpiece Aunt Catherine had called home, but by the time she parallel parked in front of it, her nerves were frayed. She looked up toward the window of what had been Aunt Catherine's bedroom, halfway hoping to see her peeking through the creamy lace curtains. Of course, they didn't move, and Natalie hurried up the short path leading to the front porch, a beauty built in the early 1800s which still exuded grandeur and southern décor even after so many years. Lakeisha opened the door, and from her face Natalie could see that the "baby-sitter," as called her, had somewhat cared for her elderly charge. She was dressed in a gray flannel shirt despite of the afternoon heat, and her usual smile was replaced by a look of somber acceptance.

"Come in, Ms. Natalie."

"Aunt Catherine said she left something for me."

Lakeisha nodded. "Yes, Miss, I will go fetch it for you."

While she waited for Lakeisha to come back, Natalie went to sit on the brown leather sofa in the library and closed her eyes. So much had happened the past two days! She had finally found a point of connection with Aunt Catherine and didn't even have the chance to explore it further; her paintings were gone, and now she had the opportunity to exhibit her work in a gallery in England. It was a lot to digest in such a short period of time.

Something else knocked at the door of consciousness, and she focused on the fleeting thought. Ryan Wheeler! She had completely forgotten about him! She wondered if he had gone by her place to see her. With Aunt Catherine being taken to the hospital in such a hurry, she hadn't thought of their scheduled meeting at all. Lakeisha interrupted her thoughts when she entered the room carrying a white envelope in her right hand. "Here you go; Miss Catherine told me she wrote it last night."

Natalie took the letter and thanked Lakeisha, who nodded and quietly left the room. A familiar scent of lavender delicately expanded throughout as soon as the envelope came open, and it momentarily overpowered the lemony aroma of the furniture polish.

Dearest Natalie,

By the time you read this letter I will probably already be gone. I suppose that I should apologize for all the years I have been unkind and quite judgmental toward you. I rest at peace as I think that once you hear my story you will understand a great deal more.

Many years ago – approximately four years before your birth – I became involved with a married man, and a child was conceived from that relationship. My family wanted nothing to do with the baby, especially since there was no possibility I could wed the father. So, they sent me away to London, and told all their friends that I had gone abroad to further my studies. I barely had the chance to see my daughter's little face before they took her away from me, and to this day I am haunted by the memory of it. I came back to the United States with no child and a broken heart, and I vowed to never fall in love again.

But love did indeed find me – once more with the wrong person. I fell in love with a young man my sister had become acquainted with, and I was swept off my feet. He was very nice and intelligent, and he was studying to become an attorney. I spent my days dreaming of the moment he would come forth and declare his love, but that day never came. Instead, he fell in love with your mother, and within a year they were married. My heart was broken again, but I kept silent and wished them to be happy. They tried to have a baby almost immediately with no luck. Unable to bear children and convinced it was her fault, your mother became quite depressed, and your father soon looked for solace elsewhere. He came to my home, one night after work, and the two of us became intimate. The next day, your father left, and we reached a silent agreement that nothing more would ever happen, and nobody would know about it.

As time passed and your mother appeared to be quickly drowning in her own despair, Phillip had to take matters into his own hands, and started looking for a child to adopt. I begged him to take my daughter in, if she hadn't yet been adopted – I left her in a convent of nuns – but he refused and said that he couldn't possibly raise the daughter of someone who had been his mistress even if only for one night.

When you arrived, you were a breath of fresh air for your mother and a death sentence for my dream of seeing my daughter again. In my heart, although it wasn't rational, I felt you robbed her of her chance to be reunited with me. That is why I resented you all these years. Every success you could possibly achieve was painful for me to witness because it could have been her success, and every time something unpleasant happened to you I always reasoned that it wasn't as bad as losing a mother.

I know I was wrong, Natalie, and I ask for your forgiveness. I am going to meet the Lord without knowing whether you will ever find in your heart the strength to understand. I never meant to hurt you, and I was secretly proud of the milestones you conquered. If you look in my closet, behind the suitcases and the extra linens, you will find a small door leading to a secret room in the house I only knew the existence of, and used as a studio. In there you will find several paintings I completed without anyone knowing. They are yours to keep, if you wish to have a small reminder of my presence in your life.

Now please allow me to move on to something that weighs heavily on my heart.

About a year ago Tom, the gentleman you will meet in London, thought he had some leads in finding my daughter, and I began to prepare for the reunion, in the event that one could become possible. I was going to give her one of my pieces of jewelry to remember me by, but as I walked in front of Hidden Treasures something drew me in. If I believed in ghosts, I would say that a spirit guided me to a very unusual rosary, and the moment I held it in my hand, I felt something strange - a sudden rush of warmth that overtook my entire being. The sensation only lasted for a moment, but it left me quite shaken. I put the rosary back down and began to look at other things, but I felt drawn to it again. I finally bought it and brought it home – it is inside a small velvet pouch in the paint closet toward the back of the studio. I was always afraid to pull it out again, and have left it untouched since. If you can find my daughter I would like for her to have it. In the event that your paths will not cross, please keep it for yourself, but never give it to anyone else, aside, maybe, to a child of your own, if you will have one.

So, this is my story. I am sure you are shocked and perhaps a bit hurt by the way things played out. I am sorry about the brief affair with your father; please know that it was a moment of weakness for both of us, and neither meant to hurt your mother. To my knowledge, she doesn't know about it, and I trust that you will spare her from a disturbing piece of truth which is nothing but ancient history. Your father truly loved her then as much as he does now, and his behavior didn't, in any way, reflect the depth of his feelings for her.

Take care Natalie, and take your art all the way to the moon. If I am reserved a place in Heaven, I promise that I will always look out for you. I disappointed you in life, but I will not do so in death.

Yours always,
Aunt Catherine.

Below the closing was Tom's full address in London and his phone number. Natalie gently folded the letter and quickly brushed away tears. Poor Aunt Catherine…only now Natalie understood how filled with pain her life had been. The baby in question was by now a thirty-something-year-old woman living in another country – good luck finding her.

She stood up from the couch, tucked the letter inside her skirt pocket, and literally ran up the stairs leading to Aunt Catherine's room. She went straight to the closet and searched with her hand behind the linens. She immediately felt a latch and her heart skipped a beat. She pushed the linens aside, opened the door, and ran her hand on the wall to find a switch or a pull cord; she was happy when she detected a small plastic knob. A sudden flood of white light washed away the darkness and exposed a sparsely furnished studio; she stepped in saw an easel situated in the center of the room, the stains of paint on it dried and filmed with dust. Some of Aunt Catherine's paintings adorned the otherwise bare walls, and a few sketches were laid out on a table nearby. Natalie ran her hand gently over the sketches, strangely worried about disturbing the layout, before heading toward the shelf adjacent to the wall. She opened one of the doors and saw a generous supply of different colors and brushes; below the paint, a stack of paintings were laid against the back of the shelf. The portrait of a child smiled at her from the shadows – the daughter Aunt Catherine lost? She pulled out the painting and looked at it. The child was happy, and was portrayed looking up toward a blue balloon, smiling gleefully.

The other paintings were mostly abstract, and Natalie felt that Aunt Catherine had used brush and canvas to express her most hidden feelings. They were all quite sad and void of bright colors, but their quality was striking. And finally she found the velvet pouch. She opened it and pulled out an exquisite rosary with gems of different colors. Instinctually she held it to her heart and she was suddenly transported back to her dream; once again she was standing in front of herself. After a moment she was back in the room, scared but also feeling strangely empowered. She put the rosary back into the pouch and slid it into her pocket near the letter, then picked up a few of the paintings and headed out.

With the paintings obliterating her view, she didn't notice Lakeisha standing quietly behind the door of the adjacent room. Lakeisha was now quite certain that finding a job at Catherine Bouvier's home was all but random. The prophecy was indeed on its way to being fulfilled.

Chapter Five

When she finally reached home and checked her messages, Natalie was mortified to hear five of them were from Ryan Wheeler. Although he tried to be polite in all of them, it was clear that he was quite annoyed with being stood up. She decided to call him back right away, and almost wished he wouldn't answer. But, of course, he did.

"Hello"

"Ryan, this is Natalie Sanders. I am so sorry about today, but there was an emergency and I had to leave in a rush."

Ryan cleared his throat before replying. "An emergency? What happened?'

"It was Aunt Catherine, Ryan. She was taken to the hospital this morning, and she passed away this afternoon. Acute congestive heart failure, the doctor said. It appears that her heart was already damaged by mild heart attacks she suffered in the past."

"Oh my God, I had no idea. Are you okay?"

Natalie swallowed the knot she felt in her throat and tried her best to remain in control of her emotions.

"I'm as good as can be expected, I guess. She was a nice lady." As she spoke those words, Natalie looked up toward the ceiling.

There you go, Aunt Catherine. I suppose you are forgiven. I never thought so before, but I really think you are a nice lady, and I wish now I could have known you better…

"I am so sorry, Natalie. Is there anything I can do?"

"Everything happened so suddenly that I am not entirely sure what needs to be done. My mother is taking care of the arrangements but I haven't heard any details yet."

And I'm sure I'll be the last one to hear. The neighbors will find out before me…

"Listen, Natalie, may I come by tomorrow? I know there is little I can do, but unless you're planning on spending time with your family I would really like to be there with you and for you."

"I would really like to have a little time to grieve on my own, Ryan. I'm sure you understand."

"Of course I do. How inconsiderate of me. Will you please call me when you find out details about the wake and the funeral?"

"Of course…."

"Take care, Natalie."

"You too, Ryan. And thank you."

She hung up and sat back on the sofa. Billy appeared from the bedroom and loudly demanded the attention he lacked throughout the afternoon. She scratched under his chin – to which he responded with a purring serenade – and closed her eyes. There was so much she needed to process that right now she felt completely overwhelmed. She glanced at the paintings she had left by the door, and felt a sharp pain shoot through her heart. Could a heart truly be broken? She thought of Aunt Catherine's one-time affair with her father, and felt her stomach lurch at the mere thought of the next family gathering. Jokes apart, Aunt Catherine's funeral was going to be arranged within the next few days, and there was no way she could escape that sentence. Not that she wanted to. If only after her death, Aunt Catherine had done something wonderful – for the first time in her life Natalie felt she belonged with someone in her family, faults and all.

What about the rosary Aunt Catherine bought for her daughter? Was there something special about it? She was well aware of her overactive imagination, but she knew that something very strange happened when she held it in her hand. Reliving the images of her dream in such vivid detail was something she hadn't expected, and the whole episode caught her by surprise and electrified her. Somehow, she knew that what happened in the dream was an omen for something real to manifest. She stood up abruptly, hoping the shift of pressure would clear her mind, and she headed to the kitchen to make some coffee. Coffee was probably not a good idea at this time in the evening, but she needed the comfort of something warm, and tea just didn't sound bold enough.

While the coffee brewed she changed into her night clothes and washed her face. When she looked up to reach for the towel, she gasped at what she saw. The woman looking back at her from the mirror didn't look as weak as she felt right now, and she instantly thought back about her dream. She closed her eyes for a moment, and when she opened them again, the strange image was gone. Her eyes were playing tricks on her – or maybe it was her mind. She remembered reading once that the human brain can only temporarily store a limited amount of information before having the opportunity to sort it during sleep. Natalie's brain had reached capacity; in fact, it was probably beginning to overflow.

She went to the kitchen to get her coffee and went straight to bed with the mug in one hand and the velvet pouch in the other. She placed the rosary under her pillow and took a few sips of coffee. Despite the caffeine, her eyelids felt suddenly very heavy, so she placed the mug on the side table, hoping that Billy would not knock it off during his night-time acrobatics. The moment her head touched the pillow, sleep whisked her away. That night, Aunt Catherine was happy that Natalie forgave her.

Melody Bennet was already in bed when she heard Mario open the main door and walk into the house. He worked exceptionally late hours lately, and she was beginning to feel the loneliness of the many evenings she spent alone at the farm. She heard him drop his keys on the small table at the entrance, and go to the kitchen to get some water. He was such a man of routine that Melody knew he was going to use the bathroom next, and then he was going to come upstairs to bed. That was the part of his routine she liked most, and she almost giggled when the shadow of his statuesque body materialized in the darkness of the room. He lay down carefully, afraid to wake her, but she reached out to grab his leg from under the covers and scared the daylights out of him.

"Melody! You're going to give me a heart attack one of these days."

She laughed and ran her arms around his chest, drawing him closer to herself, deeply inhaling the soft smell of lingering tobacco mixed with his natural scent. "God forbid. What would I do for pleasure if you had a heart attack?"

"That's exactly right, Missy. So think about it next time."

"Well, there is really only one thing I can think of right now." She winked in the darkness of the room and wondered if Mario saw that.

That thought was quickly shot down by the ripples of delight she felt cursing through her body as Mario turned around and kissed her deeply. His hot tongue pushed against the line of her teeth and she eagerly opened her mouth to taste him. His hands cupped her face and then slid down to her breast with the skill of a master. He gently squeezed her nipples between his fingers and she groaned inwardly. She reached out to touch him and shivered when her fingers touched pure steel beautifully wrapped in tanned, glistening skin. He took her nipples in his mouth, and his tongue played with them until Melody arched her body to feel closer to him. As his mouth slid down her stomach and went down to her center of pleasure, Melody felt raw fire rising up inside of her, engulfing her swollen and pulsating core. She exploded into a powerful orgasm, followed by a wave of peace, as Mario gently moved his body on top of her and entered her slowly. He rode her body with passion, and each of his small cries was one more arrow into Melody's heart. God, she loved him so! When he was finally spent, he remained on top of her for a while, his breathing still hard and his heart thumping furiously against her breasts. She wrapped her arms around him, eager to make this moment last. When he finally rolled off of her she sighed happily.

"Wow! That was some homecoming." His breathing was still hard.

"I love you Mario"

"And I love you, Melody." He kissed her lips gently, sealing a wonderful moment he hadn't expected.

"I thought you were going to be asleep; it's past two in the morning."

"I started reading a new novel and really got into the story. I had just turned off the light when I heard you coming in."

Mario smiled and his white teeth glistened in the darkness of the room. "Well, lucky me, then. I need to send that author a little thank you note."

They hugged and fell quickly asleep, their bodies happily spent and their minds thankful that in a world filled with hate, love could still be found.

It was three o'clock in the morning, but Lakeisha still could not find sleep. She accurately detailed her report to Sister Justine, and told her about the rosary. Just writing about it brought a strange sensation upon her, and she could swear she had seen *something* when Natalie took it out of the pouch, but wasn't sure what. How could Lakeisha have missed that door? The moment she saw the rosary in Natalie's hand, everything began to make sense to her – finding a job at the Bouvier's home the moment she got into town was not a coincidence as she had originally thought. What was she supposed to do now? Catherine Bouvier was dead, and Lakeisha knew she wasn't supposed to interfere with divine plans. She hoped that Sister

Justine could come up with a plan of action, because it was going to be very hard to protect something that was kept twenty miles away from where she was. She had the distinct feeling of not being alone in the room, and looked around several times to find only shadows. Suddenly she heard a sound coming from downstairs, and her heart leaped. Who, or what, could it be at this time?

She donned her robe and opened the door of her room. She called out into the darkness of the hallway. "Hello? Is someone there?"

She heard nothing. She listened quietly for a moment, and was ready to retreat back into her room when she heard it again. It sounded like a cane being tapped gently on a hard floor.

"Hello? Mr. Phillip? Is that you?"

No answer.

"Mrs. Angela? Is somebody there? Natalie?"

She ran through the list of names in her mind to see if she could think of anyone who might have a key to the house – she couldn't think of a single soul, apart from the Sanders.

She went back into her room and grabbed the fireplace poker from its stand, then went back out and stretched her arm to turn on the chandelier in the hallway. Bright light flooded the staircase, and Lakeisha felt a wave of relief wash over her -- darkness has a unique way of magnifying the spooks, especially in an old house like this one. She went slowly down the stairs and heard the tapping sound again.

Tap. Tap. Tap.

What on earth could it be?

She walked across the foyer and quickly turned on all the lights using the panel by the front door. "Who's there? Please identify yourself, I have a weapon and I will use it."

Tap. Tap. Tap.

The sound was coming from the kitchen. Oh God, had someone come in from the back door? It didn't sound good at all – why would anyone who had any legitimate business in this household come through the service door? And at three o'clock in the morning of all visiting hours!

Tap. Tap. Tap.

It was getting closer. Lakeisha felt fear slithering like a snake in her gut. She was terrified. She turned on the kitchen light and saw something on the table. She scanned the room first, to make sure no one was hiding in the corners that weren't visible from the doorway, and when she felt that the whole area was free of humans and spooks, she finally made her way to the table to identify the object that caught her eye. A strong scent of cigar filled the air, and Lakeisha could swear she heard sounds that reminded her of soft laughter coming from the library. Of course, she knew it could be auditory and olfactory illusion, influenced by being alone in an empty, old house, but even trying to rationalize what she smelled and heard didn't help. With her heart threatening to jump into her throat and with shaky legs, she looked at the small shining object on the table: A key. When she picked it up and turned it around, she saw the initials USPS…it was the key to a post office box. She held the key tight in her hand and closed her eyes, as she knew damn well it wasn't on the table before she went upstairs. *He* had been here; now there was no denying that things were in fast motion.

She put the key into the pocket of her robe, then headed back up to her room keeping the fireplace poker down at her side. She wasn't in any danger – that much she knew. As she climbed the steps, she wondered what could be in the box and where the post office was located. A morning call to the main line of the postal service would certainly clear that question, and Lakeisha felt that everything else would be answered in time. She turned off the light in the hallway and walked into her room. While she closed the door she heard the sound one final time.

Tap. Tap. Tap.

Elegba left the house.

Melody carried a basket of laundry downstairs and set it down in the kitchen while she opened windows and made some fresh iced tea. Having been raised in the south she was addicted to both – fresh air and good sweet tea. Since this early in the morning it was still cool enough to open windows and let some air in, she decided that it was a good day to treat herself to both pleasures. The phone rang and she answered it while she stirred sugar into the tea; it was Olivia, her cousin from New Orleans.

'Hey Melody, how are you?"

"I'm great, Olivia. What about you? Are you having cold feet yet?"

"Nope. My feet are nice and toasty. I can't wait! I've always wanted to go to London, but I never even dreamt that someday I would get married there."

"I'm so happy for you, Olivia! How's Graham?"

"Oh, he's excited, too. It looks more and more that we will be able to arrange for the Spencer House. I'm so excited!

"You should be. A grand wedding in a beautiful British setting – that's fairytale stuff."

"Melody, sometimes I wonder if I'm going to wake up and be disappointed that it was just a nice dream."

"Well, look at it this way, Olivia. I've been married to Mario for two years, and I'm still living the dream. I'm sure it will be the same for you and Graham."

"Dad is beside himself, Melody. He said that he has never been so sad and happy at the same time."

"Can you blame him Olivia? His little girl is growing up and getting married in London. I would be a mess in his place. I think he's actually holding up quite well, all considered."

Olivia laughed. "Yeah, of course you're right. I suppose I shouldn't worry. I'm just afraid to get hurt. I heard this expression in a song once, and I think it applies to me - sometimes *I am* happier than should be legally possible."

Olivia's happiness was nearly tangible and Melody felt it travel through the phone line and touch her own heart. She sighed and inhaled a deep lungful of fresh air coming through the window. Johnny, the new farmhand she hired after Charlie died, must have planted something that put out a strong citrus scent; she resolved to ask him later what kind of plant it was. She could even smell it in the laundry she had begun to sort out and throw in the washing machine while on the phone.

"Stop worrying Olivia. You will marry Graham, the two of you will have a wonderful wedding, and you will live happily ever after."

"I hope you are right, Melody. Did you already make reservations?"

Melody thought for a moment; she didn't remember Mario telling her that he did. "I don't think so, Olivia, but I will ask Mario when he wakes up. He got home very late last night and he is still sleeping. He is working all the time; getting a promotion is not all that it's cracked up to be. I know he is excited that he is growing in his career, but sometimes I think he was happier when he was a simple detective with the sheriff's department, rather than a big shot at the SBI."

"Tell me about it" Olivia answered, "Since I took the new job as assistant manager at the hotel I work at right now, I work constantly. Good were the days when I used to be paid hourly. Being salaried means only one thing – you work like hell and make little money per hour. Last week I worked close to sixty hours. Graham was a bit annoyed with me about it, but he understood I had no choice."

"I'm afraid Mario hasn't either. That's part of the promotion game. How's your dad, Olivia?"

"He is doing well. I think that excitement is good for him – he looks younger and he has more energy than normal."

That bit of news did Melody's heart good. Although she hadn't known her uncle Paul many years – he had left North Carolina and relocated to his native Louisiana before Melody was born – she had grown very fond of him the last couple of years. Paul was a good man, and Melody loved to talk to him on the phone. He had a rich southern accent and a baritone's voice, and he somehow reminded her of a big cuddly bear.

"That's wonderful to hear, Olivia. Well, I'd better go if I want to get some chores out of the way before lunch."

"Yeah, same here" replied Olivia, "I need to get ready for work. Take care, and make sure your reservations are secured."

"Yes Ma'am. Too bad you aren't here to do it for me." Melody still remembered how efficient Olivia was at her job when she first met her at the hotel in New Orleans.

"Oh, I can, if you want me to."

"Olivia! I'm joking. You've got plenty more to worry about, with that wedding of yours to plan and prepare for. I'll let Mario take care of it – he's just as precise as you are when it comes to things like that."

The word 'anal' had actually come to mind, but Melody didn't know Olivia that intimately, and didn't know if her cousin was good at catching hidden humor or if she was easily offended; 'precise' had seemed a better choice.

"Take care Olivia, and I will talk to you in the next few days."

"Sounds great, Melody. Tell Mario I said hello."

"Will do. Bye, Olivia."

Melody hung up the phone and went back to her laundry. The wind must have shifted, because she couldn't smell the scent in the breeze any more. While she waited for the clothes to finish washing she went to straighten out the living room and heard sounds upstairs. Mario was finally up, and Melody rushed to the kitchen to start a fresh pot of coffee for him. She loved when they had a chance to eat breakfast together, so she looked in the refrigerator to find something she could prepare. Melody was not much of a cook, but she had really tried to catch up the last few years. She wished that Grandmama's ghost could come and help her with pots and pans, sometimes – nobody else she knew could cook as good as her grandmother. Mario came into the kitchen and walked up to her from behind; he wrapped his arms around her and kissed her neck while she was still standing in front of the refrigerator trying to strategize a meal.

"Good morning, Beautiful."

"Good morning, Honey, did you sleep well?

"Not so well, really. I kept hearing sounds coming from outside, and I even got up one time to make sure nobody was there."

"Hmm, that's odd…I didn't hear anything. Maybe it was a raccoon, Grandpapa Henry always complained about them."

In reality it wasn't too odd – Melody usually slept like a rock.

She turned toward Mario to kiss him back and noticed the dark circles under his eyes.

"Oh my…you really didn't sleep, did you? You look very tired."

"I *am* tired, exhausted really, but unfortunately I have to run. I have a meeting at eleven."

"Will you be home for dinner?"

"I'll try -- that's the best I can give you at the moment." He saw the disappointment in her eyes and reached out to touch her face; she laid her head in the palm of his hand.

"I'm sorry, Melody. I promise this won't last forever. We have a big case that we have been trying to crack for months. We finally seem to be on the right track, so I have to be there. I will make it up to you."

Melody smiled at him. "I know. I don't mean to sound so needy. It's just that I miss you, that's all."

"Don't forget we are going to London in just a few weeks. Nobody will be able to stop us from having a blast together then."

Melody flashed him a huge smile. "I can't wait! I was just talking to Olivia a little while ago, and she was wondering if we have already confirmed our reservations. I told her that you are in charge."

"Everything is confirmed already. I'm going to pick up the plane tickets within two weeks. In fact, it's good that you brought it up, because we have to really get started on the paperwork to renew passports; I think we can do that by mail. Any chance you can look into that?"

"Sure. I will check on the procedures in a little while."

"You are a jewel. How did I get that lucky?" He pulled her toward himself and squeezed her affectionately. Melody giggled.

"Hmmm…everybody gets a strike of good luck in life. You were just smart enough to see your chance passing by and you jumped on the wagon before it was gone."

"Well, I'd better hurry on."

"Oh, wait, I am making coffee."

Mario glimpsed at his watch. "Can I take that to go?"

"Coming up." Melody opened one of the cupboards and took out a travel mug. She filled it with coffee and handed it to him. "Here you go. Have a great day, Honey."

Mario took the mug and brushed her lips with a kiss. "You too. I love you." And with that he was gone.

Melody poured a cup of coffee for herself and walked outside on the porch. It was a glorious morning, warm and peaceful. She sat on one of the rockers, took a sip, then looked around the front yard. Mario had mentioned hearing noises last night. Was someone here? And if they were, what could they want? She thought about Charlie, the old farmhand who was senselessly killed by a vagrant after Charlie caught him sleeping in the barn two years before. She focused her attention on the steaming cup in her hands. If someone was looking for something at the farm, she wasn't going to worry about it this morning. Right now she just wanted to enjoy the peace and know that everything was well in her world, even if she knew in her heart that the peaceful feeling wasn't going to last much longer.

Chapter Six

Lakeisha Jackson walked into the small post office near the Bouvier house, and hoped it was the right one. Since she didn't have a car, she wasn't fond of venturing across town if she had a choice in the matter. The post office was situated in an old house, and she found comfort in the fact that the postal workers standing behind the counter looked about as ancient as the building itself. She appreciated the wisdom of old people, and felt that if decisions were left more to the elderly we would live in a better world – definitely a more peaceful one. No other patrons were inside when she walked in, so she headed straight to the counter, holding the small silver key in her hand.

"Good morning Ma'am" The silver-haired gentleman nodded politely from behind the counter, "can I help you?"

"Yes. My niece sent me this key and asked me to go retrieve her mail, but I forgot what location she told me. You know how young people are…I hate to ask her again."

The man nodded in understanding, as if Lakeisha had spoken an undeniable truth.

"Could you tell me which post office would have this box, just by looking at the key?"

He took the key from Lakeisha and looked at the number.

"You are in luck, Miss. It's at this location."

Lakeisha was relieved. "For real? Oh, that's wonderful! Now I don't have to take the bus or catch a cab just to fetch my niece's mail. Where are the boxes located?"

The gentleman pointed at the hallway around the corner from the counter. "Right that way, Ma'am. You just need to find the one with a number that matches your key. Simple as pie."

Lakeisha nodded her head in respect. "Thank you so much, Sir."

He nodded and went back to weighing some packages stacked up on the side of his work station.

She walked toward the boxes and looked at the key to see the number. The matching box was to her left, so she inserted the key in the lock and turned it until the box opened to reveal a postcard from London and a travel magazine. Strangely enough, the photo on the cover of the magazine featured the London Eye, a giant Ferris wheel situated near the Thames River in London. Two apparently unrelated items indicating London…could it be coincidence? Lakeisha felt suddenly nervous. She sensed that something bigger than her was at work and she hoped it was something she could handle. She shook her head the moment doubt crossed her mind. If God put her in charge of a certain task, then she was pretty sure she also had the means to take care of it – they didn't make mistakes in their recruiting department up there. What could be happening in London? Was she supposed to go there? And if so, why? She took both the postcard and the magazine and quickly stuffed them in her handbag; then she left.

It was a beautiful morning, sunny and slightly breezy – a change of pace and a welcome relief from the muggy days of late – and Lakeisha would have loved to take a walk, but she was eager to go back home and message Sister Justine. The old

Sister would surely know if going to London was what Lakeisha was being guided to do. She walked up the uneven sidewalk, feeling under her feet the roots of the centuries-old trees that lined the street on both sides, the Spanish moss dripping from their branches a charming reminder that although she was quite far from New Orleans she was still in the south.

She got home and crossed the shady yard, hurrying up the path to the porch. She went inside and made some tea to sooth her nerves, then went up the stairs and fired up her laptop. Somehow, knowing that Sister Justine was only a few keyboard strokes away made her feel safe, so she recounted all that had happened that morning and the night before, and then hit the send button. She hoped Sister Justine wasn't too far from her computer. While she waited for the good sister's reply she went back downstairs to see if the water was boiling. She poured some in a cup over a tea bag and waited for it to steep. She was still a little shaken and wondered how long it would take Sister Justine to check her inbox. At that precise moment, her cell phone rang from inside the purse she had accidentally left on the kitchen counter upon entering and she jumped from her chair, but recomposed herself quickly before answering.

"Hello, this is Lakeisha Jackson."

"Sister Lakeisha, this is Sister Justine."

Lakeisha felt relief spread through every cell of her body. "I am blessed, Sister. I assume you got my message."

"I did. There is obviously no time to waste. The signs are coming in closer."

Lakeisha nodded automatically. "I know. I have been wondering what I need to do now."

"You are not paying attention, Sister. It seems to me the guidance is quite clear."

"With all due respect, Sister Justine, I don't understand. I am guided to go to London, but where in London, and why?"

"Sister, you appear to be thinking that your intellect has to be kept informed of all strategic plans, when you know perfectly well that not knowing is sometimes best."

Lakeisha listened carefully, and Sister Justine continued. "You mustn't ask of your purpose in the unfolding of the prophecy; you only need to humbly go where you are needed, with no questions asked."

"But who needs me in London? How can I protect someone whose identity I'm not privy of?"

"You are asking me questions I have no answer for, Sister. It will all be revealed to you in due time. Some of those truths are not for me to know, you understand. I shall wire funds to you immediately."

"I understand, Sister, and as always you are the wise one. I will pay closer attention to the signs that are sent my way, and will try to adhere to the guidance without wondering about the validity of the path I am led to follow."

"Very well, Sister Lakeisha. If anything important happens, please include it in your daily report."

"I will. Please pray for me, Sister Justine."

"You are blessed, Sister Lakeisha. Your role in this great design is one of the puzzle pieces that will complete a great vision."

"I am blessed. Thank you, Sister. I will be in touch."

Lakeisha terminated the call and went to pull the tea bag out from the cup. The bag had broken, and the tea leaves had settled on the bottom of the cup. The tea was warm and soothing and worked like a balm on her heightened senses. After taking the last sip she noticed the leaves had formed a strange shape on the bottom, something that slightly resembled the Roman number two – two identical vertical lines side by side, encased between two horizontal lines. She looked at the shape for a second and then rinsed the cup and placed it in the dishwasher.

Today, she planned on packing some of Catherine Bouvier's things, just to help the family a little, so she headed in the direction of the stairs. Her thoughts were on the prophecy, and although she knew that all that was lining up was part of a divine plan, she couldn't help feeling a little apprehensive about the days ahead. For a second, she thought she saw something moving in the drawing room beside the staircase, but when she focused her attention in that direction, everything appeared still and untouched. She wondered if the spirit of Catherine Bouvier was still in the house, and felt instantly compelled to say a prayer for the old lady. Catherine never found peace while alive – hopefully God would have pity on her tortured soul.

Catherine Bouvier looked around the room searching for a sense of familiarity. Her memories were fading fast, and although she knew she was in her own house, the place felt foreign by now, and she knew that she was close to crossing over. Upon passing, she had seen an old man; he was tall and dressed in a smart black suit, and he had a red carnation in his lapel. His extravagant attire included a Fedora hat which he pulled off his head in sign of respect when she walked through the door. His hair was gray and his skin the tone of strong mocha, but what mesmerized Catherine most was his ice-melting smile. She noticed that he limped slightly, and used a cane to move around. Strangely enough, it wasn't the first time she and this man crossed paths – even as her memory of earthly events was fading fast, she remembered seeing him browsing tables at Hidden Treasures the day that she bought the rosary for her daughter. His unusually elegant attire caught her eye, that day, but she never thought she would meet him again.

Natalie was going to London, he told her, but there was a higher purpose to her trip -- a divine one, entirely different than what Catherine believed while she was still alive. He also informed Catherine that there was one final thing for her to do before crossing over completely, and in due time she would find out the details. As he waited for her to fulfill her final task, he leaned against a wall and lit a pipe. "I'm in no hurry" he told Catherine "after all time is but a human invention."

Ryan Wheeler sat in his office and pinched the bridge of his nose in the fleeting hope to erase the bone-crunching fatigue he felt. He was up late several nights in a row, trying to figure ways to delay the unavoidable, but felt that trouble was catching up with him faster than he could run. The bank called several times already and he had instructed his secretary, Jill, to tell everyone he was out on business. He had to come up with a solution and he couldn't afford any delays. Natalie could be the name of the solution, but she was playing hard to get. Especially now that Catherine Bouvier was gone, Ryan felt that his instinct was on the right track. Natalie was certainly going to inherit the old lady's estate, as there were no other descendants in the family tree, and a merger between the Wheelers and the Sanders could make the difference between life and death.

He heard this morning that Catherine Bouvier's funeral was scheduled for Saturday afternoon at two o'clock, and he felt that it was the perfect time to get through to Natalie. The poor girl was going to be vulnerable and not quite as guarded – a golden opportunity for Ryan to work his magic on her. He jotted the time and date on his calendar to ensure that other commitments wouldn't get in the way, then had his secretary look up the number of a florist in Carolina Beach and personally ordered two dozen white roses to be delivered to Natalie Sanders.

The flower shop attendant asked him what he wished to write on the note to go with the flowers, and Ryan thought for a minute. Words were very important at this juncture, and he had to pick each of them with precision and wit. He finally came up with the perfect note – "Natalie, Aunt Catherine is forever alive in the hearts of her friends. I know she will always be proud to be alive in yours. Your friend always, Ryan."

It sounded good -- affectionate but not invasive. He had a feeling that Natalie Sanders was not a woman that could be pushed around easily, and Ryan had to play his cards right. Someone like her would accept a friend but would be weary of a romantic, eager lover. He would start with friendship; the rest would follow in time.

Belinda Allen left the shop early today, not feeling too well and fearing that she, too, was a victim of that nasty spring virus everyone talked about. Her head was pounding and her stomach was disturbed, and for the past hour she had constant chills that even the warm air of a southern afternoon in May could not push away. Business was pretty slow anyway; with the spring recital at the church, most residents had gone to attend the show, and the majority of tourists had taken advantage of the amazing weather to enjoy a day at the beach. She decided to stop by the drugstore on the way home to see if the pharmacist, Mr. Lewis, could suggest anything to kill the symptoms, and she got home with a bag of medicated saline drops, Advil and some new miracle cure for the flu that some of the other afflicted residents had sworn by.

She looked at her watch before taking the miracle medicine and saw that it was nearly dinner time – not that she could eat anything, with her stomach in knots as it was. She made a sour face as she sipped the vile red liquid which was supposed to taste like cherry but was closer in flavor to rotten plums, and she changed into her flannel pajamas in spite of the fact that the thermostat in the hallway indicated the temperature in the house as being seventy-eight degrees. Belinda wasn't sure whether the medicine she took was indeed miraculous, but she knew that it hit her faster and harder than a two-by-four. She couldn't keep her eyelids from closing, and after fighting a very short battle with her fuzzy brain, she lay down in bed and fell asleep. She never heard the phone ring, and slept right through the sirens of the police vehicles that passed right in front of her house. Had she not been drugged and unconscious, Belinda would know, by now, that someone broke into her shop.

Natalie finally got out of bed after sleeping nearly all day. She had woken up several times but lacked the strength to truly get moving, and lay there watching mindless TV, wasting a good day she could have used to paint by the shore. She stood up and stretched, and then went to shower and dress, although the day was officially almost over. After that, she made coffee and decided to call her mother to find out about funeral arrangements.

Of course everything was already in place, and Natalie could have sworn on a Bible that her mother was not even going to call her to inform her of any updates, had she not called herself. A memorial service was scheduled for Saturday at two in the afternoon, and Aunt Catherine was going to be privately buried in the Bouvier family plot with only family attending. Natalie asked if Aunt Catherine had left any specific instructions regarding funeral arrangements, but her mother blew her off, as she always did. Of course Aunt Catherine's memorial service was going to be a social affair – her mother would see to it.

She thought of calling Tom, Aunt Catherine's friend in London, but a quick calculation told her that it was night time in England, so she made a mental note to call the next day, as soon as she got up.

She went to her studio, trying to decide whether she felt like painting or just lounge around with Billy the cat. She was experiencing a "painter's block" and her mind drew an absolute blank as she stood in front of the white canvas. Rather than getting upset over the lack of inspiration, she mindlessly scanned through the paintings she had collected from Aunt Catherine's house. One of them represented an old man of color. He was wearing a suit and walked with a cane along an unpaved path at the edge of a swamp, probably near the outskirts of New Orleans. Natalie only visited Louisiana once, but she doubted she could ever forget the feel of the place. It was an artist's paradise, especially the area around Jackson Square in the French Quarter, where local painters showcased their talents to tourists in constant hope of making a sale. She remembered walking down streets that resembled the rues of Paris and the times when, sitting by the shore of the Mississippi River and watching tourists board a freshly painted red and white steamboat, she entertained the thought of possibly moving there.

She lined all the paintings against the wall and studied them one at a time – all were exquisite and conveyed a talent that was criminal to hide. She decided to ask Tom if he could display some of them at his gallery and proceeded to inspect the frames – most of them would need to be replaced. She had some extra frames in her studio, so she carefully removed the one around the painting of the old man, and was surprised to see a folded piece of paper fall on her foot. She picked it up and gently opened it – it was a handwritten note from Aunt Catherine.

The gentleman I portrayed is not a figment of my imagination...or maybe he is, but I think I saw him in a store, one day, and felt compelled to paint him.

Natalie smiled, and suddenly felt sad. She really didn't know Aunt Catherine, and she regretted not having more time with her, now that she knew they shared a common passion. She was going to try and find Aunt Catherine's daughter, regardless of how daunting the task was going to be.

"Oh my God, Belinda! You scared me to death. Why didn't you answer the phone?"

Belinda opened her eyes and tried to adjust her focus – her head still felt fuzzy from the medicine she had taken earlier. She saw her husband sitting on the edge of the bed and noticed that he wore an expression etched with deep worry. She sat up and rubbed her eyes with her fingertips. "I took some cold medicine and it must have knocked me out. What's going on?"

"Somebody broke into the shop. They forced the back door open, and got in. I don't think they took anything, though; maybe they got spooked by a passerby."

"Someone broke into *my* shop?!" Belinda felt a shot of adrenaline curse quickly through her body, and the sticky feeling of cobwebs in her head was instantly swept clean by the broom of shock. "Oh Dear, I have to go see."

Jim stopped her by gently placing a hand on her arm. "Wait, Belinda. The police secured the area, and I just left there myself. I already called a locksmith to replace the locks, so you don't have to worry about anyone else trying to get in. Why don't I make you a good cup of tea and we talk about it before you rush out? Especially since you are not feeling good."

Belinda didn't really feel sick right now – fear and deep anxiety had seemingly cured her of her ills – but when she saw the concern on Jim's face she sat back against the pillow and smiled at him. "Thank you, Jim. Thank you for taking care of everything."

Jim smiled back at her. "That's my girl. Now get a little more rest while I go make the tea."

He stood up and walked out of the room heading toward the kitchen.

Belinda wondered who could have broken into the shop - a tourist perhaps? She couldn't imagine any of the locals going after antiques. But why didn't they take anything? Even if spooked and ready to run, there were plenty of small items the thief could have easily picked up and carried out. She knew that Jim would worry if she went out there tonight, so she decided to wait until morning. He had already made sure the locks were replaced, and she could really use a little more rest if she wanted to kick this cold. Jim came back with the tea and some toast with strawberry jam. She didn't really feel hungry, but ate a few bites to please her husband. "I can't believe someone broke in. That kind of scares me a little. We don't see many break-ins in Wilmington, thank goodness."

"Well, don't forget it is almost summer, Belinda; plenty of strangers in the area this time of year."

Belinda nodded – it was the only gesture of acknowledgement she could think of while she chewed the toast. She swallowed and took a big gulp of tea. The warm liquid felt good going down her stinging and swollen throat. "I think you are right, Jim. It really sounds like the type of petty crime committed by a tourist who was trying to get his hands on something he could sell to prolong his vacation."

"Yes, I think so. But tell me more about how you feel now. What's the matter?"

Belinda groaned. "Oh, don't remind me…I had the worst headache and my body felt like I was hit by a truck. That's why I closed a little earlier and came home. I stopped by the drugstore on the way and picked up a decongestant. Boy, that killed me instantly! Nothing serious though, you should go grab something to eat yourself. I bet you haven't had dinner yet, right?"

Jim smiled. "Woman, you know me too well; it's a darn good thing that I wouldn't dream of doing you wrong, or you would catch me in a heartbeat."

Belinda laughed, "You bet I would, so you'd better behave." She winked at him and was pleased to see him blush.

"You know I would never do anything to hurt you, Belinda."

"I know that. You couldn't hurt a fly if it came to eat your last bite of food."

Jim stayed for another moment and then went to the kitchen to see if he could come up with a quick meal for himself. He moved through the house and never thought of closing the blinds. The man hiding in the shadows was very happy about that.

Chapter Seven

It was almost nine in the morning when Natalie opened her eyes. Billy was meowing madly and occasionally pawed at her face in his unique feline attempt to wake her up. She looked around the room and observed the color contrast of some of the hanging prints against the sun-washed wall, but Billy was hungry, and wouldn't allow her to waste an extra minute indulging her artistic eye.

She slowly got up and stumbled toward the kitchen to feed the cat and make coffee. While the coffee brewed she opened the blinds and looked outside. Mrs. Thompson, her neighbor across the street, was busy watering the flower boxes on her porch, and Ms. Nettie was furiously sweeping sand off the entrance of her Inn, getting ready for another day of hospitality.

Natalie smiled. The scene outside was a familiar and comforting one, yet, this time of year, it was slightly different everyday thanks to the crowds of tourists floating around. She found herself laughing out loud when a particular episode popped in her mind – just a week before, one of the families staying at Miss Nettie's place had taken advantage of the pet-friendly status, and had decided to take their pet python on vacation. Since they didn't bother telling Miss Nettie about it, she had no idea it was a pet she was facing when she went in to bring fresh linens and found a four-foot snake greeting her from the fake tree in the left corner of the room. Obviously this family didn't believe in keeping the snake locked up in its glass case while they went to soak in the sun and jump in the waves.

The brief episode cost the family a pet deposit and Miss Nettie a close call with a heart attack. To this day, anytime she walked into any of the rooms, Ms. Nettie went in with a watchful eye, stopping briefly on the doorstep before walking in.

A steamy snorting sound announced that coffee was ready, so Natalie poured herself a cup and walked into the living room to get the phone. She remembered Aunt Catherine's letter was still tucked in her skirt pocket from the day before, so she went to get it before finally settling on the sofa.

She still couldn't believe all the things she had learned about her aunt from that letter, and in so many ways she wished Aunt Catherine had told her about her life before, when Natalie still had the opportunity to draw closer. Unfortunately there was little she could do now, aside, maybe, from doing justice to Catherine Bouvier's hidden talents by convincing Tom in England to exhibit some of his old friend's paintings. Natalie was more eager to earn some recognition for her aunt than she was excited about showing her own work.

She dialed Tom's number and waited for him to answer. He finally came on the line.

"Hello, this is Tom Hadley"

"Mr. Hadley, this is Natalie Sanders, Catherine Bouvier's niece. I believe my aunt called you a few days ago to discuss the possibility of exhibiting some of my work in your gallery."

"Yes, yes, of course, Miss Sanders. How are you?"

Tom Hadley's voice – deep and quite cultured – introduced him as a man of stature, and Natalie immediately wondered what he might look like.

"Unfortunately I am mourning, Mister Hadley. I'm sure you haven't heard, but Catherine passed away in illness a few days ago."

He gasped on the other side of the line, then, he cleared his throat.

"Oh dear, I am so sorry, Miss Sanders. Please accept my condolences."

"Thank you, Mister Hadley, I really appreciate your kindness."

"I just spoke to Catherine a few days ago, Miss Sanders; when did she…when did she pass away?"

"I believe it was the day after she spoke with you, Sir. She just informed me she was going to talk to you about my work on Tuesday, and she died on Wednesday. It was a sudden thing – acute congestive heart failure, the doctors said, and unfortunately, they weren't able to save her. What kills me is that I didn't even know her condition was so dire. She had a mild heart attack last year, but I thought she had fully recovered from that episode. My mother even hired a nurse to live with Aunt Catherine, to make sure she ate a healthy diet and took her medications."

"Dear…that's awful…"

Natalie could imagine Tom Hadley sadly shaking his head many miles away. "It really is, Mister Hadley. My family is deeply saddened by the loss."

"Your aunt told me you are quite talented." Tom said, "It is very tragic about your paintings".

"It was a hard blow, Sir, but I can paint more. Loss of life is impossible to repair; paintings, no matter how amazing, can be created again."

"You're remarkably wise, young lady. The older I become, the more I realize the same."

"Losing my work felt paralyzing at first, but it stimulated me to create something new. I believe everything happens for a reason."

"So do I, Miss Sanders. I didn't always think this way, but I do now."

Natalie smiled – she was already fond of him and hadn't even met him yet.

"So tell me, Natalie – may I call you Natalie?"

"Of course you can."

"Are all of your paintings gone?"

Natalie thought for a moment. "No, not all of them; most are, but I had a few at home I was still working on when the fire occurred."

"That's great, Miss Sanders. I would like to see them if it is possible."

"I can finish them within a week or two, and send you photos of them, or e-mail them to you, if you would like."

"That would be wonderful, Natalie. E-mail might be faster."

Natalie found it touching that Mister Hadley kept switching between using her first and last names. He was accustomed to formalities, but his attachment to Aunt Catherine was evident through his will to connect with her niece on a more intimate level.

She hesitated for a moment, then decided to ask if he knew about Catherine's paintings.

"Mister Hadley, I have one more question for you, if you will allow me."

"Of course, what is it?"

"Did you know that my aunt painted as well?"

Tom Hadley was quiet for a few moments; then he spoke again, and his voice registered surprise. "Catherine painted? No, I knew nothing about it. She never mentioned anything of the sort to me. What kind of paintings?"

"Mostly portraits and some abstracts. They are quite striking. I am wondering if I could send you photos of those as well."

"Absolutely, Natalie; I would love to see them."

Natalie felt a smile originate straight from her heart and spreading to her face. "That's great! I just know you will love them."

"That will only make me appreciate Catherine more – if that's possible indeed. I am scheduling a show one month from now; do you think you could send me some beforehand, if they are of my liking after I view the photos?"

"I certainly can, Sir. I don't know how I can thank you."

"It's my pleasure, young lady."

"Aunt Catherine would certainly be pleased to know we have connected."

Natalie could hear the smile in Tom Hadley's voice. "I believe she would be, Natalie. She sounded very proud of you on the phone."

Oh, Aunt Catherine…you were proud of me?

Natalie felt a knot in her throat and swallowed quickly to stop tears from rising to her eyes. To her knowledge, nobody had ever been proud of her before. "I will finish the paintings and send the pictures to the e-mail address Aunt Catherine left me, then."

"Thank you Natalie, I look forward to seeing them."

"Thank you again, Mister Hadley. I will be in touch. Good-bye for now."

"Good-bye, Natalie."

Natalie hung up the phone and laid her head on the back of the couch. She liked Tom Hadley, and she was happy he was willing to consider hers and Aunt Catherine's paintings.

You will see, Aunt Catherine, you will no longer be second to anyone. From now on your light will shine brighter than all others.

In that precise moment the sunlight in the room appeared more vibrant, and one of the cards Natalie had purchased last week to send off after the art show and had left on the adjacent dining room table fell to the floor. Natalie walked up to it and picked it up; on it were only two words – "Thank you."

The rosary wasn't at the antique shop. He was quite angry about that, and didn't know what to do at this point. Did Celeste lie to him? He didn't think so, but then, one could only expect so much honesty from a crack whore. Or maybe the old lady at the shop had lied to him; could it be that she was hiding the rosary at home? She didn't seem stupid, and it was entirely possible that she had discovered about the power of the rosary and decided to keep it to herself. Celeste could have rambled to her the same things she told him, especially if she was hoping to strike a fat deal.

There was only one way to find out…he had to get into her house. He followed her and her husband two nights before when they strolled gingerly home after closing her shop, so he knew where she lived. He had one problem – he couldn't risk being seen. He began to explore his possibilities and thought about a variety of scenarios to ensure all bases were covered. He knew she wasn't at work today – not yet, at least – but he expected her to go back soon. He would make sure she was out of the house before going in; he was ready to take care of things as needed, but preferred to avoid unnecessary bloodshed, if at all possible. In fact, he was happy he thought of taking back the card he had given Belinda Allen the day he first walked into the store. The number he wrote on the card was of a Track Phone he had purchased on the way there, but he had to provide a land line number to register the phone, so he knew there was a chance he could be tracked down through that number, and that wouldn't do.

The Allens had the habit of not closing their blinds, so he had an opportunity to study the interiors of the house a bit, and know for sure when someone was home. He laid his head against the seat of the car and lit a cigarette. Every time he thought about the rosary, and felt close to getting his hands on it, he experienced a feeling of euphoria. He needed the power of the rosaries, for himself and for Tess, if he ever hoped to have her in his life. As true to her religion as she was, she couldn't be with a married man, even if he was divorced; in her strict belief, she was convinced that only death could rightfully separate two people that had pledged their lives to one another in front of God. If he could change the course of time, he could take himself back and not get married.

Celeste had done well by telling him. Sadly, he couldn't let her live, given what she knew. He really liked her in a way, and felt that she was a gentle soul without a purpose; unfortunately, drugs ruled her choices, and she would not hold back if someone asked her questions in exchange of cash. So he made sure she was never going to be identified – her fingertips, toes and ears were severed, and all her teeth were pulled out of her mouth. He shaved all her hair as well, and thrown her body far off shore; the fish would take care of the rest, especially after he inserted chunks of bloody meat in all her body cavities.

He doubted that anyone would be looking for her after the shuffle between Louisiana and North Carolina, and the fact that her drug habit had made her a home in the streets even before moving to a different state had certainly played in his favor. In any case, he didn't have to worry about her any further. Celeste Hudson was no more.

He only worried about Belinda Allen now; in fact, he was obsessed with her and the rosary she might be hiding. The more he thought of it, the surer he felt that she had it. Not for long though; his plans were going to be finalized within the next few days.

Sister Justine was worried. Things really seemed to follow an order much different than the one she expected. The rosary was meant to remain in care of the nuns until all prophesied signs were in place, but fate had arranged that it, like The Book of Obeah, would get lost. She needed to get the rosary back, but so far her efforts had been futile.

After discovering that Sister Serene, the original keeper of the rosary, had secretly given it to her niece Celeste, Justine went in search of Celeste to get it back. Shortly after that, Hurricane Katrina ravaged through New Orleans, and people were transported all over different states. During one of her searches, she was told that Celeste had left New Orleans on one of the buses, but nobody seemed to know where she was gone. She sent Sisters to all the locations that were announced on TV, but nobody seemed to have any information about the girl or the rosary. That was until two days ago, when Sister Lakeisha called.

Justine wondered why the old lady in North Carolina had the rosary – Did Celeste give it to her? Lakeisha kept a good watch, but she never saw Celeste around the Bouvier household – the place where Lakeisha had found work as a caregiver, strangely enough – and she doubted the old lady ever met the girl. There was a strong chance that she would never know the exact dynamics, but what mattered was that Sister Lakeisha had identified the sacred rosary as being the one now in possession of Miss Bouvier's niece, Natalie. Maybe Lakeisha could talk to the young lady and explain how important it was for the rosary to go back to its rightful order of keepers.

The Prophecy was clear – only when four pre-determined signs had taken place around the globe, would the elders know it is time. From their chanting and drumming, vibrations would be sent out to affect the realities of the keepers and to direct them – unknown to them - to a secret meeting place.

The first sign, Hurricane Katrina, had already taken place, exposing racial wounds that needed to come to the surface for healing, and The Book of Obeah, after a long and complicated journey, had finally made it into the hands of its final keeper. Of course, the keeper was not aware of this, but he would learn of his role in due time.

The second sign manifested in the global economic crash of 2008. The global financial fall affected the core of humanity and left many feeling extremely vulnerable. When the carpet of material security was pulled from under their feet, those who were meant to stay on Earth during the shift were discovering new meanings of existence, and were opening up to a new level of understanding. Those, instead, who were anchored enough to the old ways didn't agree to remain during the shift, and were quickly departing before all the signs would manifest. Justine didn't understand it all, but knew one thing – the manifestation of the second sign had the purpose to teach humans to rise above fear.

The prophecy spoke of twin rosaries, but although Justine heard of their existence, she had only seen one, and she never touched it. When Lakeisha told her about her visit from Elegba, the Cosmic Prankster, Justine knew that something big was nearing its unfolding, and although she tried her best to reassure the good Sister over the phone, she felt edgy herself. She didn't know what Lakeisha's role was within the secret layout of the plan, but she strongly felt that prayers were needed, and they were needed fast.

Ole Man Paul was ready to close his store in the Atchafalaya Basin and head home, when a strange fellow walked in. Paul was used to strange fellows in the bayou, but this one definitely took the cake. He walked in dressed in a black suit and a fancy hat, holding a gold-tipped cane he used to lean on as he walked. His skin was a deep mocha color, and the bit of hair that escaped from the hat was grey.

Paul was stocking bags of rice the moment the stranger walked in, and couldn't help but drop one of the bags on his foot when he saw him. The stranger seemed to have trouble opening the door – Paul really needed to grease those hinges – and the chime rang three times before the man finally stepped into the store. Paul tried to look past him to see what kind of car he was driving. Certainly he was on his way to a costume party or to a really fancy evening affair, and that alone was quite odd; folks around here didn't go to fancy evening parties, and it was too early – or late, depending on what side of the year one was assessing – for Mardi Gras.

The strange man walked around the store for a minute, whistling a tune Paul was sure he had heard before but couldn't think of at the moment, and he walked straight to the counter.

Paul looked him over again, crisp and polished from head to toe, and walked up to the front door to look outside, since he didn't hear the engine of a car approaching from the back of the store where he was standing.

No car. How had he gotten there? There was no public transportation here, and without a car or a boat it was quite impossible to move around.

He eyed the stranger suspiciously from under the visor of his fishing hat, and put his hands inside the pockets of his trousers while he walked toward the counter. Paul was a bulky man – over six feet tall and quite hefty – but he still moved around quite fast when he wanted, in spite of his age. Right now he didn't want to; he walked slowly, with each step taking in a little more of the stranger waiting for him.

"Can I help you?" Paul said with his hands now folded against his chest.

The stranger smiled and nodded. He pointed to a pack of Black & Mild cigars with one of his long, manicured fingers. Paul noticed a strange gold ring sparkle on the same hand, the design of which appeared that of two snakes coiled around a cross.

"Cat got your tongue?"

The old man smiled. "No Paul, I was just thinking that I would like a nice drink to go with these cigars."

Paul looked at him sideways. Did he know the strange old man? "I've got some beer in that cooler over there, if that's what you're after."

"I was actually hoping for some Rum, or even a good glass of Cinnamon or Butterscotch Schnapps."

"Buddy, you've got the wrong place. This here ain't no bar."

"I know that, Paul, or should I call you Francois?"

Paul froze in his spot. Who in hell was this man that knew his real name from before he moved to the Bayou? He changed it a long time ago to avoid a lot of questions about his family history, and everyone here knew him as Ole Man Paul. "Who are you? And what do you want from me?"

"Easy…easy…if you prefer, I will call you Paul. Happy?"

"I'll be happy when you tell me who you are and what you're doing here."

"It doesn't matter who I am, Paul. I am who I am; we all are who we are, although some aren't who we think they are."

"If you're about done with your riddles, I'm ready to close. Is there anything else you want beside those cigars?"

"Well, Paul…there is, if you are willing to hear me out."

"Okay, spit it out, and do it fast. I've got stuff to do."

In reality Paul had nothing to do. Since the death of his wife many years before, he had nobody waiting for him at home, and his daughter Olivia lived in New Orleans.

"If you call going home to an empty house having stuff to do, then you are very content with yourself. I will cheer to that."

"Listen, Man, folks around here knows patience is not my greatest virtue. You're obviously not a local because I've never seen you before, but you seem to know me personally. What do you want from me?"

"I need your help, Paul. You see, your sister, Giselle Baton, was the temporary keeper of a rosary."

Paul was speechless – who was this man that knew him and his family?

"Your great-niece, Melody, is now in possession of one of two rosaries, and she is the final keeper, but she is not to know that, because of events that have yet to take place."

Paul could not see himself in that moment, but he could swear without looking that his face was white as a ghost – the first drop of blood had begun to drain away when the stranger spoke his sister's name, and was now completely gone in a torrential flow to nowhere. His legs were shaking, and he felt faint.

"Don't be afraid, Paul. All is well, and everything is happening in perfect order. There is one thing you must do for me – convince your great-niece, Melody, to bring her rosary to London with her, and don't forget to bring your weapon."

Even in deep state of shock, Paul heard the word 'weapon' filtering through. "Why will I need a weapon?"

"Things aren't always as they seem, Paul. You have saved Melody once before, and you might have to do it again. Be careful, because who you think is, is instead who is not, and who you think isn't, is who it is."

Paul's head was spinning, and he shook it in confusion.

"Don't you go driving yourself mad with this now, Paul; you will see things clearly when the time comes. All you must do now is to ensure that Melody brings her rosary along."

"Okay. I have no idea of anything you've told me about, but I will do as you say. And don't worry about Melody, I will keep her safe."

"That's your final task, Paul; then you will be free."

The stranger waited for Paul to process his words for a moment, then he headed slowly toward the door, limping slightly as he went. Paul stopped him in his tracks.

"Wait… about that Rum…I happen to have a taste of it in my personal stash. I keep it here for emergencies, you know, in case someone goes into shock or something."

The stranger seemed pleased with Paul's words, and walked back toward the counter, not limping much anymore. He took the glass Paul offered him and bowed his head slightly, holding his hat with the other jeweled hand. Paul was about to come around the counter and walk him out, when the stranger held up a hand and motioned him to stop.

"I will take my drink outside to the bench, if you don't mind. And if it is not too much to ask, I would prefer if you don't follow me."

Paul nodded and went back around the counter. "Take care, and thank you."

"My pleasure, Paul; I'm a little sad that you didn't agree to be around after the shift, but I do understand. After all, all souls have free will, and that was your choice. But we will see each other again, my friend – this is not a good-bye, but rather a moment in time in which our paths have crossed." With that he was gone. The door closed gently after him, and the chime rang three times.

When Paul finally gathered the courage to go outside, the stranger was gone. No engine sound was heard, and the water on the other side of the store appeared undisturbed. As he looked around for clues, Paul's eyes fell on the bench near the entrance – there stood the empty glass and a half-smoked cigar, and beside those items, he saw two sets of Mardi Gras beads, red and black in color, arranged to form a cross; in the middle of the cross lay the ring the old man was wearing, with the twin snakes coiled around the cross. Two of the same coming together to trigger global healing. Paul kneeled beside the makeshift altar and cried. "I am humbled, Legba; and I am ready to fulfill my final task."

Chapter Eight

Today, Aunt Catherine was being laid to rest. When Natalie arrived at Renewed Hope Baptist church, the place was already filled to capacity, and she had to park two blocks away even if some of the parking spaces in the church lot were labeled "family only." People were either too saddened to read or too lazy to walk.

Natalie hadn't been into Renewed Hope for at least ten years; she stopped going approximately around the time when she told her family to stuff it, and she felt sad when she looked around and saw not a single thing that brought back good memories.

The two front pews on either side were wrapped with a sash indicating they also were reserved for family members, and to Natalie's disappointment, they weren't filled up like the parking spaces, so she had no excuse but sit near people she shared only a last name with. Aunt Catherine's coffin was still in the adjacent room, but when she saw her parents and a myriad of other equally obnoxious acquaintances hang around there, she decided to remain in the chapel and keep her distance. She didn't want to see Aunt Catherine that way, anyway; she preferred to hold on to the mental image of the sweet lady that had come to visit her at her place.

She tried to get close to her parents through the years, but any attempt she ever made had resulted in complete failure. Natalie was happy she never planned to be an army general – her poor strategies would have certainly lost them the war and caused her men to die an untimely death; or maybe, like her parents, they would have miserably deserted her.

She wished nobody would walk up to her and say anything, but her hopes evaporated when Ryan's voice whispered its way into her ear. "Natalie, how are you?"

Natalie turned her head and took a good look at Ryan. He was quite handsome. With his light blond hair and deep blue eyes set in a tanned cherubic face, matched with a body that held its own at six feet two inches, he was the living image of the California surfer. Although Natalie doubted he had any roots in the west coast, Ryan lived close to water all his life, and the water sports he regularly indulged had molded his figure into a well crafted masterpiece of tight muscles. He had a tiny scar on his left cheek, and luscious thick lips that brought Brad Pitt to mind; he wore a formal black suit with a very subtle tie; the dark jacket set a nice contrast with the golden, sun-kissed tone of his hair. Not bad…maybe she should give him a chance, even if in her eyes he was already guilty by association with her parents.

"Hello Ryan, thank you for coming," she stood up and shook his extended hand. She waited to see if he would try to hug her, but southern decorum had the best of him as well, so they sat together and waited for the service to begin.

When people started filing in, she braced for the moment when her parents would walk up and sit beside her, and was happy she wasn't alone. Her parents would not appear rude by preaching their accusations in front of others, especially if those others were none other than a very suitable young man they could, by the grace of God, marry their only daughter off to.

This would finally get her out of their hair; not to mention the social perks of being associated with one of the most prestigious names in the Wilmington area.

As expected, her parents were there within minutes; her mother, still a pleasant looking woman at the age of sixty-two, was dressed entirely in black, and wore a dainty hat over her blond hair which was skillfully styled into an intricate French twist. Of course her mother would include a hairstylist appointment as a part of funeral preparations. Angela's petite figure gave her a delicate, vulnerable appearance, quite different than the large boned frame her sister Catherine had been forced to live into. Her face had few wrinkles – compliments of Botox, even if Angela would go to her death bed without admitting it to a soul – and her eyes, which always reminded Natalie of cat eyes, were a light shade of amber.

Her father was tall, slim, and still sporting a head full of dark hair; attired in black suit and tie, he looked extremely distinguished and handsome. His eyes – a shade of dark chocolate – rested on Natalie for a moment, before shifting back down to appear contrite.

Natalie wondered if her father looked at Aunt Catherine lying in her coffin and thought about their one-night-fling at Catherine's house. The thought almost made her laugh out loud – what a smack to her mother's pride it would be! If it wasn't because of Aunt Catherine's wish to keep it secret, Natalie would have loved to tell her just to see her mother's self-righteous face crumble into tears of embarrassment.

Ryan nodded in the Sanders' direction, to ensure he was being seen at Natalie's side. Although his family's fortune was almost gone – and that was kept under very tight wrap indeed, the Wheelers were still a very prestigious family.

People finally stopped filing in, and before the last person sat, the music began to play. Botticelli's amazing voice filled the room, and Natalie already felt a knot in her throat. She was a little surprised by her own reaction – after all she had wished Aunt Catherine under a truck until a few days ago – but she had wanted so badly to belong that she treasured the fleeting feeling of finally connecting to one of her family members.

Mister Hodges, the minister, began the service as soon as the music died down; his imposing, thunderous voice kept everyone in a spell. He spoke of Aunt Catherine's loyalty to her family, and her selfless dedication to her aging, ailing parents, prior to their passing.

Before friends and family could walk up and speak, a bagpipe player stood up, and the sound of Amazing Grace swept everyone away on the wave of its notes. There wasn't a single dry eye in the room – except Natalie's mother's, who pretended to dab at her eyes with a white kerchief that never got wet.

Ryan took Natalie's hand, and when she turned to look at him, she saw that his eyes were burning holes in her. That momentary connection made her a little uneasy, but she felt an unexpected stirring in her lower stomach and quickly averted her eyes to avoid blushing.

Her father walked up to say a few words on behalf of the family.

"The sadness our family feels today cannot be expressed in words. Catherine was a wonderful woman, and everyone who knew her was blessed to have encountered such kindness. I remember the day we brought our daughter home for the first time…Catherine was so touched by her arrival that she went out and bought her clothes, stuffed animals and balloons. She left all her purchases in the nursery, and left before we got home. We later found out that she didn't want to intrude in our happiness, and wanted to allow us the privacy of enjoying this very special moment alone."

Sure she was, Dad…she was crushed by your decision, that's why she stayed away.

"Catherine was selfless. It showed in the way she took care of her parents, day in and day out, without ever complaining. Other women might have resented giving up their lives to look after their aging parents, but not our Catherine – for her, for her kind soul, it was an honor, and she wore that badge of self-sacrifice with pride. My wife and I will never forget her; Catherine is, and will remain, alive in our hearts."

Phillip Sanders stepped down, and took his place again beside his wife, although Natalie noticed that her mother was shifting uncomfortably. Could she really be grieving her sister's death or was she unsettled by having lost the spotlight to a dead woman? Imagining her mother having any real feelings about another human was, in Natalie's mind, synonymous to a snake feeling affection for the rats he was about to eat. No way – Natalie thought – it was all just a big act.

A few other people walked up and talked about their liaisons to Aunt Catherine, but nobody talked about the real woman behind the mask of the self-sacrificing maiden. It was time for Natalie to let the world know who Catherine Bouvier really was. She stood up and excused herself with Ryan, then went straight to the microphone. She glanced at her parents and saw that they were holding their breath – her mother looked as if she was going to have a stroke, but tried to hide it behind the façade of grief. Her discomfort gave Natalie the strength to speak.

"For many years I didn't like my aunt Catherine. She was never mean to me, or directly did anything wrong, but I suppose we were just different people…or at least I thought so until a few days ago."

She paused briefly, and scanned the crowd to see the general reaction of her audience – she had everyone's undivided attention.

"My paintings were scheduled to be exhibited at Mrs. Wilson's gallery in less than a month. I was thrilled beyond belief, and saw that as my opportunity to show the world my work, the passion, the fire I had inside. Sadly, a different fire destroyed everything – and as Mrs. Wilson's gallery went up into smoke because of an electrical malfunction, so did my paintings. I was devastated. All my work, or most of it anyway, was in that gallery. I saw my chance of being validated as an artist blow away as the marine breeze carried away the smoke from the fire. Well, on Tuesday afternoon, the day before she fell ill, Aunt Catherine came to see me. I thought she was going to admonish me about my house being a mess, or maybe she was going to drill some of her many rules of etiquette into me…but she didn't. When I snapped at her over something totally ridiculous, she told me I shouldn't give up just because some of my work was destroyed. She told me she had a friend in England who deals in art, and after hearing of the fire, she asked him about the possibility of bringing some of my paintings to him. I was flabbergasted! This wasn't the aunt that I knew...After she passed, she left instructions for me with her housekeeper to go by and pick up a letter she had written to me the day before. Reading her words opened my eyes to the wonderful person she was, and before I could finish reading, her letter directed me to some paintings she worked on herself. Aunt Catherine was an artist as well, although I doubt anyone knew that about her. She never shared her talents, because she never wanted to steal anyone's spotlight – that's how strong and wonderful she was. I can stand in front of you right now, and candidly tell you that I miss Aunt Catherine, and wish I could have one more chance to spend time with her, and get to know her better. I know it isn't possible, but I do know that her true essence lives in her paintings, and I will forever be thankful to her, and deeply honored, for having shared her secret passion with me. You are my true family, Aunt Catherine, even if we never shared the same blood...family is in the heart, and you are definitely in mine. I hope you rest in peace."

Silence reigned in the room for several moments. Nobody knew this side of Catherine Bouvier, and everyone seemed shocked into a silent stupor. Ryan took her hand the moment she sat down, and Natalie didn't fight him. She felt she needed some allies right now, and if Ryan wanted to step into the game, why shouldn't she let him?

After Natalie's speech, nobody else walked up to share their story, so the minister led the congregation into a few more prayers and the service was over after that. Her mother and father left the chapel and went quickly to the receiving room, to greet the attendees, while the pallbearers stepped in to carry the coffin outside to the waiting hearse. Natalie walked outside with Ryan, still holding hands, and she noticed that both her mother and father watched her closely. She knew that she was expected to stand by them and shake hands with those who had come to show their respects, but she needed some fresh air. She turned to look at Ryan, and was impressed by the way his blond hair glistened in the sunshine. With the church in the background he looked like an angel.

"Thank you so much for your support, Ryan. It really meant a lot to me, and I'm sure it would mean a lot to Aunt Catherine."

"Yeah, she really was a nice lady, Natalie. I feel fortunate that I got to meet her."

Formalities…empty words…Natalie hated them.

"Say, Ryan…you asked if we could go out sometimes. I would really like that."

Ryan appeared as if he got suddenly hit by a sunray - he literally glowed. "Why, that would be great, Natalie. Tomorrow, maybe, or the next day?"

"Sure. Remind me to give you my cell number before we part, today. I'm often out, and it is easier to reach me that way."

"Thank you, Natalie. I will call you later tonight, and we will figure out when is the best time to meet. Are we going to the cemetery now?"

Natalie shook her head and smiled, but Ryan couldn't detect the bitterness because of his lack of knowledge concerning her family's internal affairs.

"No, Mom arranged to keep the burial private, and we are going directly to Aunt Catherine's house for a reception."

"Great. I will follow you then."

Mostly everybody had already come outside, but her parents were still inside. Natalie realized that in her haste of getting out she had left her purse on the pew, so she walked back in to get it. She saw her mother standing by the pew, holding something, and she looked as if she was arguing with her husband. When Natalie got closer she saw that her mother had pulled Aunt Catherine's letter out from her purse – Natalie put it in there to have Tom Hadley's number handy, in case she needed to call him, but she never expected her mother would find it. Angela Sanders' face was a mask of agony, as she suddenly realized that her sister didn't always live in her shadow after all.

When her husband found her, Belinda Allen was laying in bed staring at the ceiling. Bright sunlight poured in from the large bedroom window and washed the walls a ghostly white.

He knew something was wrong from the moment he walked in, although everything seemed to be in place. He and Belinda shared a special bond, and if something was ever wrong with one, the other felt something that could be equated to a punch in the gut. Today, when he got home, Jim Allen felt as if Mike Tyson attacked him at the door.

He called her name from the entrance, and his anxiety grew by leaps and bounds each time his own voice echoed through the house. Knowing that she hadn't been well, his main concern was that she was still sick. He drove by the antique shop on his way home for lunch, and didn't think she had been in at all in the morning, although she mentioned going after he left for work. He went straight to the bedroom.

"Belinda, Honey…are you in here?"

Belinda was there, on the bed and still in her nightgown, her honey blond hair loosely spread on the pillow; her eyes were fixed on the heavens above, as if to pray for the salvation of her assailant.

Jim stood frozen on the doorstep. Certainly he had fallen asleep and was having a nightmare. This doll here, with her neck twisted in a funny, oblique position couldn't be his Belinda. Suddenly, all the sounds and smells of the moment became more intense, and he heard a faucet rhythmically dripping in the master bathroom. The window was slightly opened behind the white lace curtain, and from the sound of car doors closing he was fairly sure that their neighbors, the Smiths, a semi-retired couple, had gone home for lunch as well. The room had a strange smell lingering in, one Jim couldn't quite identify.

He felt a sharp pain in his chest and barely made it to call 911, before his legs gave out. He didn't see his wife being taken away, because by the time the emergency crews got there – alerted by the call he placed but couldn't complete – he had already lost consciousness. As he swam in the peaceful waters of nothingness, Jim Allen was ready to follow his lovely wife on her journey.

Lakeisha Jackson brought out the last few trays of food, and waited for the Sanders and their guests to arrive. With only a couple of caterers from "The Walking Fork," a lot of food drop offs, and a single day of notice, Lakeisha barely made it to get everything ready on time.

She was exhausted – the last few days had been filled with more emotional ups and downs than Lakeisha was used to handle. Being an empath didn't help, as it was extremely hard for her to be near so many raw emotions and not absorb them as her own. She planned to get everything set up and then pass the ball to the caterers to work their magic; for her own sake of mind, it was best if Lakeisha stayed up in her room during the event.

She heard the door open, and walked into the foyer to see who had arrived. Phillip and Angela Sanders came inside together, but Mrs. Sanders was acting as if her husband didn't exist. His saddened face confirmed something was up – one more reason, Lakeisha thought, to run up to her room and shut herself away from all the drama.

It wasn't long before a steady stream of visitors arrived, and by the time Lakeisha went up, there were probably close to a hundred people in the house. Thankfully, two more hired bodies showed up as well, so she saw no reason to stick around. She went into her room and closed the door, drawing a breath of relief. She could hear voices and sounds downstairs, but at least their emotional baggage didn't travel through her floor. That was until she heard sounds coming from the room adjacent to her own – Catherine's room.

She listened carefully and heard someone move things, and she wondered if one of the Sanders had gone in to look for something specific. She was too tired to get up and look, and tried to focus on the book she was reading instead. She managed to keep her concentration for a while, until she heard Miss Catherine's door open; that same moment something fell, and Lakeisha heard the voice of a man mutter profanities. She didn't think it sounded like Mr. Sanders' voice, but then one never knew – it was too low to properly discern.

She got up from her bed and went quickly to her door to see a man rushing down the stairs, but a little too late to see his face. He was tall, with black hair, around two hundred pounds, but she couldn't be sure if he was Mr. Sanders or anyone she had seen hanging around the house before coming upstairs.

"Sir" she called out to him as he went down the stairs with the padded quietness and stealth of a sleek black cat, "is there anything I can help you with?"

The stranger didn't stop or turn to look at her, nor did he reply. Lakeisha went down to the living room, where many of the guests were gathered, and looked around for a man that resembled the figure she had seen darting out of Catherine's room. She could feel his emotions still lingering in the air, but they were so mixed up with the bouquet of other emotions everyone in the room felt that she couldn't pinpoint the source. She saw the front door was open, and noticed that two of the guests were standing by it, talking. She walked right up to them.

"Excuse me, have you seen a man just going through? He is a little over six feet tall, with short black hair."

The two people – a plump lady with ginger hair and a balding man in his mid-fifties – looked at each other, and then shook their head in unison. "No, sorry, we didn't notice anyone by that description."

"Thank you anyway, he just dropped his wallet and I trying to catch him before he left." Lakeisha said, keeping a hand into her pocket to support her white lie.

She walked briskly outside, but all she saw were two older gentlemen talking about finances and sipping iced tea. She went back inside and up the stairs to Catherine's room. Everything looked tidy; only the jewelry box was open, and the door of the closet was ajar. A small statue that Miss Bouvier had kept near the door was shattered, and Lakeisha quickly thought about the sound she had heard after the stranger opened the door; he probably accidentally knocked it down on his way out. In the closet, Catherine's stuff was a bit shuffled but essentially in the same place she had seen it yesterday afternoon, when she went in there to pack a few items for the family. What could the man want in Catherine's room? A quick image of the rosary flashed before her eyes, and Lakeisha instinctually began to pray.

He was running out of patience. He dabbed a cotton swab soaked with Peroxide on the cut on his foot. He could almost hear his mother's voice admonishing him for not wearing socks. Had he learned from her teachings, he wouldn't have been injured when that blistered statue fell and shattered and one of the small pieces, fast as a bullet, hit the naked skin between the hem of his trousers and the loafers he was wearing. He hoped there weren't any blood spatters left behind to tie him to Catherine Bouvier's house.

He already had enough to worry about, after the incident with Belinda Allen. Killing her had not been a part of his plan, and when he had driven in front of the shop, on his way to her house, he was positive he saw a woman inside that looked like her; of course, the glare from the window deceived him, and because of that fatal mistake, Belinda Allen was dead. By the time he got into her room looking for the rosary, and she was getting out of bed –looking groggy and confused at the sight of someone standing in her bedroom – he knew she had recognized him from the shop. He couldn't take any chances, and his heart truly ached when he wrapped his hands around her pale throat and began to squeeze the life out of her.

He really didn't dislike Belinda – in so many ways she reminded him of his own mother, sweet and unhurried in her daily affairs. He had a moment of weakness and almost let her go when her eyes locked with his, and silently begged him to let her live. He couldn't do that; his mission was too serious to allow faulty human emotions to get in the way, but he made sure to put her out of her misery fast, and with just one skilled move he snapped her neck. He watched her ease into his grasp, her body quickly giving away as her head bobbed pitifully on one side. He gently carried her back to her bed, and laid her down with the same care a mother would use tucking her precious child in for the night.

The rosary was not there, but he did find something – a file cabinet where Belinda Allen kept receipts of all her past sales. When he found one dated back to the previous year, which identified Catherine Bouvier as the buyer, he felt so overwhelmed by emotions that a quick shot of urine trickled down and soaked his underwear.

Getting into Catherine Bouvier's house during the reception that was taking place there was a piece of cake. He had the opportunity to walk upstairs unobserved and felt quite certain that if the old lady had the rosary it would be in her room.

Thankfully, everyone was busy chatting and eating downstairs, so he could work undisturbed. Everything had gone quite well – aside from the fact that he saw no trace of the rosary – until he broke that silly statue, and heard a woman's voice calling out to him as he fled. Did she see him? What was she doing upstairs? He hoped to not have to resort to violence once again – his hands had already been washed in enough innocent blood.

Chapter Nine

"It was kind of spooky, I must say, Melody; I don't scare easily but this time I thought I was going to cry like a baby." Paul said, emphatically enough to make Melody giggle like a little girl.

Melody totally understood what Paul was trying to explain - the same spirit already appeared to her, just a few years before, on her way back home to North Carolina, after she left Louisiana.

"You don't have to tell me, Paul. I've had the pleasure to meet the very same gentleman before. When I drove home from the Basin, two years ago, I stopped at a diner on the way. Well...this very eccentric man just came up from behind me, and asked if we could have a cup of coffee together. I sat at a table with him, Paul, and I know I talked to him for a while; then, he said he had to use the restroom, and he excused himself. When I didn't see him come back I got a little worried, and I knocked on the door of the men's room. He didn't answer, so I walked in and I found an old key resting on the chipped sink. Next to the key lay a red carnation, a black fedora - which he was wearing when I met him - and some empty sugar packets. Beneath the pedestal of the sink, he had drawn a large circle on the black linoleum floor with sugar. An equal-armed cross drawn inside the circle divided it into four equal sections. In the right half of the circle was a shape similar to the skeleton key. I took the items and brought them to the waitress who served us both coffee, and she told me that I was alone at the table the whole time. She never saw the man; I guess he only needed me to see him. I must have looked very smart sitting at that table apparently talking to myself and ordering two cups of coffee." Melody laughed, as the emotional charge still connected to that past event wrapped around her heart – it had indeed been a powerful moment in her life, one she would never forget.

"Wow…you never told me that, Melody!"

"Paul, I think it really took all this time to even explain the episode to myself. I have to say that it is kind of liberating to know that someone else has encountered him, that he's not a figment of my imagination. I look at the key sometimes, and still can't fully wrap my mind around it."

Paul chuckled, "Melody, I was just thinking how funny it would have been if one the folks from around here walked in and saw me talking to myself. I still have the things he left here, too. The ring is a bit small for my fingers, so I keep it at home in the same box where I have all of my late wife's precious belongings, but I do keep the twin strings of Mardi Gras beads here at the store. Every time I look at them, I can't help shaking my head. I've seen some interesting things around here throughout the years, Melody, but this one takes the prize."

"So, are you ready for London, Paul?"

"Oh yes, I'm glad you brought it up… you know, the man we were just talking about…he told me to ask you to bring a rosary to London."

Melody's voice registered surprise.

"Are you talking about the rosary Grandmama left me with Yvette's diary?"

"That's the one, I reckon. I didn't even know you have a rosary."

"Yes. Grandmama had it at the farm. I never told you before that I have it?"

"Not that I can recall, but he insisted that you should bring it along."

"This little tidbit right here just sort of scares the shit out of me, Paul, excuse my French. The last time I was instructed to carry on a divine wish and related instructions, I found myself in the midst of a war. In the end, no matter how hard I tried to keep it safe, I lost The Book of Obeah and felt awful about it. It's not every day that people from the Vatican and some crazy old swamp guy and his grandchildren are coming after me. I almost lost my skin in that deal, Paul, and I am not sure that I'm eager to start on a new adventure."

Paul chuckled again. "Yeah, you did look kind of vulnerable when I found you in the woods that time."

That fateful night, Paul had saved Melody at the eleventh hour – after going back to Louisiana with the Book, she had nearly fallen victim to Maurice Abudah, a man living in the swamp who felt he had ownership of the sacred text. The Book was initially stolen from his mother by Melody's great-grandmother, many years before, and he believed that the only way to avenge his mother was to take the book back and kill Melody. What transpired later was that Maurice's granddaughter, Alex, was the one who had orchestrated the whole thing, wearing Maurice's mother's wedding dress to make him think she was the spirit of the deceased woman, and use his madness to claim the book as her own. In the end, Alex accidentally shot her brother, fled into the night, and Melody survived. However, the tome Melody had promised to keep safe disappeared in the shuffle and washed away with the heavy rains that ravaged the bayou that night. It was when Melody left the bayou to return home, disappointed and distraught for having lost the book, that she met Elegba, the spirit that visited Paul at his shack in the Atchafalaya Basin. The very same one Paul called 'Legba' without an 'E' at the beginning of the name, due to his loyalty to the Haitian tradition which has a big influence in that part of the bayou . She heard, later on, that Mario's brother, Federico, found the book and fled with it, only to crash his car shortly after. By the time authorities arrived, both Federico and the book were gone, so nothing was ever confirmed.

"I thought the same thing, Melody. I'm getting too old for chasing ghouls and crazy men and women. Mostly, I don't want you to get in any kind of danger...we might not be as lucky next time."

Melody felt a surge of affection for the old man on the phone. All considered, she was happy that Grandmama had steered her toward the bayou. If her grandmother's dying wish of having her ashes brought back to her native bayou hadn't taken place, Melody would have never met Paul or his daughter Olivia. "I'm a big girl too, Paul. You don't have to worry about me. In fact, let's talk about you...Olivia told me you've been dealing with some health issues."

"Nah...nothing to worry about, Child. Doc said my cholesterol is high, and my blood pressure acts up once in a while. He wanted to put me on this crazy diet that would never work – could you see me giving up fried chicken, or bread pudding, or crawfish cakes? That's nonsense, that is, for sure."

"Paul, I think you should listen to your doctor. A good diet will only give you extra energy, which you will need to travel across half the world to see your little girl say I do."

"I'll be alright, Melody. There ain't nothin' a good shot of rum won't fix."

Even if she was worried, Melody couldn't help but smile at Paul's stubbornness; in so many ways he reminded her of her beloved Grandmama Giselle. Melody had a lot of trust in Olivia, however, and she felt comfortable knowing two things: Olivia would make sure Paul remained on the right track, and Paul would do anything to please his daughter. "Well, I'd better be going, Paul. I have a lot of chores I still need to attend to."

"Go on, child. Be good and tell Mario that I'm looking forward to kicking his butt at Chess."

Melody laughed. "I will tell him, Paul, but he's been practicing with a guy from work, so he might be more of a challenge than you think."

Melody could picture Paul smiling affectionately.

"I hope so for him; that way his pride won't be hurt too badly. Bye Honey, enjoy the rest of your day."

"Bye Paul. I love you."

"I love you too, sweetheart."

When she hung up the phone, Melody felt a fleeting twinge of pain shoot through her heart. She was more worried about Paul than she allowed herself to think. How many good years did he have left? She contemplated going down to Louisiana and spend a little quality time with him when she got back from

London. Mario was always at work anyway, so she wouldn't feel too bad at the thought of leaving him to fend for himself for a few days. There was a low level of anxiety simmering below the surface of her being, and Melody didn't know if it was worry over Paul's health, or if it was something more. She wondered why she was being asked to bring the rosary to London; Grandmama asked her to safeguard both items she entrusted to her, and Melody lost the book – was the same fate awaiting the rosary? She mentally prepared for a new battle ahead.

After all the guests finally left, Angela and Philip went into the family room to have a drink. It was a hard day, and they had been successful in keeping a united front for the sake of appearances. Now, alone at last, tension was free to surface, and it took little time to bring the atmosphere in the room to a sub-zero temperature. Angela Sanders sat on one of the Queen Anne chairs at the far end of the room; her face was tight as a cord, and she looked as a tigress ready to pounce. Phillip Sanders sat as far as he possibly could, in the opposite side of the spacious living room; he appeared shrunk and pitiful, and he swallowed often, as if to stop himself from shedding tears of guilt.

Angela stood up abruptly and walked up to the bar to fill her glass with more Scotch on the rocks, breathing deeply. "That tramp! I can't believe she would do that to me, her sister…and all along she played the part of the poor, sacrificial little maiden. What nerve!"

Phillip swallowed again. "She wasn't a tramp, Angie, you know that. It was a moment of weakness for both of us. We were both at wits end, and sought each other for a moment of comfort. That's all it ever was, I swear."

But his tone wasn't convincing enough – Angela jumped at the chance to slaughter him. "Oh, so you swear, do you? You also swore that you would be faithful to me, for better and for worse, and what happened to that promise? You forfeited it for a moment of filth with a pathetic whore!"

Phillip stood up, and his half attempt at defending himself came through as an admission of guilt. "That's enough, Angie! I understand you are upset, but you are taking things out of context. Catherine and I did not have an affair, and she was not a whore. She was your sister, for God's sake, and she died a few days ago. Can't you even respect the dead? Maybe if you weren't so cold and insensitive, so selfish and judgmental, people would actually think twice before they behave certain ways around you."

"Oh my God! Are you implying that it is *my* fault *you* strayed? How dare you? I want you out of here, right now. This is the same house where you and my sister slept together, where you screwed her while I thought you were dealing with a difficult case. Get out and don't come back. I don't need you in my life!"

Phillip dropped his glass on the table so hard that he thought it would shatter in a million pieces, but it merely clung when the two surfaces collided. He strode out the door, almost knocking Natalie down as she came in. She looked at her father's drawn face, then at her mother's accusing eyes, and

121

debated with herself whether she should even ask what was happening – she was sure it had something to do with the letter her mother had found in her purse, when she accidentally left it inside the church. There was little, if anything, she could do to help her parents – they had been beyond help for a long time, and had embodied the concept of "dysfunctional family" since Natalie was a young child. She didn't want any part of their drama, and was somewhat saddened by the fact that she felt no affection, nor compassion, for the two people who raised her. To Natalie, they were no different than perfect strangers.

She did nothing to stop her father, and it only took one glance in the direction of her mother to decide it was best to stay away. She turned on her heels and marched up the staircase, heading toward Aunt Catherine's room. When she was there a few days before, she was so overwhelmed with the discovery of Catherine's artistic skills that she didn't inspect to see if there were any other things of interest in her room. The upstairs were dark, and Natalie turned on the hallway light to make sure she didn't trip anywhere, since she wasn't too familiar with Aunt Catherine's house. She passed by Lakeisha's room, and heard soft chanting filtering through the closed door. It was charming and haunting enough for Natalie to stop and listen. She couldn't understand the words, but whatever she was singing had a strange feel to it, and Natalie felt oddly relaxed and liberated by it. Suddenly, she felt compelled to knock on Lakeisha's door. She heard the chanting come to a stop, and then an assortment of small sounds as Lakeisha came to open. When the door opened, Lakeisha stood in the doorway, blocking Natalie's view of the room.

"Miss Sanders…what can I do for you?"

Natalie took in the image of the woman standing in front of her – Lakeisha was wearing a loose white gown, not a nightgown per se, but rather an attire that called to mind African garb; her head was wrapped into a white scarf, and she wore a cross pendant around her neck. Her face was void of any traces of make-up, and Natalie noticed all the rings Lakeisha normally wore had been removed from her fingers. When Lakeisha shifted slightly on her feet, Natalie saw the flickering of a candle flame. "Nothing in particular, Lakeisha. I was going to Aunt Catherine's room, and couldn't help hearing you sing; it was absolutely beautiful."

Lakeisha smiled gently. "Thank you, Miss Sanders. I've already started packing some of Miss Bouvier's things, to make it easier for you and your mother."

"Thank you so much for doing that, Lakeisha; Aunt Catherine told me just the other day how efficient you are – I see that she was right. What will you do now that Aunt Catherine is gone?"

"I'm not sure, Miss Sanders. I suppose my job here is done, and I assume I will be discharged soon."

"Lakeisha, can I talk to you about Aunt Catherine for a moment?"

"Of course, Miss Natalie. If you can give me a moment I will get dressed and come out to talk to you."

Natalie's curiosity was running in high gear, and she wondered what Lakeisha was doing in her room. In the past few years she had dabbed in alternative paths of spirituality herself, and was always eager to learn about others. "May I just come in a moment, Lakeisha? I see you are burning a candle. I do that myself often, when I pray."

Lakeisha stood on the door for a moment, her mind working fast to decide whether she should allow Natalie into her private world; she relented and stepped away from the door to allow Natalie into her room.

Natalie was wrong – there wasn't a candle burning, but eight of them, arranged on the table to resemble a Christian cross. The room was pristine clean, and Natalie could detect a slight scent in the air, but couldn't figure out what it was. A white cloth was laid out on the floor in front of the table, and another one was under the candles. Beside the candles she saw a shallow dish of water and some white Lilies. There was also a plate with something in it that looked like food, although Natalie couldn't understand what kind of food it was. The most interesting piece of Lakeisha's room was, however, a large white snake coiled around a faux tree inside a glass case.

"Oh my God, Lakeisha! I didn't know you have a snake in here. What kind is it?"

"It's an albino King snake, Miss Natalie. Please don't be afraid, it's not aggressive."

Natalie couldn't take her eyes off the magnificent animal inside the large case. "I'm not afraid at all. I find snakes to be charming and intriguing. Does my mother know you have it in here? She is terrified of snakes."

"No, Miss Natalie, I can't say that I've ever volunteered the information of its residency here. I figured nobody really needed to know, since it only leaves its case when I'm in the room."

Natalie was mesmerized by the beauty of the snake. She had seen, and held, snakes of different types before, but she had never seen an albino at such close distance.

Lakeisha sat quietly, studying Natalie as she gushed over the snake. Suddenly Natalie turned around, and looked in the direction of the altar.

"That's a beautiful set-up, Lakeisha. What is it for?"

"I'm just praying, Miss Natalie. I normally do this on Sundays, but I needed guidance tonight."

"Whatever you're doing must be very peaceful, Lakeisha. It feels amazing in here. I've only ever been into another place that felt this good, before. It was the home of a lady I went to see to get a Tarot reading. Her house felt so peaceful, that I didn't want to leave."

Lakeisha smiled. "Obatala is the most gentle and peaceful of all Orishas; maybe your friend had a little bit of His essence in her house."

Natalie was a bit puzzled. "What's an Orisha?"

"An Orisha is one of God's aides. Catholics call them Saints."

"So Obatala is a Saint?"

"Obatala is more than just a saint, Miss Natalie. The other Orishas lived earthly lives and were raised to sainthood after their death. Obatala is the closest Orisha to God – He embodies the energy of the Christ."

Natalie was totally mesmerized. "Wow! Really? That's awesome."

"There is a dual energy around you, Miss Natalie. If I could humbly assess my impression, I would say that you are guided through this life by the Ibeji, the cosmic twins."

"What do you mean when you say I'm surrounded by energy, Lakeisha?"

"Each of us is crowned by an Orisha; He or She is like our guardian angel. You have two over you, but they are of the same essence."

"How cool!"

"The Twins represent the duality of the Universe. They are good and evil, constructive and destructive, protective and vengeful, all at the same time. If you ever wish to ask for their protection, or their assistance, you must bring two small offerings near a playground, or anywhere where children normally abound. But, don't forget to always bring exactly two of the same, as they can get a little jealous of each other and competitive at times. The last thing you want to do is to get them fighting with one another." Lakeisha smiled, and she suddenly appeared older, wiser.

And then something happened. The snake began to furiously tap on the glass case. When Lakeisha took him out to see why it was so unsettled, it stretched toward Natalie. Rather than being afraid, Natalie moved toward it and extended her hand to touch it. The snake immediately wrapped around her arm and inched in midair toward her face. Natalie held her breath – although she loved snakes, she was completely surprised when it slithered against her cheek, touching her skin ever so gently. An explosion of images shot through her mind. She saw herself holding the rosary, walking down the street from her dream, before entering a building. Suddenly she was no longer holding one rosary, but two, and they were twisted together. She felt she was floating somewhere that wasn't Earth, but had no idea where she was. And then, as fast as it started, the vision was over. She woke up on the white cloth Lakeisha had laid in front of her altar; the snake had detached from her and was now drinking out of the shallow dish. Lakeisha picked it up reverently and placed it back in its case.

Natalie looked at Lakeisha and hoped to get some sort of explanation, but Lakeisha was instead asking her questions. "What did you see, Natalie?"

"I'm not sure...I saw myself, holding a rosary I found in Aunt Catherine's room, and then I saw another rosary. In the vision, the rosaries became infused with light. I can't remember anything else."

"You were sent a message, Natalie. Maybe it is time we sit down and talk."

He woke up in a sweat. The nightmare had been so vivid he struggled to come back to the reality of his room. In the dream, Belinda was back to take him with her. She looked different than she had when she was alive - her blond hair was now black, and she was wearing a tight-fitting black dress; she was walking slowly toward him, coming from the shadows, and when she got closer she stood in front of him and grew in size, until she could almost touch the ceiling. Her head spun around in a full circle, and her voice was strange, deep yet melodious. "You can't get away from me now. Your game has lasted long enough, and it is about to end. I can see you wherever you go, and I will always be nearby."

Something on her chest glowed – a strange red circle that emanated a bright red light and slowly opened to let something out. Suddenly spiders were crawling out of the opening and rushed toward him. He ran and ran, but the spiders were faster than he was. They caught up with him and crawled up his legs, and into his eyes and mouth. He tried to scream but words stuck to the back of his throat, trapped into the silky thread of sticky webs. He collapsed to the ground and felt the spiders' venom shoot through him. As his consciousness began to slip away, he heard the woman laugh and when he turned his head to look at her, her mouth was so close that he could smell her fetid breath.

When he woke up and realized he was only dreaming, he took a deep breath to steady himself; he got out of bed, walked quickly into the bathroom and turned on the light. When he looked at himself in the mirror he saw strange red bumps on his face, and the haunting sound of Belinda's voice, spreading quickly through his feverish mind, turned his blood to pure ice.

Chapter Ten

"The rosary your aunt left in your possession is one of the four key elements necessary to trigger the unfolding of an ancient prophecy, Natalie."

Natalie was now sitting on the bed sipping water from a glass Lakeisha handed to her, still a bit shaken by what happened but intrigued beyond belief.

"I don't doubt it, Lakeisha. When I took the rosary home, something strange happened; I just pulled it out of the pouch to look at it, since I didn't really have the time while I was here, and held it in my hand for a moment…well, I can't really explain what took place next; suddenly I saw myself holding the rosary, and I also saw a street I have seen before in a dream, but I don't think I've ever been there in real life."

"What happened after the vision?"

"Nothing, really. I freaked out and put the rosary back into its pouch. I can't exactly put any of this into words, but in those few moments I felt as if I knew everything – past, present and future. What does the prophecy predict, Lakeisha?"

"Nobody really knows for sure. All we have are transcripts of the oral knowledge that was passed down from one generation to another. When the Nuns came to America, many didn't trust sharing their knowledge with new people, and some of the information was lost. However, we do know that it revolves around the meeting point of a sacred cross which extends to the four cardinal points from the center of the Atlantic Ocean. The elders mapped those points as New

Orleans, London UK, Carolina in Brazil and Benin in Africa. According to them, each of those cities is meant to provide solid ground for the unfolding of one of the four quadrants of the prophecy. There has been speculation among different traditions that the meeting point of the cross marks the exact location of Atlantis, although nobody really knows for sure or has any factual evidence of it. Also, there are supposed to be four signs that precede the shift of consciousness predicted by the prophecy. The first two have already taken place – Hurricane Katrina and the catastrophic financial meltdown we are experiencing on a global level. No one really knows what the next sign will be, or if the next location to be a catalyst will be one of those the elders predicted. All we know is that the prophecy is due to manifest on Earth in, or a few years after, the year 2012."

"I've heard a lot of predictions about 2012." Natalie said, entirely captured by Lakeisha's words.

"So have I, Natalie, but few of them reflect the truth. People think that 2012 is the year when we will all die, and very few, if any, have understood that it is the year we will finally begin to live. With each of the prophesied signs, a wound in societal history is revealed and brought to the surface to be healed. In the case of Katrina, racial divides were brought out in the light, and although mankind still has some ways to go, things are getting better under the surface – people are talking and raising issues, thus looking for ways to fix problems and heal old hurts. With the economic crash, many people had no choice but to go within and brush off the dust from their priority lists. They were forced to make hard choices, and through those choices they have learned to identify with important feelings such as hope, humility and compassion, and they have felt compelled to reach out to others. As the blanket of security woven with threads of material possession unravels, many are connecting to the self and to the collective."

Natalie was suddenly pensive. "Lakeisha...you mentioned London as one of the key cities – I'm scheduled to go to London next month."

Lakeisha's heart skipped a beat. "Why are you going to London, Natalie?" Surprise mixed with a sensation of euphoria – was this the epiphany of the second sign? Could it be that this was the reason Elegba directed her to go to London?

"Aunt Catherine didn't give me the rosary to keep. She told me to find her daughter and give it to her. According to the letter Aunt Catherine wrote the day before she died, she felt compelled to buy it last year, when she visited a local antique store to buy a little token for the daughter she hoped to meet. Another reason why I am going is because one of Aunt Catherine's friends, Tom Hadley, is willing to allow some of my work into his gallery."

"Catherine Bouvier had a daughter? I knew nothing of it."

"She allegedly gave birth secretly, over thirty-odd years ago, in London, and the baby was left at a convent of nuns. Supposedly, the father of the child was a married man who wanted nothing to do with her or her offspring, so her family sent her away to get rid of the baby, worried about their reputation in the eyes of society."

Lakeisha listened intently. "Hmmm...worry is one of the ills that affect the world. We worry too much about the perception of others – not the truth, mind you; only their perception, their illusion."

Natalie nodded emphatically. "Boy, don't I know that? My family – or I should say the family that adopted me – lives for appearances, and their perception is often faulty."

"That's one of the main levels of consciousness that will shift. Those who are too anchored to the old material ways have one of two soul choices – they can adjust their perception or they can go back to the Source before the shift occurs."

"By going back to the Source, do you mean they will die?"

"It is believed that those choices were made prior to our birth; some people agreed to adapt to the new consciousness, and others didn't. Those who didn't are going back – have you noticed how many more people seem to be dying unexpectedly, lately?"

"Now that you mention it, Lakeisha, I think you are right. I have wondered often what is happening. Too bad Aunt Catherine didn't sign up to be here when the shift occurs."

"Maybe her role was different, Natalie, maybe her task was to oversee you doing your part. Or, on the flip side, perhaps she really didn't agree to adjust – her attachment to societal rules and etiquette was paramount."

"It really was." Natalie smiled, thinking about the last day she had seen the old lady. "Aunt Catherine could have written the ultimate Book of Manners; I'm quite sure nobody knew the rules of our societal game better than she did."

"Natalie…maybe Catherine's daughter is the final keeper of the rosary. If so, we need to find her. Nobody knows who the final keepers of all four objects are."

"We…?"

"I was told I must go to London to protect the chain of events leading to the unfolding."

"Who told you that?"

"Natalie, if I tell you how I found out you wouldn't believe me, so let's leave it at that…you are going to London; I'm led to go there myself; why don't we travel together and see what happens?"

Natalie pondered over Lakeisha's suggestion for a moment; then she smiled. "I think that's a terrific idea, Lakeisha. I would feel so much better going with someone I know already."

"Then it is set. Call me as soon as you have some of the details of the trip in place, so I can buy a ticket on the same flight you will be on."

"I will, Lakeisha. Thank you for your loyalty to Aunt Catherine – I know that despite her vinegary exterior, Catherine really respected your opinion. It was after talking to you that she finally warmed up to me. Not a second too soon, either."

"Everything happens in its own time, Natalie, and that timing is not always aligned with what we perceive as being the right moment."

"But if we have free will, Lakeisha, how does everything really work? Do we only have the illusion of choosing, if everything is pre-destined, or is fate changed by what we choose?"

Lakeisha laughed. "You just asked a million dollar question, Natalie. Some believe that the reason we feel we have a choice in what we do is because we don't understand time. Time in itself doesn't really exist - it is one of the many human fabrications to make life on Earth easier. What happens now and what will happen in the future already happened – we just don't know it yet, because our minds aren't ready to accept that our ability to control our circumstances is nothing more than illusion we keep alive to feed our ego. Although our goal in the ascension process is that of overcoming the ego, we can't do so completely without causing the destruction of our earthly selves. That's why there are only a few truly enlightened people that pop up in history from time to time. Most of us continue to create the drama necessary for the collective soul to learn of itself. The prophecy predicts that everyone will reach the same level of consciousness by the time the shift has come to pass; those who struggle to adjust to concepts of unity, equality, oneness, or true meaning of worth will be experiencing great hardship between now and the time of the unfolding."

Natalie was stunned. "Wow, when you put it that way, it really brings home a lot of things I never considered…"

"This is only the tip of the iceberg, Natalie. There is no telling just how much we all will learn when the shift occurs."

I'm not sure if I should be eager or scared."

"I guess we all should be a bit of both. Once everyone reaches the same level of consciousness, there will be nothing new to learn. Life as we know it will be different, and souls will have progressively less reasons to incarnate on Earth."

"Lakeisha…is that what the Bible described as Armageddon?"

"The fight between good and evil, the eternal conflict between the Divine and the earthly bodies…yes, Natalie, I believe it is. Of course, that's only my opinion, so take it for what it's worth to you."

"Actually, your opinion is worth a lot to me, Lakeisha. You have explained, in just a few moments, things I have spent entire nights wondering about."

"I'm sure we'll get more chances to talk, Natalie, especially on our trip. Now we should start thinking of retiring for the night; this has been a full day."

"I think you're right. Well, goodnight, then."

Natalie got up from Lakeisha's bed, and headed for the door. Before leaving she turned around and ran to hug her new friend. "Thank you Lakeisha. I look forward to learning more."

Lakeisha hugged her back and smiled. "Me too, Child, me too."

Jim Allen woke up to the sound of his own heartbeats coming from the monitor he was hooked up to. He looked around the room and tried to understand where he was – nothing looked familiar. Even if the dim lights were making it hard for him to discern details of his surroundings, he knew he wasn't at home. Where was Belinda? He had no earthly idea of what happened; as hard as he tried, his mind was a blank slate – no recollection of anything that happened the past day or so; the last thing he remembered was leaving home in the morning after breakfast.

Certainly Belinda was on her way back; she would explain everything and it all would make sense – Belinda could rationalize even the craziest things. He felt very tired, and struggled to keep awake. Part of him demanded to know what happened, but he didn't even have the strength to push the button for the nurse. He realized, by now, that he was in a hospital room. He had tubes in his nose, both arms infused with an IV, and wires attached to his chest that connected him to the heart monitor. Somehow, whatever happened had to do with his heart.

He was ready to fall into slumber again when he heard the door open, and the eagerness to know what happened jolted him awake. It wasn't Belinda, but a very young nurse.

"Mr. Allen, you are awake." She looked at the clock on the wall and then at his chart. "You slept almost eight hours. Your vitals are strong again, so you should be out of danger, but I can't really say much more. The doctor will be in shortly to talk to you."

"What happened to me?"

"You had a mild heart attack. By the time they brought you in, you had lost consciousness, and your vitals were extremely low, but you responded to treatment very well."

"Well, let's thank God for the small things."

"This was not a small thing, Sir. You would have died if you didn't call 911."

"I called 911 myself? I cannot remember anything. Is my wife outside?"

"Your wife? What do you mean?"

"My wife Belinda. Did she go home? Does she know I'm here?"

The nurse's face grew darker with concern. She suddenly felt tremendous compassion toward this kind old gentleman who obviously didn't remember his wife died. She knew she could not say anything to him – a strong emotion in his precarious state of health could be fatal. "She stepped out for a while, Mr. Allen. She will be back soon. Why don't you rest for a little longer? By the time you wake up she should be here."

"Sounds good to me. I'm very tired."

The nurse noted a few things on his chart, and then left the room.

Jim, now appeased by the fact that he knew what happened, fell asleep again. As soon as his eyes closed, he and Belinda were walking together in a field of sunflowers.

Melody woke up in the middle of the night gasping for air. She was sobbing and asking Grandmama for forgiveness. In her dream she had just lost the book all over again, and was trying to explain the circumstances to her grandmother. Finally, Grandmama asked her to safeguard the rosary, but in the dream Melody didn't know where it was. She looked everywhere in the farmhouse, and could feel her grandmother's irritation rise with each passing minute. She saw someone darting through the front yard from the bedroom window, and she was certain she had seen him before – he was one of the priests that had come to see her when she was looking for the book at the farmhouse, the very same priest that turned out to be Federico Hernandez, Mario's estranged brother. He had the rosary around his neck, and was laughing as he ran. Melody ran downstairs and flew outside to stop him, but he was faster than she. Before she could get to him, he fled with Grandmama's precious rosary, the one she had begged Melody to keep safe. Melody had let her down once again, and she would have to live with that guilt the rest of her life.

She sat up in bed and turned on the bedside lamp. She was glad that it was just a dream. Mario wasn't home yet, and when she looked at the alarm clock on her dresser she almost jumped – three-thirty in the morning! She picked up the phone and dialed his cell number; it rang four times before he picked up.

"Jesus, Mario. I was worried sick!" She exhaled as relief pumped through her veins.

"I'm sorry, Honey. What time is it? I fell asleep in my office. I lay back one minute and closed my eyes to rest them for a second, and I guess I was more tired than I thought."

"I thought something happened, Mario. You really have to review your work schedule to allow yourself some time to sleep."

"I know, Melody. It will all change soon. We are almost ready to close in on the biggest case I've ever worked on."

Melody sighed. There was no arguing with him when it came down to police work. "I understand, Sweetheart. Can you come home now?"

"I'm on my way. I'll be home in less than thirty minutes."

"Okay. See you then."

She doubted she was going back to sleep after that dream, so she got up and went to check on the rosary for her own sake of mind. She was aware that she only had a bad dream, but the guilt of losing Grandmama's book was still haunting her from time to time. She couldn't bear the thought of losing the rosary as well. To make sure nobody's life would be in danger, and to keep the promise she made to Grandmama, she told nobody about the rosary. To her knowledge, the only one who knew about it was Paul. She didn't even tell Mario. All she had said to him was that Grandmama left her The Book and a few other little knick-knacks that had sentimental value for her. He never pushed the issue, and for two years Melody kept her secret.

She went downstairs and walked into the kitchen. She opened the little secret compartment behind the flour container and pulled out the velvet pouch that contained the rosary. She didn't really look at it much the past couple of years, and was still mesmerized by the beauty of it. It was crafted out of different gemstones, and the cross at the end of it was equal-armed.

Thinking back of her dream caused her to shift uncomfortably. Could Federico, Mario's younger brother, be after the rosary? Having been raised into a family that delved into Voodoo, he might have known about it. He obviously knew about the book, but then, due to his religious education into priesthood, she wasn't too surprised.

The thought made her shiver – would the Vatican be after the rosary, too? Memories of that awful Cardinal Bonelli made her blood run cold for a moment. And what was of Federico, anyway? After his car was found empty following a terrible crash on the highway, witnesses had come forth. Someone from Cardinal Bonelli's office called and identified the car as belonging to Father Gervasi, one of the cardinal's aides.

When the police investigated, they were told that Father Gervasi had stolen a priceless manuscript that Cardinal Bonelli had unearthed down in Louisiana – a priceless tome that belonged to the Vatican. The authorities asked for a photo of Father Gervasi, and since he looked like Mario's double – the investigator knew Mario personally – a copy of the suspect's photo was faxed to Mario's office. Mario almost fell out when he realized that Father Gervasi was none other than his estranged little brother he hadn't seen in at least a decade.

Where was Federico now? The simple facts that he was alive and well somewhere unnerved Melody and made her wish that her husband was here with her. Being alone in the farmhouse was okay during the daytime hours, but at night time it was a little scary. The old walls creaked and moaned, and an occasional mouse scurrying around in the attic had the power to make her jump out of her skin. She kissed the rosary and put it back into the velvet pouch, before placing it back into its hiding spot. *I won't let you down this time, Grandmama. I promise.*

Phillip Sanders laid his head against the soft leather seat of his Mercedes, and took another swig from the bottle he was holding. Angela could be a real bitch sometimes – actually, she was a real bitch *all* the time, and was only nice when it fit her purpose.

Phillip didn't care about her, not any more at any rate. He used to, until he laid eyes on his pretty young secretary. How could he resist her gorgeous blue eyes and silky blond hair? She probably had no idea of the effect she had on him, but he had surely enjoyed working long hours lately. She didn't seem to really acknowledge his advances, but she didn't do anything to discourage him either. She almost seemed to find pleasure in teasing him, and rubbed her braless breasts against him every time she leaned over the desk to show him something. He searched for the best word to describe her in the foggy dictionary of his inebriated mind. She was a cock-tease…yeah, that's what she was. But he wanted her nonetheless – every day more than the one before. If she just said the word he would have no remorse leaving Angela and her bratty tantrums.

He drank some more, and looked at the box under his passenger seat, his "box of disguises," as he called it. The box contained some items of clothing and even a fake moustache he used when he went to look for cheap pleasure, since he had a reputation to maintain and Wilmington wasn't exactly New York City. God bless the small towns of America, where everybody knows your name!

By now, Phillip felt like throwing up. He hadn't eaten much, and the alcohol was sloshing around in his gut. He heaved a few times and pressed the button to lower the window of the car. He was drunk but not stupid – if he had to throw up he could do so without ruining the upholstery of a fifty thousand dollar car.

The fresh air did him good. He was still dizzy, but his stomach seemed to have settled a bit. He left the window open and leaned back against the headrest. Suddenly, he thought of Catherine. Sweet, lovely Catherine. Phillip should have married her, instead than her evil sister.

They had only spent one night together, but that had been enough for Phillip to fall in love. That was why he couldn't take in her daughter – the thought of looking at a child that reminded him of his true love would have been the sure death of his already shaky marriage.

He really tried to love Angela after that, but something was missing. Now that he looked at the situation from a different perspective, he knew that something was always missing. He had been physically attracted to Angela in his younger years, but that was all. She was good looking, and was comfortably rich; exactly what Phillip needed at the time to build a respectable law firm. Now he hated her, and as the grip of alcohol tightened around his mind, he entertained, for a moment, the thought of killing her for kicking him out of her life. Phillip Sanders knew the law enough to get away with it.

It was past five in the morning when Natalie finally fell asleep. From the time she got home from Aunt Catherine's house, her mind was running eighty miles per hour. She thought of some of the things that Lakeisha told her, and felt her head spin as she tried to rationalize some of those concepts. Lakeisha talked about the duality of the Universe, of all things having a positive and a negative, of everything being good and evil at the same time. Could that be true?

She mentally scanned through some of the things and people she was familiar with, and no matter which of them she tested, the concept of duality applied to all of them. Starting from even the most basic and elemental forces, everything had a dual nature. Water could be nurturing if applied as a trickle or with the power of a gentle stream, but it could be deadly in other manifestations. The same was with fire, wind, earth.

Thinking about the elements triggered another thought – the meeting point of all cardinal directions. Did the middle point embody the power of all elements? If it did, and vibrations poured in from each cardinal direction inward, the power of the middle point had to be tremendous, and there was no doubt in Natalie's mind that an earth-shattering shift could occur.

She thought of the prophecy Lakeisha told her about. The middle point, she said, was in the center of the Atlantic Ocean; Natalie wondered what mysteries lay under the deep blanket of those waters, and her mind wandered to the concept of fate vs. free will.

According to Lakeisha, everything that happened was already pre-destined. So, Natalie wondered, what was the point of making choices? She remembered an old lady she met several years ago during a weekend trip to New York. This lady claimed to be a wise woman following what she called the "Old Ways". She told Natalie that people waste time doing works of magic to attract things into their lives, when instead they should do things to see what's already there. The blessings, the lady explained – Rosina, that was her name – are already around us and don't need to be attracted. "You can't attract something that's already there. God gets confused when you ask for blessings you already have at your disposal." She told Natalie as the two shared a cup of espresso. "If you want to see real magic," she continued, "give yourself permission to see the blessings. If you can't see them it is not because they are not there, but rather because, deep down, you don't feel you deserve them in your life."

Natalie thought about the old lady's words many times, and tried to apply what she learned to her own life. In fact, she often wondered if her adoptive parents' rejection was caused by her own feelings of low self-worth. Maybe, deep down she thought that if even her birth mother rejected her, there was something wrong with her, and she couldn't fully accept herself. It was easier to identify the blocks than it was to heal from them. How could she ever get over the trauma of being rejected by her own mother?

When she was little, her father explained to her that every situation is unique, and if her mother had to give her up, she surely had a good reason for doing so. Intellectually, the concept was an easy one to absorb, but putting the knowledge to work toward personal acceptance was not as easy. Although she understood that her mother certainly had a reason for giving her up, being abandoned by the person who should love her most caused a wound so deep that it would be nearly impossible to heal from it.

She decided to light up a candle and put a healing wish on it – she was sure she still had some small tapers in her emergency cabinet. She found a small stash of them and reached her hand inside the enclosure to grab one, but changed her mind and pulled out two. Lakeisha told her about the Ibeji, the cosmic twins, and Natalie really needed some balance in her life, especially if it came from happy children. Maybe honoring them would help her on her quest to heal her own childhood, so she lit both candles, side by side, and placed a handful of candy in front of each. She closed her eyes and tried to tune in to her inner guide, and just then she felt as if someone else beside her was there – the sound of children's laughter filled the room, and although she was sure it was only in her head, Natalie felt like giggling. The Ibeji had come to play.

Chapter Eleven

When he opened his e-mail and saw a message from Natalie Sanders, Tom Hadley's heart skipped a beat. He couldn't wait to see Catherine's paintings, and once he opened the attachment, he was genuinely surprised at the quality of his friend's work. In fact, Catherine's paintings reminded him of others he had seen before at a gallery in Washington DC, during his last trip to America. He believed the name of the artist was Marcie Walker, although he would need to do a little research to be sure. He remembered this American artist was quite famous, so it would probably be easy enough to find some of her work online to compare the style to Catherine's.

He scanned through the photos of the paintings – most of them were about little children, and Tom felt a deep wave of compassion tug at his heart as he thought that Catherine never really got over the emotional pain of giving up her daughter. One of them, particularly, caught his attention. It was the portrait of a little girl with golden hair and tiny pig tails. The little girl looked happy as she climbed on a piece of playground equipment, but the woods behind her were dark and ominous. A face – a pale and drawn spectral apparition – watched the little girl from the thick forest; a small pond was right below the ghostly face, fed by her tears of sadness. It was a haunting piece, the fruit of inner pain at work. Tom felt his heart tug as he tried to imagine Catherine's raw emotions through delightful and superior display of color.

A lot of the paintings were portraits of different people, including one that she had entitled "The Spirit." It had a cheerful tone to it, much different than the other ones; it showed a flamboyant old gentleman of color, dressed to impress and holding a walking cane to steady himself. He stood near a crossroads and appeared to look over his shoulder, smiling mischievously.

There was something about the tone and techniques used that still looked vaguely familiar; if he didn't know for a fact that Catherine had never shown her paintings to anyone, he would swear he had seen them before. The name Marcie Walker continued to flash in his mind, and he decided to get to the bottom of it. He searched the name online, and was surprised to see many entries -Marcie Walker was even more popular than he initially thought. He found photos of some of her work, and once again he was struck by the similarities between the two. Then, he found an article that tickled his curiosity.

Marcie Walker's simplest paintings are now estimated to be worth anywhere in between $10,000 and $100,000. Her descriptive style and passion for scenes inspired by daily life are a breath of fresh air, and her paintings are expected to continue rising in value. Nobody has ever been able to interview Miss Walker, as she appears to be very adamant about keeping her private life shielded away from the public eye. 100% of proceeds from the sale of her paintings are handled by Jane Wiley, the director of the Marcie Walker Foundation, an entity which benefits women shelters and provides needed supplies to children going into foster care.

Despite searching, Tom could not locate any interviews with the artist. Even stranger, he could not find a picture of Marcie Walker. A small voice inside his head pushed him to investigate further. His imagination was probably working overtime, but he wondered for a moment if Catherine and Marcie Walker were one and the same.

Some of Marcie's work was exhibited in a gallery in Birmingham, and Catherine's niece was planning on sending the paintings for the show scheduled on the following month. He didn't want to jump to conclusions, but he instinctually felt that he was dealing with something odd, and he wondered for a moment what he would do if it turned out that the mysterious Marcie Walker was his friend – would he give away her secret?

Catherine was gone now, so there was no reason to keep things under wraps. After all, Marcie Walker was a benefactor, and her family would certainly be amenable to bringing her name out. Never mind the fact that with her death the value of the paintings would skyrocket overnight. He looked at the photos again. The more he studied them, the stronger he felt that these were originals from Marcie Walker, and the thought excited him. Then, he remembered something...

It happened about a week before Catherine went into labor. She had asked Tom to go for a walk at Hyde Park and they planned to meet at Clarendon Gate. When Catherine arrived, her face glowed with a special light and she seemed happy, in spite of the fact that she was only days away from losing her child. Considering how tortured she had been since Tom met her three months before, he was sure something happened to cause this dramatic change of attitude in his friend. They strolled together to the Hudson Memorial. Catherine smiled as she walked, occasionally tossing her head back and closing her eyes, soaking in the sun rays.

"Something happened yesterday, Tom", she said with a suddenly serious face. "I came here alone and sat in the sanctuary, hoping to get my mind off what's happening by doing a little bird watching. A bird was sitting on the ground, near there, and it seemed to have trouble flying off; when I looked closer, I saw that it had a small net wrapped around one of its legs. I approached it slowly not to scare it more, and held it in my hand while I carefully slid off the net. It looked at me, and in that moment I felt I could understand what the bird was feeling – it wasn't scared any more, but rather relieved that someone had gotten there at the right time to set it free. I opened my hands and it spread its wings; it paused for a second, and then it flew away toward the dying sun. Watching it take off made me think about my unborn child. I realized I am helping it come into the world, but it has a destiny of its own; no matter what, even if the circumstances around the birth are not optimal, and the start is rough, one day he or she will also spread wings and fly toward the sun. All I have to do is find a way to provide something that will give hope to lost children, and will facilitate their flight. God gave me a talent, Tom, and I will use it, someday, to free the abandoned children."

He asked what she had in mind, but Catherine smiled sweetly and changed the subject.

After so many years, Tom had forgotten about that conversation but now it echoed in his soul. He couldn't wait to analyze Catherine's paintings, and determine if she was Marcie Walker.

He decided to place a call to Natalie and see if she could expedite the delivery of the paintings to the gallery.

Angela Sanders sat at her vanity table and inspected her face closely -- that bastard was giving her wrinkles. She lightly ran a finger above her cheekbone where she thought she saw two lines. Just thinking about Phillip made her blood boil, and she felt her blood pressure shoot up.

How dare he? Has he forgotten he was nobody before he married her? When Angela met him the first time at Café Express, he was a student in law school, barely making ends meet, and scraping tuition with grants, loans and a pitiful night job washing dishes in a cheap restaurant. Angela fought her parents when they tried to dissuade her from seeing him, and secretly gave him money to supplement his meager income. After he graduated from law school she introduced him to the right people, advanced him funds to open a practice, and gave up many of her interests to be a good wife, and always be by his side.

And instead of thanking her, look at what that insensitive son of a bitch was doing while she sat at home crying over their inability to conceive a child of their own! He screwed her mousy sister, and pretended to be a loving husband. And what did he say at the funeral service?

"…everyone who knew her was blessed to have encountered such kindness." That asshole! She shivered at the thought of people finding out – they would all remember those final words, his way of subtly salivating after Catherine, and they would laugh at Angela.

She couldn't allow that to happen, no matter what it took to make sure the secret wouldn't leave the family. She needed to talk to Natalie, and explain to her the importance of this matter. Natalie didn't always understand the necessity of keeping up appearances, but Angela was confident that she could make her daughter see things her way. After all, what would anyone gain from airing out old, dirty laundry? She resolved to call Natalie that same afternoon.

She hadn't seen Phillip at all since the day she told him to stay away, two weeks before, and had only spoken to him twice regarding some issues with a rental property they owned in Asheville. It wasn't going to be long until people would start wondering if something was wrong. Until now she told everybody that her husband was staying at their Raleigh apartment to follow new leads in a difficult case, and driving back and forth to his office in downtown Wilmington.

Perhaps she had moved too fast, without thinking things through, and it would be best to maintain a united front even if they lived separate lives behind closed doors. She picked up the phone to call him, but her hands shook as she dialed the number. She felt a knot in her throat and hung up quickly, before his secretary picked up. She realized tears were flowing down her cheeks – what hurt more? Was it her sister's betrayal, her husband's philandering, or the fact that for once she didn't feel like the star of the show?

Angela was always the star, even when she and her sister were children; her father doted on her and made her every wish come true. Catherine, instead, was the odd child, the one that never stood out in the crowd. Daddy always joked about Catherine being the only debutante who couldn't find a suitor. And how could she? She was mousy and uninteresting, and was never blessed with striking looks – a real plain Jane.

But Phillip liked her enough…

She pushed that thought aside and began to apply make-up. She was still a beautiful woman, one that men looked at with interest in spite of her age; if she wanted to, she could get Phillip to come back. In fact, she would do just that, and hopefully the old bastard would come back to restore her spotless reputation. She smiled at herself in the mirror, suddenly pleased with her plan. She dialed the number again, this time with increased strength. A woman answered the phone but didn't sound like Mrs. Barnes. Angela wondered who she was.

"Sanders Law Offices"

"Yes, this is Mrs. Sanders; I would like to speak to my husband, please."

"Hold on, please, Mrs. Sanders."

She was on hold for a few seconds, before Phillip picked up.

"What do you want?"

"Phillip, I was sort of hoping to be greeted with a 'how are you', or maybe even a 'I missed you, Angie". We haven't seen each other in two weeks."

"I'm thinking you should be jumping up and down with joy, Angela. Isn't it what you wanted?"

Angela squirted a little extra liquid sugar into her voice. "Phillip, you know I love you."

Phillip kept quiet.

"I mean it, Phillip, I love you. I am sorry about the things I said at my sister's house. I was still overwhelmed from the funeral, and reading that letter sent me over the edge. I guess I was just surprised, that's all. Let's bygones be bygones."

Phillip still didn't say anything, but when he cleared his throat Angela knew she had gotten through to him – he always cleared his throat when he was overcome by emotion. So she continued her soft drilling. "Phillip, listen, I am really sorry. Please have dinner with me. We go back a long way, Honey, we can't let something like this destroy all we've built throughout these years."

Phillip sighed loudly. When he spoke, his words sounded heavy and tired. "I'm the one who should apologize, Angela. If you are willing to put this one single mistake behind us, I can only be thankful."

Although she hated to admit it, Angela felt relieved of the outcome of the conversation. It wasn't just about pride…after all these years she couldn't envision being alone. In so many ways Angela was an insecure woman who needed constant reassurance. Maybe she should get a lover, she thought, laughing at her own private joke. She couldn't do that because, deep inside, she still truly loved Phillip.

Happy that her evening was shaping up to be a rewarding one, she dressed quickly and headed to Catherine's house. Now that the funeral was over, and Catherine's will was scheduled to be read tomorrow, there was no reason to keep a housekeeper with a nursing degree. It was time for Lakeisha Jackson to go.

It was nearly ten in the morning when Ryan Wheeler woke up. Natalie was still sleeping beside him, and groaned softly when he sat up in bed. He got up and went to the kitchen to make coffee and possibly cook a little something for breakfast. He opened the refrigerator, but all he could find were cold cuts and tomatoes, along with half a bottle of white wine and two small containers of flavored coffee creamer. He started the coffee and peeked in the bedroom to see if Natalie was still asleep, then threw on some clothes and left to go out to fetch some breakfast. If his memory didn't fail him, he remembered a donut store not too far from there.

He slipped out of the house, got in his car and drove around a few blocks until, discouraged, he gave up looking and stopped by a convenience store to ask for directions. Thankfully, the donut store was nearby. He parked the car and headed to the boardwalk, and suddenly, the aroma of freshly fried dough assaulted his senses, and became stronger as he got closer to the store.

He wasn't sure how much Natalie normally ate for breakfast, so he decided to buy a whole dozen – better too many than not enough. The white bag he walked out with was more tempting than a siren singing for sailors, and he had to exercise some serious self-discipline to avoid stopping somewhere and eat half of the contents. When he got back, Natalie was just stirring, her coffee sensors on full alert. He poured two cups of coffee, added some sugar and cream, and brought one to Natalie, along with two donuts laid side by side on a plate. He passed the coffee and donuts under her nose and waited for a reaction.

"Oh my God! Is that coffee and donuts I smell?"

He laughed heartily, and sat on the bed beside her, while she adjusted her pillows.

"Wow! That was sweet of you, Ryan."

"Anything for you, beautiful lady."

"Do you know how long it has been since someone called me pretty? And, brought me coffee and breakfast in bed? Wait; let me think…oh yeah…never."

Ryan laughed again and stamped a kiss on her forehead. "Well, somebody should…everyday."

Natalie smiled and placed her coffee on the bedside table. "Come here, you. I might get used to this, which might be a scary, dangerous thing for you, because I may come to expect it every day."

"Oh, so do you think I should run?"

Natalie was about to take the plate of donuts but she changed her mind and reached her hand out to touch Ryan's chest instead. "Maybe you should, Ryan. The more you keep hanging around, the harder it will be to let you go if you decide this is not what you want."

The light in Ryan's eyes changed, and they suddenly looked fluid and aroused. "Don't worry about that, Natalie. Let me be the one who decides what I want."

He ran his hand gently on her cheek, and slid it back behind her head, drawing her close to his face. His breath was hot and inviting, and even if she was lying down, Natalie felt her legs wobble and a seed of yearning settled in her lower abdomen. He kissed her then, and his tongue snaked into her parted lips and teased the inside of her mouth. Her body responded by instinctively arching toward him, the light cotton sheet dropping off her naked skin as she pushed up toward him. He ran his hand down toward her breasts and cupped one firmly, lightly squeezing her nipple between thumb and forefinger, until his mouth found the exposed treat.

Natalie moaned and threw her head back, her hands blindly reached for him, a drowning woman seeking to hang on to anything that would prevent her from being swept away by the wave of passion that was threatening to swallow her. Ryan's mouth traveled down, his tongue drawing circles around the pulsating center of her feminine being. He tortured her until she begged him to take her, and right when she thought she would die, he entered her slowly, and began to rhythmically push deeper and deeper inside of her.

Their breathing increased in unison, and finally graduated into a simultaneous scream as both reached orgasm and lay over the crumpled sheets, their souls dancing together above their heavy, spent bodies. It took Ryan a full two minutes before his breathing finally slowed down and his heart stopped thumping. He rolled off of her, and pulled himself up on an elbow looking at her while she sat up. Beads of sweat were still adorning his upper lip and more were glazing his chest.

"Natalie…I don't think I ever want to leave, if you don't want me to."

Natalie's face lit up. She smiled at him and planted a kiss on his lips. "That's good. I don't want you to leave."

"Really? You don't say that to all the guys you sleep with, do you?"

"All the guys I sleep with? Ha! You give me too much credit…seriously, Ryan, I don't date much and I don't usually get this close to people. You are…you are kind of special, I guess."

"Well, that statement could be interpreted in a number of ways…some not too flattering."

She playfully punched his chest. "You know what I mean, Ryan."

He laughed with her. "I'm just messing with you, Sweetie. Listen…what do you think your family is going to say when we tell them we are together?"

Natalie raised her eyebrow. "I'm not sure. Are we *together?* What do you mean by being together, exactly?"

Ryan cleared his throat before he continued. "I was thinking that maybe we could get to know each other better, and if things work out, maybe we could go out exclusively. I know I'm rushing a little, but I am a grown man, Natalie, and I know what I want; I don't see how waiting would help anything."

Natalie was blown away – she stared at him without speaking, and took a sip of her cold coffee to wet her suddenly parched throat. After a moment of heavy silence she replied. "Wow…Ryan…I don't know. We barely know each other. I think maybe it would be best to keep our relationship to ourselves and not involve families, at least until we have a chance to see if we are compatible."

"I thought it was pretty obvious we are compatible." Ryan said, winking.

Natalie felt dizzy. Her head was spinning and her heart was beating at crazy speed. "It's obvious we are attracted to each other physically, Ryan, but we can't be sure we'll get along. Also, I'm getting ready to go to London. I don't know how long I will be gone."

Ryan looked at her a bit puzzled. "And why does that matter? Are you planning on meeting someone else there?"

"Of course not. That's not the point."

"Look, why don't you take a couple of days and give it some thought? I know it's a big thing to decide right now, but please promise me that you will think about it."

"Oh…ok…I promise I will think about it."

"That's all I'm asking. Now, what about seconds?"

Natalie laughed,"Seconds? I'm still tired…"

"I was talking about coffee, Natalie. The rest will come later."

She laid her head against the fluffy pillows and wallowed into that moment of bliss, while Ryan went to fill their cups. Why not? She thought as her mind floated on a sea of wellness. Maybe being in a relationship with Ryan was the right thing to do.

Chapter Twelve

Catherine Bouvier's Last Will and Testament stunned everybody.

Through the years, Angela and Phillip never saw Catherine show an ounce of affection toward their adopted daughter, Natalie, so when they heard that Natalie was named executrix of the will, everybody's mouth dropped.

The will stated that Natalie should search for Catherine's natural daughter. If she was successful, and could find her, the daughter would inherit her mother's estate; in the event, instead, that the daughter could not be found, Natalie would be the sole beneficiary.

Nobody in the room was more surprised than Natalie. She sat in one of the burgundy leather chairs and swallowed hard. She already knew that Aunt Catherine had hoped Natalie would find the daughter she had to give up over thirty years ago, but she wasn't prepared to be second in line in inheriting such a vast estate.

"Natalie doesn't know the first thing about executing a will, Mr. Dillard. Is there anything that can be done to turn that power over to my husband?"

"I'm sorry, Mrs. Sanders, but Ms. Bouvier's instructions are quite clear. If Ms. Sanders has any questions, I'll be here to help her."

Natalie smiled. Mr. Dillard's tone was southern-bred and firm enough to shut Angela up.

"Well, this is about all, Ladies and Gentleman" Mr. Dillard said with the flare of a story teller, "Ms. Sanders, I will probably need you for a few extra minutes to sign all the papers. Of course, if that's inconvenient, we can schedule another appointment to finalize everything."

"Oh no, Mr. Dillard; I will stay and finish. Thank you for your consideration."

"Very well, then." The old attorney stood up and saw Natalie's parents out before coming back to sit in front of her. He closed the door, and waited a few moments, before he dropped another bomb. "Natalie, you are an artist...have you ever heard of a painter by the name of Marcie Walker?"

Natalie looked at Mr. Dillard a bit surprised – this was the last question she expected from him. "I've heard of her, but I don't think I've ever seen her work. Why do you ask?"

Mr. Dillard took off his glasses and focused his old myopic eyes on Natalie's. "Well, no reason to beat around the bush. I might as well come out and say it...Catherine Bouvier was Marcie Walker."

It took Natalie a moment to process the information. "Is this a joke? Are you telling me that my old, spinster aunt was a world-known artist?"

"That's exactly what I'm telling you, Young Lady."

"Did Aunt Catherine tell you that?'

"She did more than just tell me, Natalie. I have cared for her affairs as Marcie Walker for years. She didn't want anyone to know until now. She called me the night before she died to finalize her will and to ask me to tell you." The attorney shook his head, "It's almost as if she knew she was leaving this earth.

Your aunt was a lot more intuitive than any of us ever gave her credit for."

"I don't know that I could handle any more surprises for today, Mr. Dillard."

The attorney laughed. "Don't worry, Natalie. There won't be any more, at least from me. It will be hard to find Ms. Bouvier's daughter, but if I can help with anything let me know. Catherine and I were friends, aside from having a professional relationship. As far as Marcie Walker is concerned, there is a foundation in place to manage the proceeds from the sale of the paintings and donate the money to charitable venues."

Natalie stood up and reached out to shake hands with Mr. Dillard. "Thank you Sir. I will do my best to honor Aunt Catherine's will. I promise that I will begin to search for her daughter immediately. Aunt Catherine has left her a little something more she would like her to have – a rosary which, I discovered, is very old and priceless."

Mr. Dillard walked her out and he went back to his desk. Neither of them noticed his secretary scramble away from the door where she had stood listening to their conversation. As soon as he closed his door, she picked up the phone and dialed a number. The man on the other side of the line listened eagerly.

"Natalie Sanders has the rosary" she said almost in a whisper, "that's the information you were looking for, right?"

Ryan was equally surprised by the news Natalie shared while they ate lunch together. "Wow! Who would have known?"

"No kidding! Now I am suddenly in charge of securing the terms of a will, finding some mysterious woman who was left in foster care in a different country over thirty years ago, and making sure she gets what's rightfully hers, including that damn rosary which looks like an ordinary rosary to me, but it is not, unless Lakeisha is making all this up."

"Whoa! Wait up…you lost me…what rosary are you talking about?"

"A rosary my aunt bought at some antique store last year, when she thought she was going to meet her daughter - I found it hidden in her studio after she passed. Lakeisha, my aunt's former nurse, who claims to belong to a secret order of nuns, told me it is an important piece necessary for the unfolding of some ancient prophecy."

Ryan looked at Natalie over the rim of his water glass. "And you believe her?"

"Hmmm…I sort of do. She seems to know things we common humans don't know."

"I see. Is this rosary worth money?"

"According to Lakeisha the rosary is worth more than money. Allegedly, the keeper will have power to see past, present and future. Yes, I guess it's worth money too. "

"Natalie…I hate to burst your bubble, but it sounds like Aunt Catherine's nurse might have indulged her share of swamp water." He circled his right forefinger around near his temple to indicate that Lakeisha was crazy.

"She's not crazy, Ryan. She told me things that really made a lot of sense, and she explained some concepts I have struggled with my whole life."

"I would really take everything she says with a grain of salt, Sweetie."

"Oh, I will. She really is a pleasant person to talk to, though. I think she is planning on going to London with me."

Ryan pulled his head back and looked at Natalie. "Really? Why would she do that?"

"I think she has some personal loose ends to tie up there, so we are taking the opportunity to travel together."

"That should get pretty interesting – ancient prophecies and crazy swamp ladies."

Natalie really was beginning to resent Ryan's preconceived attitude toward Lakeisha, but she let it go to not spoil the moment. "Yes, it might. Well, look, I actually have to run. I have some phone calls to make, and I want to make sure I have enough time to stop by the grocery store as well."

"Okay Sweetie; I have to roll out of here and get back to work too. See you tonight?"

"Sounds great. I will call you later."

Ryan watched Natalie walk out, and followed her with his eyes until she got into her car. He wondered just how much that rosary was really worth. If it was something really sought after, he might be able to sell it for a good amount and patch up his family's misfortunes without having to marry Natalie. He planned to spend the night at her house again, although he didn't remember seeing a rosary there. Maybe Natalie didn't take it out of Catherine's house yet. If he got lucky, and found the rosary, tomorrow he could just come up with an excuse to stay away, save his family and start seeing Ashton again. It really looked like things were shaping up in his favor.

When Tom Hadley's phone rang he was just thinking of calling Natalie. Hearing her voice on the other side of the line was definitely welcome news.

"Natalie, it's great to hear from you. I was going to call you tonight. Given the time difference I was going to try after dinner my time, to make sure I would find you."

"Tom – you don't mind if I call you by your first name, right?"

"Not at all."

"I discovered something crazy about my aunt today…"

"Yes, I think I did too. From the photos you sent me, I have reasons to believe that Catherine has painted before, under a different name."

"Marcie Walker, right?'

Tom was stunned. "You knew?'

"No, actually I didn't, but her attorney informed me of that today. Catherine Bouvier and Marcie Walker were the same person."

"That's an amazing thing, Natalie. Marcie Walker's paintings are highly sought. I can't imagine what their value will rise to if word leaks out that she passed away."

"I know, Tom; to tell you the truth, I've heard the name, but I've never really seen the paintings. I think I will do a little research tonight."

"When are you planning on sending Catherine's paintings to me, Natalie?"

"I have to pack them and ship them – probably a few days. I'm hoping to get to London myself, within the next two weeks. I'm calling the travel agency this afternoon, or tomorrow at the latest. My passport is already in order."

"You are welcome to stay with me, Natalie, if you are comfortable with the idea. I have a fairly large home, and I am rarely there. Of course, if that makes you uncomfortable, I can book a hotel for you."

"Staying with you would be fine with me, but I am not traveling alone, so I will have to ask my friend if she is amenable to it."

"Inquire with her, and then let me know. It would be a great pleasure to have you stay at my house. I live within walking distance from the gallery, and it would make it easier for you to go back and forth, especially if you don't have transportation."

"Thank you, Tom. I really appreciate the offer. I will call my friend today and we will discuss the possibility."

"Natalie, go ahead and also ship your own paintings, the ones you have ready."

Natalie's heart skipped. "I will, Tom. I have a few more I'm still working on, but I can certainly finish them before I ship the others."

"Very well. Let me know if there is anything I can do to facilitate the shipping. You have my address, I assume?"

"I do, thank you. Aunt Catherine wrote it down for me."

"That's great. I look forward to receiving them."

"Bye for now, Tom."

"Good-bye, Natalie."

She hung up the phone and looked at her watch – almost three in the afternoon. She decided to go home right away and skip the grocery store, but first she figured she would give Lakeisha a call. There was no answer at Aunt Catherine's house, so she assumed that Lakeisha had gone out to run errands. She went home and pulled out the paintings that needed more work, determined to finish all five of them before packing Aunt Catherine's. She had just started setting out the colors, when someone rang her doorbell. She wiped her hands on a cloth and went to open the door, surprised to see Lakeisha standing in front of her.

"Lakeisha! What are you doing here? I just tried to call you a short while ago."

Lakeisha shook her head. "I'm not staying at the Bouvier's house any longer. Your mother discharged me."

"Really? Wow, that was fast…come in, come in." She moved out of the way, to allow Lakeisha inside. "When did she let you go?"

"Just this morning. I haven't taken all my things yet, but I'm staying at the Rest Inn on Market Street."

"Not for long, Lakeisha. I would like for you to stay with me, if you will; at least until we go to London."

Lakeisha was taken aback by the offer. "Why, Natalie, that's very kind of you. I just took the bus here because I wanted to talk to you in person; I didn't expect your generous offer."

"It's no bother for me, Lakeisha. In fact, I could really use the company, and maybe you can teach me a few more things.

You really gave me some food for thought the last time we talked."

Lakeisha smiled. "That's good, Natalie. That shows your thoughts run deep. I would love to accept your offer, but I will have to go back to Wilmington to fetch my things from the hotel, and go back to the house to get the rest."

"I have an idea…why don't you go take a walk on the beach while I work on this for a little while, and then we'll get some dinner and head back to Wilmington together? I will drive you back to Aunt Catherine's house on my way to get a few supplies. Then, I can wait for you, if you want me to."

"I would love to ride back into town with you, Natalie. The bus system in North Carolina is really not the best there is. You can just drop me off to your aunt's house. I'll just pack the rest of my belongings and then I will walk back to the hotel – it's quite near."

"That's settled, then. Go on and kick some sand around those toes, and I will be done in a jiffy. Of course, if you prefer to stick around and have some tea, feel free to do so. I will just be in my own little world for a while."

"No, actually a nice walk will do me good. I will be back in a bit."

Lakeisha left, and Natalie dove right into painting. She was happy to be working again, and immediately felt invigorated. She wondered if she had jumped into things a bit too fast – she barely knew Lakeisha. Would she work out as a roommate? Well, it wasn't forever anyway; just until they went to London, which was going to be within the next couple of weeks, hopefully.

When she heard knocking at the door, she jumped and looked at clock on the wall – seven o'clock! It had been two hours since Lakeisha had come and gone. As it always happened when she painted, Natalie had lost track of time. She opened the door to a smiling Lakeisha. "I really needed that walk. The beach is quite nice here."

Natalie smiled back. "Yeah, I think it is, too. Well, I'm just about done here. Are you ready to go grab a bite?"

"Sure. Walking made me hungry."

"Let's go, then" Natalie said as she moved the easel away from any jumping platform – Billy seemed to have a fatal attraction to wet paint. "Oh, you know what? I never called Ryan. Give me a moment, Lakeisha, and we'll be out the door."

Lakeisha nodded and sat on the loveseat in the family room. It only took a few minutes for Natalie to wrap up the conversation, and by the time she got back into the family room, Lakeisha appeared a bit unsettled.

"Is everything okay, Lakeisha?"

"I think so…I just got this funny feeling about deception, a few minutes ago, but I think I'm just tired after a long day."

"Well, let's go eat something; then, I will give you a ride back into town to tie up all the loose ends. When you come back, you can have the guest room all to yourself."

He moved through the house in the dark, afraid the neighbors might get alerted by lights in the house. Time was really running out – he knew it, he could feel it in his bones.

168

After he spoke with Lisa, the attorney's secretary, he found out that Catherine Bouvier left the rosary to her niece, but it was never made clear whether it was taken out of the Bouvier home already, or if it was still hidden somewhere in the house.

Accidentally meeting Lisa at the Sweet Carolina Café, the day before, was, in his opinion, another sign – getting in her pants so quickly was just an added benefit.

Lisa was completely unaware of the impact her words had on him when she told him of her annoyance at having to change her employer's appointments to accommodate the reading of a Will and Testament. He was fairly sure that client confidentiality forbade the young woman to disclose names, but she was so heated up about having to stay late that afternoon, and missing her niece's birthday party to make phone calls, that she angrily blurted out Catherine's name as she discussed the situation.

Of course, he was all ears. He turned on his charm and told Lisa that Ms. Bouvier owned a rosary his own mother would love to have. His mother was ill, he explained, and owning that rosary was her greatest wish; if he could find out whom Ms. Bouvier left it to, he could maybe talk to the new owner about purchasing the piece. Lisa knew nothing about the rosary, so she had no reasons to doubt his words.

They met again that same evening, and after a few drinks and some coaxing on his part, they sealed the deal: Lisa would listen in, the next day, and she would keep him informed if she found out any details about the coveted rosary. When she finally called, Lisa informed him that Catherine's niece planned to take the rosary to London – when did that plan materialize?

He slipped quietly into Catherine's closet, careful to not turn on the flashlight until the door was closed. There were several boxes on the ground, and he wondered if the rosary could be into one of them. It would take him a while to go through all the boxes in there, but he should have enough time. It was certainly a plus that the housekeeper was gone.

He went through the first box and all he saw were old photographs of days gone by, yellowed by time and bent at the corners. He got through the second box and he found a small case of costume jewelry. At the bottom of the case was a velvet pouch that felt as if it contained a necklace. It was tied with several knots and he sweat profusely as he tried to undo the tie, his fingers shaking so badly that it was torture to focus on such a patient task. He studied the contents through the material of the pouch – the small beads were about the same size as he expected the rosary's to be, and he thought he felt something sturdy at the end of the bag…a small cross, maybe?

His heart was thumping furiously; he heard blood rushing through his ears, and he suddenly felt faint. He laughed out loud, and kissed the pouch. He was ready to get out of there now; he turned off the flashlight before he opened the door, and slipped quietly out of Catherine's room. And that's when he heard voices…

At first, he thought they were just in his head – fear tricking him into hearing what wasn't there – but when he listened closely, he distinctly heard the voices of two women. He went back into the room and into the closet, and literally prayed that they wouldn't come upstairs. He heard one of them asking why the back door was open, and the other one assuring her friend that it was her mother who had likely left it unlocked this morning on her way out. One of the women was Natalie Sanders. To his dismay, he heard her tell her the other woman "I'm going to check all the doors while you fetch your things. Knowing Mom, she probably left a few more unlocked. After that I'll be on my way, then. I'll see you tomorrow. Call me if you need a ride."

He hoped that wherever *her things* were, they were nowhere near Catherine's room. He heard the woman come up the stairs and open the door to the room adjacent to the one he was in.

The housekeeper! He thought she had been discharged already…why was she here? He heard her moving around, his breath catching in his throat every time the sounds stopped. Then, he heard silence for a minute – where was she? He was sweating profusely, and almost gave in to the temptation of using one of Catherine's clean garments to wipe his face. He bit down on his lower lip, the way he did when he was really nervous, and he cursed himself when he tasted blood.

He heard Lakeisha's footsteps leaving the room, and heading toward the stairs. She suddenly stopped and turned around. The footsteps got closer and closer to Catherine's room, until the door opened and she walked in. He hid behind two long satin nightgowns, and waited.

Lakeisha moved some things around the room, then, obviously not finding what she was looking for, she opened the closet door, and he was ready to pounce on her. He hit her with the back of his gun, and watched her collapse on the floor, her face an instant mask of blood. She didn't move, and he touched her throat to see if he could find a heartbeat – he didn't. He wondered if she was the same woman who had called after him the day of the funeral, but in the darkness of the room, and with all the blood that covered her face, he could not make out what she looked like. Even if he had seen her before, he would not be able to recognize her now. He put the pouch safely into his pocket and quickly fled the house and disappeared into the night.

Natalie was ready to take the ramp to get on 421 S after getting her supplies at the 24-hrs store, when she realized she accidentally left with the spare key she had used to lock the doors -- the one that Aunt Catherine always kept outside. Unsure of when she would go back, and certain that her mother would have a fit if she went to check on the house and the key was not there, she turned around and headed back toward Princess Street.

She wondered if Lakeisha was still in the house, so she went in and called her name. No answer. Lakeisha had already left. She wasn't too tired, so she thought of going up to Aunt Catherine's room and maybe box up a few things to make her mother's job a little easier. Lakeisha had already packed most of Aunt Catherine's personal belongings, but she was sure there was plenty more.

She went up the stairs and headed straight to Catherine's room. Although it was almost summertime, she felt cold, and couldn't decide whether the temperature was low, or if this old house was just giving her the willies. She walked in and turned on the light.

Most of the room had been packed up already, aside from the contents of the bedside table. She went to the closet to see if she could find a large bag or a small box to pack those items, and when she opened the door and went to turn on the light, she saw something. At first, she thought it was an old coat that had fallen off the hanger and had bunched up on the ground, but then she saw that the coat had a face, and the face was covered in blood. She screamed and stood frozen in place for what seemed like an eternity. She forced herself to look again. It was Lakeisha, a motionless ebony doll abandoned to its fate.

She instinctually tried to find a heartbeat – it was faint, nearly undetectable, but there was definitely a beat. She burst into tears of relief, and ran out of the closet to grab the phone on Aunt Catherine's bedside table. She prayed that Lakeisha would hang on. The wound on her forehead was bleeding profusely, and Natalie shivered at the thought of what would have happened to Lakeisha if she hadn't decided to stop back by after she left the store.

The rescue team and the police arrived, and in minutes, the room was overtaken by medics and uniformed officers. Lakeisha was quickly whisked away, more dead than alive. The officers took Natalie's statement, and told her that a detective would get in touch with her the next day. She wondered if what happened to Lakeisha had anything to do with the rosary. She didn't even know what led her to think of that, but it sounded like pure madness even as she formulated the thought. And yet, as she drove away from the old, dark house, she knew something evil was at play. That night, Natalie Sanders was truly afraid.

Chapter Thirteen

Jim Allen sat on his recliner and stared into space. Gone were the days when he would sit and do a crossword puzzle, or turned on the TV set to listen to the latest news. Without Belinda, life was not worth living, and he hoped every day that it would be his last.

His children and their families had come and gone; the police scraped every square inch of his home looking for clues, and found none. Same with the store – the perpetrator seemed to have vanished into thin air. He was pretty sure that the break-in at the store and Belinda's death were related, but he didn't think the police took him seriously when he tried to direct their attention to the possibility. They thanked him for his input, and for his cooperation with authorities, but as there hadn't been any updates in over two weeks now, he was beginning to lose hope. And what if there were any updates? Even if the culprit was caught, Belinda would still be dead. Although he willed the son of a bitch to melt in the flames of hell, his capture could only fix the problem the way a band-aid would dress a slashed throat – a very small consolation indeed.

Jim wanted to die. In simple words, and without beating around the bush, that was his only wish from the heart. He stopped taking his heart medications three days before. Being a religious man, he considered suicide a sin, but if he looked at the issue with the twisted perception of a broken heart, he came to the conclusion that stopping artificial treatment aimed at preventing the course of nature wasn't really suicide. If it was

175

God's will for him to live a tortured life without his Belinda, then he should be able to do it without chemical help, but he was simply not going to extend his own journey on borrowed time just to suffer.

One of his sons was still in town, working out details Jim had no will to deal with, so he had to be careful not to raise any suspicion. When asked if he took his medications regularly, he always replied that he did, and his son never questioned him.

He closed his eyes, and saw Belinda's smiling face. There were times he saw her as he found her on that fateful day when she died, but he always opened his eyes immediately and pushed those memories away. He wanted to see her the way she looked while she was alive; when the two of them were together; when Jim was still happy to walk the streets of Earth.

"Really, Natalie, what was that woman doing in my sister's house? She had no reason to be there after I discharged her."

"Mother, I think I've told you that five times already."

"Don't you use that tone with me, young lady!"

Natalie sighed – there was no winning a battle against her mother; the most one could hope was that Angela would soon tire of her adversary and focus on the next enemy.

"I'm not using a tone, Mom. I told you – Some of Lakeisha's belongings were still at the house; she doesn't drive, so she can only carry so much on foot or on a bus. I gave her a ride to Aunt Catherine's place. She was going to get her things, and walk back to her hotel. The perpetrator must have been already in the house when we got there. In fact, I know he was, since we found one of the doors unlocked. My first thought was that maybe you or dad went by the house earlier in the day and forgot to lock up."

Angela took a deep, exasperated breath. "Maybe it is as you say, Natalie, but we've never had anyone breaking in before -- until that woman lived there, that is. Maybe she called some thugs from that God-forsaken place she is from...there is no telling. You know how those people are...don't you, dear? We've heard all kinds of scary things on the television about violence down there where she is from."

"Mom, the violence in New Orleans is due to gangs that moved into the run-down parts of town that were abandoned. Not everybody is violent 'down there where she is from'. I know you've heard that too, from the television."

Angela blushed – the impertinence of that child! She stood up and left. Natalie, relieved by the unexpected retreat of enemy troops, drew a big breath and prepared to go back to the hospital to see if Lakeisha's condition had improved at all. Two hours ago, Lakeisha was still unconscious; the doctor said that whatever hit her cracked her cranium only slightly, but the brain was still badly swollen and bruised, so she would be kept in an induced coma until the swelling decreased.

She called Ryan on the way there. "Hey, I'm on my way to Jackson Memorial. Someone broke into Aunt Catherine's house last night, and Lakeisha was there gathering her belongings. The perpetrator attacked her and she is now in ICU"

"Oh my God, Natalie...that's awful!"

"I should be there in just a few minutes, if you would like to meet me for coffee."

"Definitely, Sweetie. I'm on my way."

"Okay, Ryan; thank you, I can really use the support – my mom is being a bitch, as always."

"She's probably upset too, Natalie"

"Nah, my mother doesn't get upset; she's pure Tuscan marble under the skin."

Ryan laughed. "You're hard on her. What would she say if she heard you?"

"She would say that I am a hopeless brat, and that my attitude probably comes from some bad, unrefined gene I inherited from my real mother. And for your information, she would say it, or at least think about it, whether I say anything or not – it's her favorite mantra."

"Well, don't worry about it, Sweetie. There is nothing bratty or unrefined about you. You're 100% winner."

"See? That's why I need you there. You walked into my life to restore my self-esteem."

"I'll be there in about thirty minutes, Natalie. I only need to finish reading a few paragraphs of a contract that came in this morning."

"That's fine, Ryan, see you there."

She ended the call and laid the phone on the passenger seat. The hospital loomed ahead and she slowed down to make sure she wouldn't miss the right entrance. She hurried upstairs to the ICU and went straight to Lakeisha's room, hoping to talk to one of the doctors in charge of her care. She saw a nurse leaving the room, and sped up her step toward her.

"Excuse me, Miss,"

The young nurse turned to see who called her and smiled at Natalie. "Yes, can I help you?"

"I was wondering if there have been any changes with Miss Jackson."

"I'm not at liberty to discuss that, Miss. You're not family, right?"

Natalie almost laughed – She was white, Lakeisha was black, and although they shared a soul bond of some type, they were not blood-tied or related in any way. Did soul family ties qualify one to get information in a hospital setting?

"No, I'm not related to her, but she was my aunt's nurse and a personal friend. She was injured when a perpetrator broke into my aunt's house and attacked her. I already explained this last night to another set of nurses and to the doctor on duty."

The nurse warmed up a little. "Of course, Miss. If you'll have a seat in the waiting area I will send the doctor who checked on her this morning. I'm afraid this is a restricted area, so I cannot let you go into the room."

"I understand. I will be in the waiting room."

When the nurse left to find the doctor, Natalie walked into the waiting area and picked up a magazine. In the light of day, things didn't seem quite so ominous; the police believed that whoever attacked Lakeisha was probably a simple burglar who knew the house was empty after hearing of Aunt Catherine's death. Ryan arrived within minutes, kissed her forehead and sat down beside her. "Hi Sweetie, are you okay?"

"Yes; a little shaken, maybe, but I'm okay."

"Do the police have any leads?"

"None they are sharing, if they do. Someone is supposed to call me today, but I haven't heard anything yet."

"Most likely she happened to walk in on the burglar and he panicked. Wilmington is not what it used to be. I've heard that the same thing happened to Mrs. Allen, the owner of the antique shop."

Natalie arched her eyebrow. "What happened to Mrs. Allen?"

Ryan took in the surprised look on her face and proceeded to deliver the news of Belinda Allen's death as gently as he could. Unfortunately, there just wasn't a way to soften the blow. "You haven't heard? Her husband found her strangled in their bed when he got home from lunch, a couple of weeks ago. The whole house was ransacked. The police are pretty sure the person who broke in thought Mrs. Allen was gone when in fact she was in bed sick."

"Oh dear God..." Natalie was at a loss for words.

"I know – that's pretty bad, huh? I remember when we still lived in a quaint small town. We have lots of strangers around at all times now, and a really bad economy. Things have changed from what they used to be, and not for better."

"I didn't even know, Ryan. I've known the Allens since I was a little girl...Mr. Allen was my teacher, for crying out loud!"

A young doctor walked in and interrupted the conversation. "Are you Ms. Sanders?"

"Yes. Any improvements?"

"Surprisingly yes." The young doctor replied with a smile, "Ms. Jackson's condition is still listed as critical, but the swelling has begun to recede. If all proceeds well, she might be able to awaken within the next day or two and her condition will be upgraded to serious."

Natalie smiled in relief. "That's wonderful news, doctor. Thank you. Would it be possible to see her for just a moment?"

The young doctor ran a hand through his extremely short blond hair, and nodded. He had gentle eyes – eyes of a healer, Natalie thought. She liked him immediately.

"Just for a moment, though. She won't be able to hear you, you know."

"I know. I will only stay for a few seconds."

The doctor was ready to leave the room, when Natalie called him back.

"Will I get notified if anything changes? Ms. Jackson has no family, to my knowledge. I'm her only family."

The doctor – Dr. Barnes, as his name tag indicated – pulled out a pen from his coat pocket. "What is your number? We probably already have it on the chart, but I want to make sure we have a way of getting in touch with you."

Natalie took the pen and wrote her number on the back of a business card the doctor handed to her. "Here you go. Thanks for bending the rules a little." She gave him the card and sat back down while the doctor left the room.

"Well, I'd better go in and see Lakeisha for a moment. Will you be here when I get back?"

"Actually" Ryan said, looking at his watch, "I'm supposed to meet my father in a short while, so I'd better be going." He stood up and kissed her gently, before both of them walked out in opposite directions.

181

When she stepped into Lakeisha's room, and saw her lying there, with an oxygen mask and her forehead bandaged, she hardly recognized the vibrant woman she knew Lakeisha to be. She was covered by a light white sheet, and her eyes were swollen shut. The most reassuring sight of all was to see her chest rising up and down. Natalie got closer to be bed and gently touched Lakeisha's hand.

"You will be okay, Lakeisha. My guest room is waiting for you, and we will go to London together. You've got to pull through this."

Lakeisha remained motionless; the only sound in the room that of the monitor which recorded her vital signs. Natalie blew her a light kiss, and then gently left the room.

After leaving the hospital she went by Aunt Catherine's house, and saw that it had been cordoned off by the police. She saw an officer standing by the door, and her mother talking heatedly with an older man in civilian clothes. After seeing her mother there she changed her mind about stopping by, and hoped that her mother didn't see her driving by.

She went home instead, and walked straight to the fireproof safe in the closet to fetch the pouch with the rosary. When she undid the tie, and reached inside the pouch, she felt that under the rosary was a small piece of paper, so she pulled it out. It was a receipt of purchase. When she saw where Aunt Catherine bought the piece, her heart stopped…the rosary was bought the previous year from Hidden Treasures, Mrs. Allen's antique shop.

She sat down on the floor for a moment, hoping that her head would stop spinning. Mrs. Allen was dead, murdered senselessly by a burglar, and Lakeisha was unconscious in a hospital bed, after being attacked by a burglar at Aunt Catherine's house. Both women handled the rosary, or were tied to it somehow. Natalie put her head between her knees, and silently prayed for the nightmare to end.

He was mad, utterly mad. Actually no, he was furious. It was indeed a better way to describe how he felt. When he got back from Catherine Bouvier's house, last night, he felt as if he had won a lottery. All the way home he touched the pouch in his pocket, savoring the precious and endless minutes that separated him from claiming the rosary's power as his own.

When he arrived home, he could barely contain his excitement; he had a hard on, for Christ's sake! He sat at the table and touched the velvet pouch; his fingers ran over the soft material, and he fantasized about the moment he would pull the rosary out; each knot he untied was a step stone to glory. And then, the knots were untied, the mouth of the bag came open, and he felt faint. He gently tipped the bag over his hand, eager to see the rosary's beady magnificence. A rosary fell out, and its crowning was welcome by a litany of curse words. It couldn't be...

Although it was of exquisite craftsmanship, what lay on the table in front of his eyes was not *the* rosary. It was a rosary, but not the right one. This one was bluish in color, with a Christian crucifix at the end – the real rosary was allegedly crafted out of different gemstones, mostly garnet and onyx, and had an equally-armed cross at the end to represent the meeting point of all energy.

According to what he learned from Celeste -- as she related what her dying aunt told her -- red and black gemstones were presented to the Ibeji twins, who wanted to craft a necklace to give to their mother. They couldn't decide which color the necklace should be, and since they weren't able to find a compromise, Olodumare sent Elegba, the patron of children, crossroads and doors, to settle the dispute. Elegba decided that in order to be fair, the necklace would be crafted using a special pattern – black and red stones would be alternated equally three times, and would be separated from the next set by a white diamond, symbol of purity and eternal light. The seventh stone represented the seventh plane of God that one could only reach through acceptance of the other lower planes. In order to remind them that true power can only come to those who take time to understand the importance of all directions leading into one, He instructed them to craft an equal-armed cross to represent the meeting point at the center of all. With the combined power of all energies connected, the keeper of the rosary would be able to see beyond the barriers of time.

He felt a damnable urge to hurl the rosary against the wall, but his strong religious views prevented him from doing so. Instead, he stood up, and slammed the chair back, leaving the unwanted string of beads on the table. He needed some fresh air. Two people were dead already, and the rosary was still at large. Acting on impulse hadn't served him well, so far. From now on he would need to seriously think things through before taking another step. For now, a mind clearing drive was just what the doctor ordered.

Natalie wasn't going to take any more chances. The circle was closing in, and she felt quite sure that the person who was after the rosary would come for her next.

She drove into Wilmington, keeping an eye on her rearview mirror for anyone following her. She thought she spotted her father's car, a few vehicles behind, but when she looked again he wasn't there. Her parents were the last people she was hoping to meet, so she drew a sigh of relief.

She went to the bank where she held an account and asked the teller for a safe deposit box. After carefully laying the velvet pouch into it, she quickly closed it and handed it back to the woman who was patiently waiting by the steel cage. As she walked out of the bank, she felt liberated. The intruder may still try to break into her place, but at least the rosary was safe.

Her cell phone rang. "Hello, Natalie, this is Dr. Barnes."

Natalie wasn't sure whether this was going to be a welcome call or one she should dread. "Yes, Dr. Barnes; are there any changes?"

"Yes, Natalie. We just ran some tests, and the swelling has subsided. To tell you the truth, we consider Ms. Jackson's fast improvement quite remarkable and surprising. Last night's tests showed swelling of the brain, and there was evidence of light intracranial bleeding. Of course, that fact alone caused a lot of concern, because if the blood does not drain, it can put pressure on the already swollen cerebral tissue and cause considerable damage. Well…I just ran those tests again, and the amount of blood has also decreased. If she continues to improve at this rate, we might be able to terminate the chemically induced coma as early as this evening."

" That's wonderful news, Doctor!"

"I'm as stunned as anyone else, Natalie. It really looks like Lakeisha has someone watching over her from above."

Cute and spiritual…WOW!

"Anyway, I just wanted to give you the update. I figured you'd be thrilled."

"I am, Doctor; I'm speechless, in fact."

"I'll be here until eleven tonight, Natalie. If I witness another miracle I will let you know right away."

"Thank you, Dr. Barnes. Your kindness is appreciated more than you might think." She wrapped up the call and smiled happily – Lakeisha was going to be okay. Maybe Aunt Catherine was watching over her; after all, it was her home that was broken into, and according to all manuals of southern etiquette, entering one's property without being invited is definitely a no-no. Thinking about Aunt Catherine being mad at the intruder because he broke rules of basic respect tickled Natalie's funny bone.

Oh, Aunt Catherine…I would give a leg to hear some of those etiquette rules from you, right now…

She thought of going home, but the prospect of going back to her empty house filled her with a sense of loneliness. She wanted to be around other people, even the busybodies of Wilmington. Connection and familiarity were very strong concepts with Natalie at this juncture, and she suddenly felt very alone.

She drove to a packing supply store on Market St. to get some supplies to start packing the paintings. It was nice to be surrounded by other humans on a day like this. Although she normally craved solitude, right now she needed companionship. She picked up new brushes and some fresh oils, determined to jump in and finish the last couple of paintings tonight. Little did she know that painting would soon be the last thing on her mind.

Robert Allen called his father multiple times, and when he didn't answer, he assumed that the old man was taking a late afternoon nap. He left several messages on the answering machine, but didn't get a return call. He almost cursed himself for flying back to Indiana today; if he were in Wilmington, he could go and check on him personally. Not knowing where his father was unnerved him to no end.

Jim Allen sat in his recliner, eyes staring into a void only he could see. His arms had come to rest on his lap, after he stopped breathing. His level of discomfort had not been too bad, and his transition was greatly facilitated by his will to move on. No more medicines for Jim Allen; no longer a life without his beloved Belinda; no more days spent lying like a vegetable on a chair waiting to rot. Jim Allen was free, and Belinda was waiting for him, right around the bend.

Chapter Fourteen

With the trip to London quickly approaching, Natalie had much to do before leaving town. The paintings were finally sent yesterday through a courier service, which cost an arm and a leg but offered a speedier delivery and higher security.

Lakeisha was at Natalie's house, resting for long stretches at a time, and trying to recuperate as much strength as possible before the departure date, which was set for the thirtieth of June, only a week away.

She had no recollection of what happened the night she was attacked – her brain had somehow erased all memories connected to the event. She remembered going upstairs, and being in her former room, but from that moment until she woke up at the hospital, her mind was like a blank slate. Her long term memory was intact, but the assailant's face was completely erased from recollection. She didn't know if she had seen him, since she could not remember even being struck.

Natalie was taking great care of her. After being discharged from the hospital, she had picked her up and taken her to her place, in spite of her mother's warnings. Lakeisha didn't know why Mrs. Sanders was so abrasive toward her, since they barely knew each other, but she assumed that the older lady was simply erring on the side of caution.

Today, Natalie spoiled her by bringing her coffee in bed. "Good morning Lakeisha. How are you feeling today?"

"Oh Natalie, you really shouldn't do this. I don't think I've ever been so pampered in my entire life; it makes me feel awkward."

"Well, then stop feeling that way, because I need to know you are making a full recovery for our upcoming trip. In fact, I will be taking your breakfast order now – you have to eat if you hope to regain your strength."

Lakeisha smiled." Yes, Ma'am, but I think a little oatmeal is all my stomach can take first thing in the morning."

"Oatmeal is on the way. Would you prefer maple syrup and brown sugar, or baked apples?"

"Maple syrup and brown sugar sounds wonderful, thank you."

When Natalie went to the kitchen to prepare her breakfast, Lakeisha fluffed up her pillows and lay back down. She still had horrific headaches, and got dizzy if she stood up too fast, but she otherwise she felt well, getting stronger with each passing day.

Natalie had no internet connection at home, so Lakeisha decided to go by the library later, to send a message to Sister Justine. Her cell phone, which was in her back pocket the night of the attack, was missing, and to make matters worse, she could not remember Sister Justine's number.

Natalie walked in with her oatmeal and more coffee, and set the tray on the bedside table while she helped Lakeisha sit up.

"Natalie, stop fussing over me."

"No complaining – my ears are deaf to complaints."

She laid the tray on Lakeisha's lap and walked over to open the curtains and window a bit, to let in a little morning breeze.

"So, Natalie, how are things going with Ryan?"

"They are going, I suppose. I haven't had much of a chance to see him these past few days, with preparations of the trip and all, but I really enjoy being with him."

"He is not sincere, Natalie." There, she had said it. She had planned to keep out of it, but there was something about Ryan that didn't feel right, and Lakeisha didn't want her new friend to be hurt by a player.

"What makes you think that, Lakeisha?"

"It's nothing in particular, really, and definitely nothing he has done. He's quite suave, that one is."

"So why do you feel he is not being honest? You are a very perceptive woman, Lakeisha – is there something about him I'm not seeing?"

"I don't know, Natalie. If that's of any consolation I can't see it either and that's what worries me. I can normally read through people, and there is something I don't like about the story his soul is telling. I think Ryan is in financial trouble."

"The Wheeler family? I really think you are misreading your instincts on this one, Lakeisha. They are old money, and that kind of financial stability usually lasts through time. The Wheelers own a great portion of Wilmington. I doubt they will ever be in any type of financial trouble."

But the seed was planted. Even after Lakeisha got out of bed and went to shower, Natalie wondered if there was any truth to her claims. There was no time to think about that right now; she had to go by the agency to pick up the itinerary of the trip, and stop by Aunt Catherine's attorney to sign some papers to give him temporary power of attorney while she was gone.

Ryan called while she was getting dressed. "Good morning Sweetheart, did you sleep well?"

"I did, Ryan; what about you?"

"Just peachy, but I really miss you. I've hardly seen you this week."

"I'm totally bogged down, Ryan. Hopefully I can get all my ducks in a row within the next few days and create a little time for us to spend together before I leave."

"I hope so, Natalie. Sometimes I worry that you don't feel the same about our relationship as I do. Did you give any thought to what we talked about last week?"

"About being exclusive you mean? I have, Ryan, but I really would prefer to not think about it too much until I get back."

"Oh…I was really hoping you would consider talking to your family before you go to London, Natalie."

Hmmm…why all the hurry?

She pushed that thought away quickly. She didn't have to make any decisions yet, no matter how hard he pushed her.

"I think it is best if we take a little more time, Ryan. I like you, but I've been burned by relationships before, and I really would feel more comfortable if we wait a while."

Ryan swallowed hard, which increased Natalie's suspicions even more, before he spoke. "I understand, Natalie. I guess I'm a romantic fool, and I was hoping that you were as swept away as I am."

Iced tea in a southern country kitchen wasn't even as sugary as this. She suddenly felt that Lakeisha's feelings might be hiding more truth than she initially gave them credit for.

"I'm as involved as you are, Ryan, but right now my focus is not in the right place to be fair about this. I really would like to wait a while before I make any commitments."

Ryan kept silent for a few moments.

"Ryan, are you still there?"

"I'm here, Natalie." He was in control of his tone of voice once again. "Okay, I will leave you to your plans, then. Call me later."

"I will. And Ryan…thank you for understanding."

"No problem, Natalie. Have a great day." No 'I love you"; no 'I'll think about you today' – Ryan was pissed.

She thought of their conversation while she got ready to go out. He really was sort of pushy…was there more to his demands than what met the eye? She decided she would poke around about the Wheelers' financial status a bit later. For now she had to concentrate on the tasks at hand and take care of the trip details that still needed to be finalized.

Melody was getting excited and was counting days before their trip to England. She needed the time with her husband, and Mario looked like he could definitely use a break, after all the long hours he had worked lately. She was actually a bit worried about him – he was involved in a case that his department had been trying to wrap up for several months, and the fever of his professional passion was burning on high-octane. He never got enough sleep, rarely ate a decent meal at regular hours, and his face was beginning to show signs of the neglect. He lost weight and was often irritable, snapping at little insignificant things and pacing restlessly when he was at home.

She fixed herself a cup of coffee and went out to sit on one of the front porch rockers. It was a glorious morning; one of those days when she was elated to live in North Carolina – the temperature was warm, the skies blue, and birds were everywhere. To this day she was very happy with her decision to buy her mother's part of Grandmama's farm. She couldn't imagine living anywhere else, and truly felt at home in her country setting.

Today was promising to be a lazy day; she made mental plans to go by the travel agency to pick up the itinerary and then, maybe, a little shopping. She occasionally missed her job as a paralegal, but the drive was simply too long, and the farm was entirely too big, for her to be gone all day and still take proper care of it. When Mario suggested she stay home, she was thrilled – in her mind she saw herself being a bit like Grandmama, taking care of animals and spending a lot of time meditating with nature. But Mario wasn't like Grandpapa who stayed home and took care of things at the farm, providing constant visual companionship even when he was scurrying around working on this and that. Mario was constantly working, and Melody was beginning to feel lonely. Maybe, upon returning from their trip, she would think of finding a part-time job in Johnston County, to keep her occupied in the daytime hours.

Something in the yard caught her attention – everything she looked at appeared to be in pairs. She saw two doves cooing on a branch nearby, two squirrels chasing each other on the tree beside the barn, and even a couple of lemon-colored finches eating from the bread crumbs she threw in the yard the night before after dinner. Everything at the farm seemed to work as a couple – that awareness made her feel even lonelier, and she missed the days when Mario was around more.

She got up from the rocker and went inside to get dressed, eager to snap out of the funk that was threatening to take over her mind. She needed to be around people, to hear music and maybe get a little lunch in town; in fact, it was the perfect day to call her friend Isabel, and see if they could get together and catch up a little.

When she thought of Isabel, Melody was almost thankful for Hurricane Katrina, the terrible storm that had ravaged through New Orleans four years before and had forced several residents to relocate to other parts of the country. Without Katrina, she might have never met Isabel.

The thought of getting together with someone she liked and respected as much as Isabel cheered her up, and sped her along as she got ready to go. She would tell Isabel about Paul's encounter, and about her trip. She couldn't wait to hear her friend's thoughts about it all. Suddenly she felt elated, and took one final glance at the sky before going inside – now that she had a plan for the day, the sun felt warmer and brighter.

"I'm sorry, Mr. Wheeler, but we have to adhere to bank regulations. The terms of the loan were quite clear, and as much as we would love to work out a compromise, our hands are tied. We need to receive a payment within thirty business days, or the properties will go into foreclosure."

"William, we have always paid off loans on time. I'm sure there are some strings you can pull to give us a little slack."

"I'm afraid not, Mr. Wheeler. Unless you can provide us with something solid beside the good reputation of your company, we won't have any options but enforce the terms of the loan. We need a payment within thirty business days. Believe me when I tell you that we are already stretching our regulations by allowing you the extra time."

Ryan couldn't think of anything to reply. He simply nodded and looked down at the notice William Schuler had personally come to deliver. The bank always reserved a special treatment for the Wheeler family, even when the transaction was one that would declare the death of the family's financial empire.

Ryan stood up and held out his hand to shake William Schuler's. "Thank you Mr. Schuler. I'm certain we will be able to find a solution." Gone was the first-name basis that had created a slight camaraderie until today.

As he walked William Schuler to the door, Ryan knew he had to think of something fast. Suddenly an idea flashed in his mind. "Mr. Schuler, would you be able to extend the terms of the loan if I provide you with something that will prove beyond any doubt that the loan will be paid off in a timely manner?"

"What exactly are we talking about Mr. Wheeler?"

"I'm working toward a merger, Mr. Schuler."

"What kind of merger?"

"It's still under wraps, and really I shouldn't be talking about it, but Natalie Sanders and I have gotten engaged. You probably haven't heard yet, but my fiancée just became the sole beneficiary of Catherine Bouvier's estate, which is valued in the millions. We spoke of it last night, and she is definitely willing to help me fulfill our family's financial obligations. Her attorney has advised her to wait until all the property transfers are finalized before paying off our loans. Technical details, you know?"

Ryan watched William Schuler's face brighten as he thought of what he just heard.

"Well, of course this fact alone changes things greatly, Mr. Wheeler. I will let my superiors know and we will discuss the situation this afternoon in our meeting. I assure you that I will keep your disclosure private, and will allow you and Ms. Sanders to announce the happy news to the world."

"That's wonderful, Mr. Schuler. I am delighted we were able to find a point of agreement."

"So am I, Mr. Wheeler. Our bank has served the needs of your family for decades. I would like to see that relationship continue through time. Good day."

"Good day, Mr. Schuler. I will be in touch."

Right after William Schuler left, Ryan returned to his desk, and began to think about strategies. He had thirty days to convince Natalie to marry him, since he didn't find the blasted rosary yet – maybe he could surprise her by secretly going to London and showering her with attention while she introduced her artistic skills to the world.

Armed with a new plan – and secure victory was right around the corner and across the Atlantic – Ryan told his secretary he was going to be out for the day. Ashton had finally agreed to meet him, and he was as nervous as a school boy on his first date. He could save his family from financial destruction and spend the day with his true love. Life was very good indeed.

"I have been so busy, lately, it's not even funny." Isabel told Melody as they sat at one of the outdoor tables of the Silver Spoon and waited for the waitress to bring the entrees they had ordered.

"So, what have you been up to this past month, Isabel?"

"I started a new job. I was laid off from my other place of employment, and was getting a little discouraged when nothing else seemed to come along, but at the time I didn't realize that it was only a nudge from God toward the realization that I needed to do something else. I decided to sign up for nursing school, and almost immediately found a job taking care of an elderly lady who needed a companion more than anything; she also needs light medical assistance, but her daughter feels comfortable enough to let me take care of her, even if I am not licensed yet. It's like advanced training that I'm being paid for."

Isabel was exuding happiness and peace – her good energy was exactly what Melody needed today.

"I'm so happy for you, Isabel! In this tough economy it is hard to find a job of any kind. You were smart to weigh your options and consider a new course of action."

"I know...I have watched so many around me lose everything they own. Houses are in foreclosure everywhere, and things are getting tougher by the day. Never mind the prices of everything constantly going up."

Melody nodded." I've seen it too. Sometimes I even worry about Mario's job. I hear they are cutting positions due to the tough economic times."

"You will be alright, Melody, we all will. You know this is part of the plan."

"It is? What do you mean?'

"We have become too attached to earthly security, Melody. We can't approach a collective shift of consciousness until more people get with the program. Look around – because of the economic crash families are drawing closer, people are venturing out less, and are going within to look for happiness instead, rather than endlessly searching for a constant flow of sensory stimulation. We are going back to the simple joys of life, the ones that truly make us happy."

Melody thought about Isabel's words for a moment, and then asked, "But what about the desperation, the increased number of suicides, the gloomy thoughts that are spreading like wildfire?"

"That's fear, Melody, and resistance to the shift. It's a blow to the ego, and a complete release of control over unfolding events. Even if our spirit knows it is exactly what we need, our ego doesn't want to let go. That's why prayers are needed now more than ever. Once we realize that we don't need to be afraid because we will be taken care of, everything will fall into place. And Melody, not everybody has agreed to be here for the shift;

that's why we are witnessing so many deaths. The souls that weren't willing to go through the hardship necessary to prepare for the transition are going back before things get really rough."

"Do you mean things will get worse than they are now?"

"It's possible, but don't forget that it is after the worst storms that Nature really thrives."

As always, Isabel had worked her magic. Melody felt better about things, and was able to find answers to some of the many questions that loomed at the edge of her mind.

"And something else, Melody…although we are drawing closer together to really understand more about the oneness of all, we are also encouraged to seek that connection within ourselves, though prayer and meditation. We will be witnessing more relationships falling apart, so that folks can learn how to find love within rather than always looking for completion through the energy of others."

Those last words really impacted Melody. Was this what was happening to her? Did she rely on Mario too much and had lost touch with her own spirit? If she had to be entirely honest, she hadn't really done much to heal her own insecurities by finding beauty within – she had let Mario be her band-aid.

The waitress finally arrived with their food, and they began to eat while they continued their conversation.

"What about you, Melody? What's new in your life?"

"Well, I have big news too – exciting ones! I'm going to England next week, to attend my cousin Olivia's wedding. Finally Mario and I will be able to spend some time together. He's really put in a lot of hours at work lately, and we haven't seen each other much."

Isabel stopped eating for a moment and looked at Melody, but said nothing, so Melody continued.

"Oh, and something crazy happened to Paul, my great-uncle. He said he is sure Elegba paid him a visit at his store in the Atchafalaya Basin."

Isabel's attention was piqued.

"Really? Now, that's not a fellow that pays visits for nothing. What did He say?"

"He told Paul that he had a task to attend to, and also gave him a message for me - I'm supposed to take the rosary Grandmama left me to London."

"One of *the* rosaries??!"

"The *rosaries*? You mean there is more than one out there?"

Isabel weighed her words, unsure of how much information she should disclose without affecting the way things were meant to unfold. She had no direct information, but knew from one of her grandmothers whose sister was part of a secret order of nuns, that there were indeed two sacred rosaries. Isabel didn't know all the details, so she preferred to keep quiet.

"That's what I know about them, Melody, which is really not much information. But no matter what, we can't really argue with the Big Man's instructions, can we?" She said hoping to lighten up the conversation.

Melody smiled, "I guess not. I will take it with me to London for sure; let's just hope this is going to be a restful vacation."

"Let's hope so, Melody; let's definitely hope so."

They finished eating, and then Isabel excused herself. "I'd better be rolling, Sugar. My sweet old lady is waiting."

Melody stood up and hugged her, before she said good-bye. She didn't really want to go back to the farm yet, so she decided to surprise Mario at work.

On her way back to Clayton, she took a detour and drove to the SBI headquarters. When she walked in, she was surprised to see many new faces around, and went straight to Mario's office. He wasn't in, so she wandered to one of the desks closest to the office and asked a pretty blond girl of his whereabouts. She looked young but very professional, with her hair pulled tight into a bun and wearing conservative attire which still showed her fabulous body underneath. Her name tag read "T. Booker".

"Hi, would you by any chance know if Mario Hernandez is coming back soon?"

The pretty blonde looked up from the forms she was working on and smiled. "I'm sorry, I'm afraid he will be gone on duty most of the day. May I take a message?"

"I'm Melody, his wife. Nothing important – I was just in the area and figured I'd surprise him with a visit. I guess I should have called first."

"Oh, that's right. I should have recognized you from the photo he keeps on his desk. It's nice to finally meet you."

"Likewise. Well, I suppose I will be going then. Please just let him know I stopped by."

"Absolutely, Mrs. Hernandez. Have a wonderful day."

"You too. Bye."

Melody left and walked back to her car, a little disappointed. She decided she wasn't going to let something so small ruin her day, after the great time she had with Isabel. She and Mario would have plenty of time to spend together once they got to London. Or so she hoped.

Chapter Fifteen

"Dad, are you ready? Cover your eyes…"

Paul nervously shifted his massive body on one of the fancy chairs in Bridal Dreams, as he waited for his daughter Olivia to come out of the dressing room.

"I'm ready, Olivia. I've been ready, Child. How long does it take to put on a dress?"

He heard Olivia giggle like a little girl, and couldn't help smiling, although the smile was quickly replaced by hanging lips the moment she stepped out – she looked like an angel, and Paul's breath channeled into a gasp. The romantic satin gown had a dropped torso waist with gentle pleated tucks, and a gathered bustier adorned with rhinestone crystals and beads. She looked absolutely stunning, and Paul feared that tears would show up at any moment and make him look like an old sentimental fool.

Olivia smiled when she saw the look of pure awe in her father's face. How many times she had dreamt of this moment when she was a little girl and didn't know who her father was! They didn't reunite until she was an adult, and by then she had given up her childhood fantasies of being given away in marriage by her biological father. Being here today, dressed as a bride, able to stare at the stunned face of the man she had come to adore, was more than Olivia ever dared to dream. She wanted this moment to be etched in her memory, and her heart leaped as her father desperately scrambled for words.

"The cat got your tongue, Dad?'

"Olivia…you are beautiful!"

And she felt beautiful. She gently curtsied in front of him and smiled happily.

"Do you think Graham will like it?"

"Sweetheart, how could he not like it? You look stunning."

"My hair will be up in a bun, and I will be wearing a small tiara. I wanted to stick to a simple design. So, you really like it?"

"Olivia, I don't just like it; I think the dress is absolutely amazing; I think you are absolutely amazing, and I can't think of anything that could make me any more proud than walking you to that altar."

"Four days away, Dad…are you ready for the trip?"

"As ready as I'm ever going to be, Olivia, and considering that I'm not getting any younger, I'm glad that you didn't wait too long. I would have hated to miss this."

Olivia wrapped her arms around him and laid her head on his chest.

"I couldn't imagine doing this without you, Daddy. If you weren't here I probably would have gotten married in a courthouse."

Paul smiled. "Graham is a lucky man, Olivia. I hope he knows just how fortunate he is."

"You and Graham share the same mind, Dad. He continues to say the same thing."

She spun around gently, and couldn't take her eyes off the image reflected in the mirror.

"Did you already send out the dresses for the bridesmaids, Honey?"

"I did. Melody already received hers, and she called to let me know that it only needed to be hemmed a little; other than that, it fit her perfectly."

"Melody must be very excited to go, Olivia. When I talked to her, last week, she said she couldn't wait."

"Yes, she told me the same thing, but I think part of her excitement comes from the prospect of spending a little one-on-one time with Mario. He's been working long hours lately and I really think she is getting lonely at that farm of hers."

"I think you are right, Olivia. I had the same feeling when I spoke with her – she lingered on the phone talking about anything under the sun. It sounded like she needed someone to talk to."

"Well, they will have plenty of time to spend together once they get there."

"Olivia…I know you don't believe in much of the same stuff we swamp folks believe in, but would you believe me if I told you that a spirit came to see me? I wasn't going to say anything, but I don't like to hide anything from you."

"A spirit? Like…a ghost??!"

"Sort of…he looked like a black man on his way to a party."

"You saw a spirit, Daddy?" Olivia arched her eyebrow. She loved her father and believed in his sincerity, but she couldn't help being a bit skeptical sometimes.

"Yes, I think so. Well, Melody saw him, too, on her way back to North Carolina, a couple of years ago."

"Tell me this has nothing to do with the trip to England, Dad…In fact, can you promise me that you and Melody won't be talking about ghouls and spooks in front of Graham? I think he would be totally freaked out by something like that."

"In so many ways, this is part of your family legacy, Olivia. Graham may like to be privy of it."

"I don't think so, Daddy. Graham would probably begin to wonder what kind of mess he has gotten himself tangled into. He doesn't believe in anything, as far as I know."

"He's an atheist, you mean?"

"I think so."

"Oh wow! He'll be the missing piece to complete our family puzzle, Olivia," Paul chuckled. "Seriously, though, if there is one thing I have learned in my long life here on earth is that people fight over things they shouldn't fight about; faith is definitely one of them. The history of mankind is bathed in blood over accounts of religious wars, and few folks have ever understood something very simple – There is only one vision, and many paths to get there. People just look at the wrong side of faith, the one that brings them down; they rarely look at what being a person of faith really means. They are like children, for the most part – "My God is better than yours; mine is more merciful; mine is more powerful and vindictive.' – there are only two powers, Olivia, no matter what one chooses to call them, and they are the powers of good and evil. Choosing between the two is really the only decision humans must make."

"I don't think I ever looked at it quite that way, Dad, but it does make a lot of sense. Graham is one of the kindest souls I have ever encountered, although he claims to believe in nothing."

"He believes in being a good person, Olivia. His heart is in the right place, and to me it's all that counts. Look at how many people claim being religious but don't follow the core teachings they preach to others. To them, religion is nothing more than a tool of judgment and the easy path to social acceptance."

"So, what do you think, Ms. Beauchamp? How is the dress fitting you?" The high-pitched voice of the attendant broke the spell of the conversation.

"Oh, it fits wonderfully. I think my father is quite impressed."

The attendant, a short plump lady in her mid-fifties, with a head full of red curls and pouty red lipstick, turned toward Paul and smiled.

"She is beautiful, isn't she?"

"Stunning." Answered Paul, unable to hide a twinkle in his eyes.

"I couldn't help overhearing the conversation you were having…I agree with you. My family is predominantly Jewish, and they were appalled when my daughter married a young man of Muslim faith. My brother won't even talk to her, and cringes every time I even bring up her name. His take is that she has sided with monsters that have been fighting our way of living for centuries, and in his mind, if you team up with the enemy, you are the enemy."

"Unfortunately it is a widespread sentiment" Olivia interjected, "most only focus on what separates us spiritually, rather than honing in on what connects us."

"You're just as wise as you are beautiful, young lady. You should be mighty proud, Sir."

"I am. Olivia is one of a kind, and I am the proudest dad in the whole wide world."

Olivia smiled and felt a little awkward being the unexpected center of such high praise. "Well, I'd better get changed. Do you think the dress can be ready to be picked up by tomorrow?"

"I'll have it ready by tonight" the attendant said cheerfully, before smiling once again in Paul's direction and heading toward the front of the store to greet another young lady eager to find the dress of her dreams.

Paul waited until Olivia came out of the dressing room and then stood up from the undersized chair and hugged her.

"Take care, Sweetheart. I will see you tomorrow."

"Okay, Dad. You got your passport, right?"

"Yep. It arrived in the mail last week."

"Perfect. See you tomorrow for the fitting of the tuxedos."

Paul walked slowly out of the store, at peace with the world, and headed down the street to get to his truck. His mind was still floating among images of his beautiful Olivia in her wedding dress, and he didn't see the old man sitting on a door step with his face buried into a newspaper, right outside the bridal shop. Although his attire was quite unique, nobody seemed to pay any attention to him, and continued walking as if they hadn't seen him. The man smiled, and took off the dark shades he was wearing, staring after Paul as he disappeared around the corner and blended with the thick crowd. "Congratulations, Paul. See you in London."

When someone knocked on the door, Lakeisha was still in a deep slumber. Last night she had trouble sleeping, and felt as if some important piece of information was pushing to surface to consciousness; rather than trying to relax, she attempted to remember what happened, but nothing came up. Her memory was still failing her, and the headaches were ferocious. She thought of the upcoming trip, and hoped to be strong enough.

Sister Justine warned her of danger looming ahead, in a letter that just arrived yesterday. She instructed Lakeisha to bring along her book of secret prayers, the ones the nuns of their order only used in extreme cases and were mostly unknown to other religious groups, aside from, maybe, a few selected members of the Vatican.

Lakeisha hoped that her superior was going to give her more detailed instructions, but all Sister Justine said was that Lakeisha needed to trust her intuition and follow the signs. In Sister Justine's opinion the devil rules the rational mind, and when one tries to understand things in human terms, the channel of true knowledge becomes blocked and doesn't allow the true voice of God to come through. "The more you keep things away from your mind, the more you become a true vessel of the Divine – pure and able to serve" Sister Justine told her.

Lakeisha got out of bed and stumbled, as quickly as she could, toward the door before whoever knocked left. When she opened, the heavenly scent coming from a vase full of long stemmed red roses filled the doorway; Lakeisha looked around the flowery wonder to see a an acne-ridden teenager with a bored look in his eyes.

"I'm sorry it took me so long to open the door. Here, I'll take these – I assume they are for Ms. Sanders?"

The boy nodded and handed the vase to Lakeisha, before producing a receipt booklet and a pen. Lakeisha signed the receipt, thanked the young boy who reminded her of Ritchie in "Happy Days" and brought the roses to the kitchen, where she arranged them in the middle of the table. She saw a small card, but even without reading it, she knew Ryan Wheeler sent the flowers.

That man gave her the creeps, and she felt sure he had an agenda of his own, but she couldn't get involved more than so much. She really liked Natalie, and in her heart she knew that she was in charge of protecting her, but Ryan Wheeler was the least of her worries. Something bigger, mightier, and scarier, was lurking in the dark, waiting for Natalie to go to London, away from her home base and thus, more vulnerable. She felt a shiver run up and down her spine, and she sighed. A few more days of rest, and then all bets would be down.

"It's nothing more than a business transaction, Sweetie, you know that."

"I don't know anything, Ryan. All I know is what you are telling me." Ashton Logan swept a rebellious strand of silky blond hair away from her face and stared at Ryan with her soft blue eyes, the ghost of youthful insecurity making her luscious lips tremble.

Ryan ran his appreciative eyes along her naked body and drank the beauty of her long, slim legs with the same eagerness of an alcoholic staring at a bottle of pricey alcohol. "Marrying Natalie Sanders will save my family from misery and shame. I'm sure you understand that."

Ashton's eyes darkened with doubt. "I'm not sure, Ryan. I love you, and all I want is to be with you, but you are asking me to be a lifetime mistress, and I don't know if I can commit to it. I want to get married, have children, have a husband I can call my own."

"But you will have all that, Ashton. We can still have children, and have the life we dream of. The only difference is that we won't be able to tell the world of our love, but who cares? We don't need a wedding to be true to one another. Marriage is nothing but a contract – it kills love."

Ashton looked at Ryan, her childhood dreams of being a bride quickly slipping away as she fell deeper and deeper into the well of Ryan's smooth words. Ryan saw from the look in her eyes that his technique was having an effect on her, so he continued relentlessly. "I love you, Ashton, but you know my family would never accept you. My parents are old school. They would never accept you, a waitress, as one of their own. Can you imagine my mother, the queen of Bridge, telling her friends about the little servant her son has rescued from misery? I don't want you to go through that kind of humiliation, Ashton, and feel as if my parents are giving you a handout. You are my baby bird, and I just want to keep you safe, tucked away from the cruel world, pampered and spoiled. If you say the magic word we will go together to find a little nest for just the two of us, and you can pick out all the furniture."

Ashton was in deep thought and Ryan could see she was seriously weighing his offer. He touched her cheek gently and drew her toward him, sweeping her off her feet with a deep, sensual kiss that stole a soft moan from her heart.

She lay back on the motel bed and received him eagerly, knowing full well that she wasn't strong enough to stand her ground. She loved Ryan. She tried to date other men when he refused to introduce her to his parents, but none of them measured up to him. At least in her dreams, when they fell asleep after making furious, passionate love, Ryan was only hers, and he smiled as she walked toward the altar dressed as a bride.

"I really shouldn't be having this conversation with you, Natalie…I have no facts – just hearsay, which might not be entirely reliable."

"Mr. Dillard, it is very important that I find out if Ryan Wheeler is in trouble, financially speaking. I am considering a relationship with him, but I have reasons to believe his interest might not be as romantic as I initially thought."

Mr. Dillard sighed heavily; then he spoke. "The older Wheeler, Ryan's father, is an avid gambler, Natalie. They are very good about keeping things under wraps, but I've heard that in order to maintain his habit, Mr. Wheeler has eroded the family fortune."

"Gambling debt? How bad can it be?'

"Very bad. Banks are after them, and are threatening foreclosure of many of their properties."

"What would it mean for the Wheelers?"

"Well," Mr. Dillard said as he took off his glasses, "it could mean different things, depending on what one considers most important. They would lose their financial stability, but first of all they would lose the impeccable reputation the family has sported as a badge for generations."

"And that would be unthinkable to some. I can just look at my mother and know that she would probably rather die than be shamed in the eyes of society."

"Then your mother and Mrs. Wheeler should meet, Natalie. I've only met Mrs. Wheeler twice, both times at charity functions, and I can assure you the woman lives in her own world. If you watch her long enough at parties, you get a feeling that you're witnessing a queen holding court – she sweats self-righteousness and thinks she is sitting a few notches above everyone else. Her husband, the culprit of the imperial fall, follows her like a puppy, unable to stand up to her."

Natalie laughed. "Ryan and I have been unknowingly living twin lives."

"If Ryan doesn't find a solution to their impending doom, they will lose everything, Natalie, even the house he grew up into. They will be forced to file bankruptcy and all their properties will be auctioned off."

"Oh my God…I had no idea. From the outside looking in they are the portrait of opulence."

"It's a front, Natalie, nothing but smoke and mirrors. In reality, the Wheelers are on their way out."

Natalie was stunned. Lakeisha's words had set the seed of doubt, but reality was far worse than she expected. "Thank you,

Mr. Dillard. I promise you that I will not breathe a word of this to anyone; I am aware that it is strictly confidential."

Mr. Dillard nodded and smiled at Natalie the way a father would. "I know you will, Natalie. Catherine was no old fool."

Natalie's cell phone always rang when she couldn't answer it promptly. Today, of course, was no different, and the blasted thing started ringing while she was driving.

Still keeping her eyes on the road, she dug her hand into her oversized bag on the passenger seat and fished for the elusive phone, all the while missing the good old days when cell phones were as big as bricks. She found it before it stopped ringing and answered without even looking at the name of the caller. When she heard her father's voice, she wished she had checked the caller ID before picking up. "Hello?"

"Natalie! It's Dad, Honey."

"Yes, Dad, how are you?"

"I'm great, Natalie, but what's this that I'm hearing? I ran into Lakeisha yesterday, and she told me the two of you are going to London for an art show. How come I didn't know anything about it?"

Maybe because you never gave a rat's ass about what's important to me, "Daddy."

"I'm sorry, Dad. Life has been crazy these past two weeks, and I still have to catch up with phone calls."

"Shame on you, Darling. Anyway, I'm calling to let you know that I'm planning to go to your show."

Natalie almost slammed on the brakes in the middle of the highway. "Dad, you do know the show is in England, right?"

"Of course, Honey. Your mother and I are thinking of going. It will give us the opportunity to get away for a little while, and maybe work through some of the rough spots we've encountered."

Natalie sighed and dropped the bomb. "Dad, some of the paintings in the show are not mine...they are Aunt Catherine's. Are you sure it would be healthy for you and Mom to try healing your marriage there?"

"I never thought she would bring those paintings out of her closet, Natalie. She never wanted anyone to know."

Oh my God! Dad knew?

"I suppose she changed her mind at some point, because she left precise instructions with her attorney to let me know she was Marcie Walker."

"Natalie...I contribute money to the Marcie Walker Foundation every year. Nobody needs to know Marcie Walker and Catherine were the same person."

"I'm sorry dad, but it's time for Aunt Catherine's light to shine."

Phillip swallowed loudly and said goodbye. Catherine made several mistakes in her life, but this one was probably one of the gravest – exposing her secret identity to the world meant the end of his marriage. Maybe that had been Catherine's plan of revenge all along.

By going to London he was going to kill two birds with one stone. Getting the rosary was, of course, his main goal, but this trip was necessary to get his life back on the right track. He had made many mistakes - and really never meant to hurt anyone - but unfortunately circumstances sometimes have a will of their own. Going on the trip was certainly a good idea; he just had to make sure all his ducks were aligned. Victory was indeed very near.

Chapter Sixteen

Olivia's wedding was set for tomorrow evening. When she first woke up in their hotel room in London, it took Melody a few minutes to even remember where she was. She stared at the pretty papered wall – a creamy background and a pattern of gold and sage curls – and listened for sounds coming from the street. Compared to her farm in Clayton, London sounded like a zoo. She got up and went to the window to take a look – several buildings were directly across from the hotel, and the street right below was congested with traffic.

She looked at her watch and gasped. It was almost twelve! She hadn't slept this late in years. Mario was still asleep but started stirring after she got out of bed, so she headed to the small coffee pot she had spotted inside a shelf the day before, and turned it on. As soon as the coffee started dripping, Mario woke up.

"Good morning Sunshine."

Melody smiled when she heard his voice. "Good morning! Did you sleep well?"

Mario lifted himself on his elbow and used the free hand to rub his eyes. "Boy, talk about jet-lag. What time is it?"

"It's past noon. We slept through breakfast, unfortunately. I suppose we'll have to find something to eat when we leave the hotel."

"Sounds good to me, even if I could sleep all day; I'm too tired to even move."

"Me too, but I guess we'll have to get up if we want to see the city a little."

"Yes Ma'am. Any special plans for today?"

"Absolutely. We are meeting Paul and Olivia for the rehearsal dinner - Graham's family is going to be there; I also told Olivia that we would probably go out on the town with her and Graham after dinner, if you feel up to it."

"Oh God, that's a full day!" Mario pretended to cry and fell back against the fluffy white pillows.

"Come on, you lazy thing…get up!'

She threw a small cushion at him, before going to fix a cup of coffee for both.

They were dressed and out of the room within the hour, still on time to wander around a bit and get some lunch. Their hotel was on the second block of St. James's Street, only around the corner from the Spencer House on James's Place, so they decided to take a walk and see the place before tonight's rehearsal. They ran into Paul, who was doing his own share of sightseeing.

"Paul! So, what do you think of London?"

Paul touched the side of his fishing hat, resting his index and middle finger on the hook threaded through the visor. "Well…It's about as crazy as New Orleans here, and people drive on the wrong side of the road."

Melody laughed – in a distant flash she remembered thinking exactly the same thing about driving on the left side of the road, when she came to London with her parents as a child.

"I remember my parents took me to a really neat little pub on Kings Road once. We took one of the red buses and rode on the top. Would you guys like to go with me to see if the pub is still there?"

Both Mario and Paul looked at her sideways.

"We will need to meet Graham's parents at five" Paul said, "what if we get lost?"

"With Melody as a navigator we have no chance of getting lost, Paul. She googled the map of this place for hours back at home; I'm sure she could take us anywhere in town and know exactly where she is at all times." Mario replied.

"You guys are probably right, though," she allowed, "we don't have much time before we have to go back and get ready for the rehearsal. Let's just get some lunch around here. Then we can maybe walk a bit around Piccadilly or go see Knightsbridge."

"It sounds like a good plan, Melody. Lead and we'll follow."

They ate lunch and walked along St. James's Place, then went back to the hotel to get ready. So far, although they were still exhausted from the trip, their stay in London had been great, and Melody was thrilled to be here and partake of her cousin's joy. She hugged Mario while they walked up the stairs to their room. "I'm really happy to be here, Mario; after Olivia's wedding tomorrow, we will finally be able to enjoy a little rest and relaxation."

When they exited the gate at the airport in London, Natalie and Lakeisha followed the rest of the passengers, hoping they wouldn't miss Tom at the baggage claim. The queue of people flowed smoothly and hurriedly like toys on an assembly line, only occasionally interrupted by a few staff members pushing wheelchairs. The line came to a halt at a security desk, where people were asked to show their passports and other documentation. The British nationals veered to a much faster line, leaving the visitors to fend for themselves in the slower lane.

After leaving the passport check point, they finally arrived at the baggage claim area, and noticed an older gentleman sitting in one of the chairs near the belt. From the description he had given her by e-mail, Natalie was fairly sure the man was Tom. She and Lakeisha headed in his direction, and he stood up immediately.

"Natalie?" The man asked with a soft voice.

"You must be Tom. It's great to meet you." Natalie replied. "And this is my friend Lakeisha. She is such a great supporter of my work that I insisted she should come with me."

"Of course; it's very nice to meet you, Lakeisha."

"Likewise" Lakeisha shook Tom's extended hand.

"It is so good to see you, both. Did you have a good trip?"

"We had a *long* trip, Tom! I didn't think we were ever gonna make it here."

"Well, let's get on our way, then. Do you have your luggage?"

Natalie nodded and quickly picked up the two suitcases on the floor by her feet.

They left the airport and went straight to Tom's house. Although most people usually took the train from London

Gatwick Airport into Victoria Station, Tom had decided to pick them up by car.

When they arrived at Tom's townhouse, both Lakeisha and Natalie took in the first few images of the street with wonder-filled eyes. Like children taking their first taste of green beans, they apprehensively but excitedly looked out of the car window to test their initial impression of the unfamiliar surroundings. The street looked very clean and appeared to be a perfect geometrical design, with white row houses and small decorative trees symmetrically aligned, their layout only interrupted by a quaint neighborhood grocery store. Natalie didn't know which house was Tom's but she assumed that it was the one directly across the spot where he had parked the car. Tom took their luggage out of the trunk and led the way toward the three front stairs.

Although she was tired, Natalie appreciated the fine décor of the simple home: a stern cast iron rail matched the glossy black of the front door, and created a strong contrast with the stark white walls of the house. Before walking in and closing the door, Natalie paused on the front step for a moment, feeling as if she was about to cross an invisible portal to a whole new world. Once she turned her attention to the interior of the house, she immediately noticed the white tiled floor and the high ceiling in the small foyer. The walls were painted a soft buttercup yellow and created a lovely contrast with the thick cherry doors past the corridor. The home was clean and not very frivolous, with only a few portraits and paintings hung sparingly as to not overwhelm the space. The furniture was simple and definitely antique, although Natalie could not determine the style or époque. Tom went to the kitchen to set a kettle of water on the stove for tea, and Natalie and Lakeisha followed him.

"Let's have some tea, ladies, and then you can freshen up a bit, if you wish. I prepared the guest room for you; it has double beds."

Lakeisha liked Tom – his energy was clean and sincere. Maybe he would become an ally in the days to come.

Paul was restless, and as time ticked away he was getting more agitated by the minute. Deep down he knew his apprehension was not only due to his daughter getting married – there was more, something he couldn't quite identify, which was bothering him at the core.

Paul had never been the most psychically gifted member of his family – his sister Giselle and his great-niece Melody certainly had him beaten when it came to that – but he did occasionally have premonitions that never failed to manifest; they often came in dreams, but once in a while they surprised him while he was awake, and scared the daylights out of him.

By the time he got back to his hotel room from meeting Melody and Mario, he lay down for a while before the rehearsal dinner, and as soon as he closed his eyes, he saw Melody walking on an unfamiliar street. He saw shadows everywhere, trying to reach out to her, but Melody didn't see them. She kept walking, until she saw a woman running. The two women looked at one another, and right at that moment one of the shadows separated from the rest and went after Melody! Paul screamed for Melody to run, but she just stood there. One of the streetlights flickered and he heard a clock ticking.

The daydream probably lasted only a few seconds, but Paul came out of feeling as if it had lasted a lifetime. His hands were shaking, and his throat was parched. He thought of the man who walked into his store back in Louisiana, and he remembered his words. "Protect Melody, Paul. That is your final task."

"Natalie, it's me, Dad. Mother and I will leave tomorrow afternoon, and we'll be in London the day after tomorrow. We will be staying at the Ritz in Piccadilly. I will call you when we get settled in."

Natalie played the message on her cell phone and rolled her eyes. It was just like her parents to not even ask if they were welcome. "Wow! Talk about being invasive!" She told Lakeisha as her friend was preparing for bed.

"Well, Natalie, maybe your parents had a change of heart, like your aunt did."

Natalie laughed bitterly. "Yeah, it will be a cold day in hell when that happens. My father said that he and my mother are trying to work kinks out of their marriage. I guess he has to do something to win her back, after she found out he cheated on her with Aunt Catherine."

"What? That's just messed up, Natalie. Are you kidding?"

"Not at all, Lakeisha. I wish I was."

"People make mistakes, Sugar. We are all only human, all here to learn."

"Oh, I know…but with my mom's sister? You have to admit that it is a little rotten, no matter what angle one looks at it from."

Lakeisha nodded, and went back to organizing the few belongings she had brought with her into one of the drawers of the antique dresser. "Natalie, where is the rosary?"

"It's still packed in my suitcase, I believe."

"You put the rosary in the suitcase??"

"Yes. I figured it would be safer there than in any carry-on bag, in case we got robbed or something."

"Goodness, Natalie; we need to make sure it is still in there. Please find it and give it to me."

Natalie was surprised at Lakeisha's tone of voice, but didn't argue with her. She found the pouch under her undergarments and handed it over.

"Thank you. I just need it for a moment." Lakeisha appeared relieved. She dug into her own carry-on bag and pulled out the book of secret prayers. "After I finish with this, you will need to wear the rosary, Natalie, and not take it off under any circumstance."

"Okay…what are you doing now?"

"The rosary must be charged now. The elders taught us that it must be kept dormant until it comes into possession of the final keeper. I didn't activate it until now, because I thought the final keeper was Catherine's daughter, but now I know it is you."

"But…why? How do you know?"

"I was told so by the girl herself, Natalie."

"What girl? Lakeisha, are you feeling okay?"

"I'm feeling great; in fact, I'm better now than I have felt in years – feel the heat coming out of my hands." She didn't explain who the girl was and Natalie didn't pressure her any further. She wasn't sure if Lakeisha was joking around to spook her, or if the kind woman was experiencing some late side effects of the concussion she had suffered, but Natalie decided to keep her concerns to herself.

"That's okay, Lakeisha. Why don't you go ahead and do what you must, while I go look for Tom and see if I can get a little more tea? The plane ride left me dehydrated."

Lakeisha nodded and went back to leaf through the pages of the book, while Natalie silently slipped out of the room and went downstairs. Tom was still in the kitchen, cutting up some vegetables.

"Tom, would it be okay if I have another cup of tea?"

"Of course, Natalie," he said pointing toward the kettle on the stove, "help yourself."

She poured hot water into a cup, and dropped a tea bag into it; then, she took the cup and waited for the tea to steep. Tom was still busy chopping carrots.

"I have a question for you, Tom…"

"Sure, Natalie, what is it?"

"Aunt Catherine wanted me to find her daughter. She said in her letter to me that you had some leads."

Tom stopped chopping and kept his eyes lowered to the cutting board, then turned the knife in his hand a few times, as if he was checking the blade for sharpness. Natalie waited for a moment before repeating the question.

"Do you know how to find Aunt Catherine's daughter, Tom?"

"Catherine's daughter is dead, Natalie. I had leads, and I figured I would find her to surprise my friend, but when I started digging deeper, I discovered that she had run away from home when she was a teenager, and no one knew of her whereabouts until she was found dead in a seedy apartment in East London. Her adoptive mother said that Suzanne never felt like she really belonged, and that even as a young girl she attempted to take her life a few times. When she began using heroin, her parents tightened down on her, and she ran off. An autopsy revealed that she was pregnant when she died and the cause of death was an overdose."

"Oh my God…that's so sad…"

"It was heartbreaking, Natalie, and I never found the courage to tell Catherine."

"Oh Tom, I am so sorry…"

"I am too, Natalie. Catherine's greatest wish was to find her daughter. The truth would have destroyed her."

Suddenly, what Lakeisha said upstairs hit home.

The girl herself told me…

"Excuse me Tom, I forgot something upstairs."

She dashed back up, two steps at a time until she got in front of the room she shared with Lakeisha. She didn't hear any sounds inside, so she knocked gently before opening the door. Lakeisha was sitting down at the small desk, her eyes closed and a peaceful expression on her face. When Natalie walked in, she opened her eyes and smiled in her direction.

"Everything is working out according to the plan." She said in a low voice.

"Lakeisha, how did you know Aunt Catherine's daughter is dead? She is the girl you were talking about, isn't she?"

Lakeisha nodded. "She knew you were coming, Natalie, and she is watching over things."

Natalie was too shaken to ask anything else.

"Here you go, Natalie." Lakeisha said as she handed her the rosary. "She said you must wear it at all times, and never take it off, no matter what happens. The rest will unfold on its own."

Natalie wanted to know what the rest was, but she was secretly too afraid to voice out her curiosity. She took the rosary and placed it over her head and around her neck. She didn't feel anything in particular when she did, and wondered for a moment if this wasn't just a nice fairytale. She thought she heard the sound of distant whispering, but it was gone before she could consciously listen.

Ryan kissed Ashton on the forehead, before walking out of the room where she was sleeping peacefully. He didn't have the nerve to tell her about the trip to England, and preferred to just slip out and say nothing. He would call her later and tell her that he had to go on an emergency trip to Colorado for a week – she would never find out about his plans to join Natalie in London for the art show. His secretary would tell anyone who called that Ryan was on a business trip, so even if Ashton called there his tracks would be covered. He hated to lie to her like this, but at this point of the game, he felt like he had no choice.

Chapter Seventeen

The Spencer House was all that Melody expected and more. The ceremony was being held in the Great Room, and she and the rest of the bridesmaids had gotten ready in Lady Spencer's Room, a large chamber adjacent to the Great Room.

When Olivia walked in, accompanied by a very nervous Paul, she looked stunning. Melody felt tears welling up in her eyes, and swallowed the knot she felt in her throat. Graham was standing by his best man and looked anxiously across the room toward the door. When Olivia made her grand entrance, his face lit up and Melody gave up her fight to keep tears at bay. The ceremony was not too long, nor short, but Melody felt as if they were suspended in time.

After formally giving his daughter away, Paul took his place beside Melody, and watched spellbound as Olivia and Graham declared eternal love to one another. By the time the pastor finally announced that it was time to kiss the bride, Olivia threw all semblance of etiquette to the wind, and clung to Graham's neck with both arms, kissing him passionately and making him blush a deep shade of crimson. Her spontaneous gesture drew collective laughter among the crowd – mostly friends and extended family of the groom.

The reception was delightful and graced by the classy touch of London's finest caterers. The food was amazing and the service superb. After the bride and father dance, Melody stole Paul away and took him out to the dance floor.

"So, old Papa Bear, how do you feel?"

228

"I don't know how to feel right now, Melody. It was an incredible day."

"It really was. Olivia was as beautiful as a princess. Graham really did the right thing by renting this place."

"This house is something else, ain't it? I didn't even know places like this exist."

"Yeah…Europe has some fine treasures."

"I never thought I would travel this far, Melody. I guess it took the love I have for my daughter to make me get on a plane before I get to fly off with my own wings."

Melody laughed, but Paul's last comment made her a little uneasy. "Are you feeling okay, Paul? This has been quite tiring for you…the trip, and then the strong emotions…did you see your doctor before you left?"

"Yes, yes…I sure did…Damn, Melody, you're worse than Olivia. Being a worry wart must be a family trait."

The music ended, and Melody kissed Paul before going off in search of Mario. She found him talking on the phone on one of the balconies. Since he spoke in a low tone, she waited at the door, not wanting to disturb him.

"I think you will really like it" she heard him say, "No, it wasn't. I just wanted to bring back a little something."

Melody wondered whom Mario was talking to, but she remained where she was, waiting for him to end the conversation.

"Look" he continued, "I will call you tomorrow, okay? There is so much we need to discuss, but I don't want to rush you. I prefer to take things slowly rather than to risk losing you."

He closed the conversation and stood on the balcony, staring off into the horizon. When Melody walked outside, he jumped at the sound of her footsteps.

"Mario, I was looking for you."

"I'm right here, Honey. I was talking to Branson, at the office."

"Oh…did you buy him a souvenir?"

"What? Oh yes, I forgot to tell you. When you were out with Paul, yesterday, I saw a book on fox hunting that I'm sure he will love; you know how crazy he is about hunting."

"I thought Branson hunts for deer, not foxes."

"He does, but he loves hunting in general, and I thought…what would please my old pal more than a book about a type of hunting that is so British?"

*There is so much we need to discuss, but I don't want to rush you; I prefer to take things slowly rather than to risk losing you…*Melody could not silence the deafening sound of those words. "You guys must have gotten really close while working on this case. Is he planning on retiring early?"

Mario hesitated. "Yes…um….he mentioned the possibility. I couldn't imagine him not being there as my partner."

"That's great, Mario. I'm glad you two tied up so closely. Are you ready to go in now? I think Olivia and Graham are getting ready to leave."

"Of course. Let's go."

They went back inside together, and said their goodbyes to the newlyweds. Melody saw Paul hug Olivia and went over to put a hand on his shoulder when his daughter gently broke off from the embrace and left with her new husband. "Are you ready to go, Paul? You can walk with us, if you want; we thought of catching a cab, but it is really pleasant outside and a little fresh air can only do us some good."

Melody really needed the fresh air to clear her thoughts. The last words she heard Mario tell the person on the phone were playing over and over in her mind.

"...I don't want to rush you; I'd rather take things slowly rather than lose you."

Who was Mario really talking to? As she walked out of the reception hall, where a union had just begun, Melody hoped her own wasn't coming to an end.

"We are here at the hotel, Natalie. We just checked in and your mother is freshening up a bit, but we can meet you for dinner."

She couldn't believe it...they were really here. For a while, after her father told her he and her mother were going to come to London, she hoped he was joking – the man never attended anything she did...why start now, and why with an event that was taking place four thousand miles away from home?

"I need to check with Lakeisha and Tom, Dad. They are both at the house – I just went out for a minute to fetch some sugar."

"Lakeisha? You mean Catherine's housekeeper? Oh, that's right...she did tell me the two of you were going. I am still a little puzzled that you became friends."

"It's a long story, Dad, and she wasn't a housekeeper. She was Aunt Catherine's nurse and caretaker. I will call you back a little later."

Before he could say anything back, Natalie hung up. The show was tomorrow, and she was nervous enough already. Not only would she have to face the world when Tom finally unveiled who Marcie Walker really was, now she had to do the unveiling in front of her mom and dad. Could things get any worse? And what would they say about her paintings? Even if she pretended not to care, Natalie knew that she always longed to be admired by her parents. Appreciation would make her happy. A discouraging word, right now, could be detrimental to her confidence.

She placed the cell phone in the front pocket of her jeans, and suddenly realized that she probably took the wrong turn while she talked to her father. She looked around and saw nothing familiar at first, then something surfaced from her memory – she had seen this street before, but couldn't remember where...maybe she had gone through this area the last time she was in London. Although she couldn't really bring the recollection into focus, she knew she was experiencing a deja-vu. When she turned at the next corner, desperate to find even the shred of a referral point, her awareness exploded. The street she was walking on was the one she had seen in the dream a few weeks ago. Fear washed over her, thick and palpable, as she remembered the man she was running from when she met her other self.

He really liked London. If it wasn't for the fact that his focus was directed on other more important tasks, he would not have minded to do a little sightseeing of his own, away from the tourist traps – that's how one can really taste the full flavor of the place.

He went through Trafalgar Square, and stood now in Piccadilly Circus, staring at the multitude of strangers walking by him without even seeing him. Power was close at hand – he could smell it in the air, and that alone was enough to get his blood pumping. His official goal – the excuse he used to go - was to spend some quality time with his wife, but there was so much more connected to his decision! The rosary was near. His whole body was electrified at the mere thought of holding it, and he savored the moments that separated him from victory; he grinned with the same arrogant satisfaction of the hare sure to reach the finish line.

By the time they arrived back at the hotel, Melody's emotions were tangled into a knot, and she didn't know what to think. She trusted Mario with her life, yet every cell of her being was screaming that something was wrong. Her mind was too terrified to conceive the possibility he could be unfaithful to her.

He lay down the moment they got to the room. "Wow! This was quite a day, wasn't it?" He said with a smile, more as an affirmation to himself than as a question to Melody.

"It really was," Melody answered, her heart still flip-flopping uneasily in her chest, "Olivia and Graham seemed very happy. It's always good to see couples in love."

"Hopefully they will be as happy as we are." Mario interjected with a smile.

"Are you happy with me, Mario?"

He looked at her with a halfway amused look in his face. "Of course I'm happy with you. What on earth would make you ask something like that? I've never been this happy in my life, Honey."

Mario's reassuring words were a balm for Melody's trembling heart. "I'm just asking, Mario, no reason at all." She didn't say anything more for a minute, which caused Mario to look at her with a mixture of confusion and worry painted on his handsome face.

"Is something wrong Melody? What's bothering you?"

Melody tried her hardest to stop tears from rising up and spilling out, but the urge to cry out her frustration was too strong, and she quickly gave in to the need of releasing the pressure she felt. "Have you ever cheated on me, Mario?"

"What are you talking about, Melody? Of course not."

By now tears were streaming freely down Melody's face. "You are never home, Mario, and then I hear you telling someone that there is a lot you need to explain but you are afraid. Were you really talking to Branson earlier?"

Mario got up quickly and rushed to hug Melody, who was now standing by the bathroom door looking at him with pleading eyes filled with tears.

"Oh, Sweetheart…Branson is having some issues with someone at the office, but even if he has every right to be angry, the situation must be handled by internal affairs and it takes time. I discovered some interesting things right before leaving for this trip which I haven't shared with him yet, but I have to be careful about what I say because Branson can be quite impulsive and would probably rush into things and talk to the wrong people. I don't want to lose Branson."

As Mario's soft words filled the space between them, Melody felt relief pouring through her whole body and spreading down to her limbs. "I'm so sorry, Mario…I don't know why I am so insecure. I have dealt with betrayal before I met you; I suppose some of those wounds are still not fully healed."

Mario held her tight and Melody buried her face into his chest, deeply inhaling his masculine scent mixed with a touch of Eternity. "It's all good, Sweetheart. We've been so busy we haven't had the chance to talk much lately. I love you, Melody, you are the only woman I've ever wanted." He picked her up and carried her to the bed, laying her down gently on the white, cool sheets. They made love for a long time, and all along Mario whispered how much he loved her. After they were spent, and sleep finally claimed Mario, Melody lay awake in the darkness of the room, unable to switch off.

Although Mario's words and obvious physical attraction had set her mind at ease, she couldn't let go of the nagging feeling that kept her heart in a tight squeeze, so she got out of bed, and tiptoed to Mario's suitcase in the closet. She listened to his breathing to be sure he was asleep before she quietly took the bag out of the closet and into the bathroom.

Her heart was pounding against the confines of her chest, and her hands were shaking as she rummaged carefully through his things. Her sense of unease increased by the minute, as her frantic search didn't produce any books, but her hand finally closed around something rectangular in shape, rigid and velvety to the touch. She pulled out her find and saw that she was holding a jewelry case; when she opened it, she stared at a beautiful necklace of fine white gold and sparkling sapphires.

I just wanted to bring back something...

Melody's heart sank. Suddenly Mario's reassuring words and his gentle lovemaking felt as if they took place light years before, in a time when Mario still loved her and she was the happiest woman in the world.

Phillip Sanders leafed through the hotel's directory trying to decide what he and Angela should do the next day. They briefly met Natalie after dinner, but couldn't visit with her for very long since she had several things to finalize before the art show, and for the first time in years he regretted not being closer to his daughter while she grew up. They had become estranged over time, or maybe, as the sad realization of it suddenly hit him, they had always been. Perhaps never consciously, Phillip knew that his affection toward Natalie hurt Catherine, and he had gradually eased himself off the ties that connected him to his daughter. It was time to make amends to her, and also to Angela, even if he couldn't shake the attraction he felt for his beautiful, young secretary. The list of his priorities really needed to be rearranged – Phillip was suddenly aware of what he needed to do, as he watched Angela sleeping peacefully. He still had time to change the cards on the table.

Natalie worked late into the night, which wasn't really a problem since she couldn't sleep anyway. Her big chance of being recognized as an artist was only two days away, and her excitement was mixed with a growing anxiety. One of the things that pleased her most was that her paintings were going to be exhibited right beside Aunt Catherine's – for the first time in her life, Natalie felt like she finally belonged with at least one person in her family. Even if she and Aunt Catherine never had the opportunity to develop a relationship while her aunt was alive, their mutual love for the fine arts would unite them forever.

Lakeisha sat in her bedroom while Natalie worked, staring at the dancing flame of the candle as its occasional flickering broke the continuity of darkness. The ghost of Catherine's daughter was present. Some of the earthly pain the young woman felt before her death was still lingering in the energy that surrounded her manifestation. Lakeisha knew that for spirits – even those who have a hard time crossing over – it takes tremendous effort to appear to humans. Their vibrations are higher than those of incarnated beings, and although they move within the confines of the same space, they function in different dimensions, and are usually unable to communicate across the barrier that separates the two worlds.

Suzanne – such was the name of the lovely creature sitting across from Lakeisha – described how sadly painful her earthly life had been, and how much resentment she had toward her mother for abandoning her, the whole time she was alive. After dying she learned that her mother was also leading a tortured existence, and had never chosen to abandon her of her own will. As her feelings of resentment evaporated she was now free to cross over, but something held her back; she didn't know the reason, but accepted the wait as part of the process. She was energetically attracted to Tom's house, and had no idea what her task there could be; all the old man in a pinstriped suit told her was that her role would become apparent to her as things continued to unfold. As she sat across from Lakeisha right now, Suzanne felt that something blocked the woman and she felt compelled to touch her head.

The moment Suzanne touched her, Lakeisha felt something she never felt before – a door was suddenly opened, and she saw Suzanne's life flash in front of her eyes. She saw her as a little girl, shy and severely lonely, playing in her room alone while her adoptive mother read book after book on child rearing, also alone in the living room. She saw Suzanne as a teenager ready to enter Grammar school, and felt the crushing sense of overall rejection the young girl experienced; she lived the first day Suzanne used drugs, and the haunting feeling of numbness that ensued from that experience.

As Suzanne's life continued to flash in front of her eyes, Lakeisha saw a young boy - Suzanne's first boyfriend most likely - and was overwhelmed by the fleeting sense of belonging they hungrily shared. And suddenly, she felt something stirring in her womb, a baby gently fluttering its tiny limbs in its first home, and was overcome with a feeling of deep love and anguish. Suzanne had wanted her baby, but knew her parents would never accept her choice. She couldn't let the baby go, and decided that if they couldn't be together in life, then they would be together in death. The answer to her problem came in the form of a disposable syringe.

Lakeisha wept. She cried for the two children who never had the chance to spread their wings and fly away. She cried for Catherine, who experienced the same pain her own daughter lived through, and she cried for herself, for she would never know the incredible love of feeling a child of her own grow in her womb. And suddenly, something else happened. The fog that entrapped her mind in the past weeks lifted and she saw the face of her attacker, the anger and fear in his eyes. In a moment that felt like an eternity, Lakeisha stared into the face of pure evil. The worst part of all was that she knew him all too well.

Chapter Eighteen

The day of the show finally arrived. It was a day Natalie would not soon forget, for various reasons. She could hardly sleep the night before, too exhilarated to relax, her mind past the realm of nervous. Before the gallery opened that morning, she walked back and forth in front of the paintings, mentally preparing for any questions that might arise. The press had been alerted about new, previously unreleased paintings by Marcie Walker, so the buzz was on and Natalie was a tangle of jumping nerves.

"So, are you ready young lady?" Tom surprised her from behind, "That's an unusual necklace you're wearing."

"Yes, it was Aunt Catherine's," she replied, "She bought it when she thought she was going to meet her daughter, and instructed me to give it to her if I found her. Unfortunately, as you know, that will not be possible."

"It's alright, Natalie. I'm sure that Catherine would be proud to know you are wearing it on such a special day."

Natalie touched the rosary gently, stroking the cross, "I hope so, Tom. I'm just sorry I can't honor her last wish."

In that moment, a large spider crept out from behind one of the sheets that covered the paintings, and Natalie jumped. It stopped halfway across the floor and remained still for a few seconds, before it resumed its journey toward the other side of the room and disappeared out of sight.

"Ugh! That was so gross! I don't like spiders," she told Tom crunching her nose.

240

"My late wife believed spiders are magical creatures, and always allowed them to go free in our home. She would never kill one or let anyone else do so, for that matter. It was almost as if she welcomed them wherever she was," he said, "I can almost hear her now…"Spiders are the power that keeps us all in balance, they weave the fibers of energy that enable circumstances; Insects believe the web is a flower as they fly around, and they don't know that what they perceive as sustenance will mark the end of their existence."

"That's kind of sad," Natalie interjected softly.

"It is, but like everything else, it is part of the cycle of life, Natalie."

"I guess that's true…think of all the people who run around always wanting to achieve more – what they believe will buy them happiness will likely be the same thing that will lead them to an early death."

"Exactly. Well, let's get those paintings ready, Love; the show will start before you know it."

"Oh God, Tom, I don't know that I can go through with this…just thinking about people looking at my paintings makes my stomach flutter; the thought of art critics lurking in the crowd makes me want to throw up."

Tom laughed heartily, "You will be fine, Natalie. Your paintings are wonderful, and today will mark your debut into the world of fine arts."

"My grandmother always said that a good breakfast will chase the demons that cause anxiety, Natalie," Lakeisha said entering the beautifully adorned door. "You really need to get something to eat and, maybe even get a little rest before the show. I'm sure you have checked those paintings a hundred times by now -- they are fine."

"Lakeisha! I'm so glad to see you here. Do you have any funny feelings about tonight?"

Tom raised his eyebrow in confusion. "Is Lakeisha psychic?"

"Hmmm…not technically," replied Natalie, "but she feels things. So, Lakeisha, do you pick anything up?" She nudged and touched Lakeisha's arm, the rosary sweeping across her chest and fleetingly touching Lakeisha's shoulder. A vision exploded into Lakeisha's head, and she struggled to keep from gasping. "No, I don't feel anything right now; all I'm feeling is that you are hungry and stressed. You're shielding me from reading anything else." She said averting her eyes as Natalie's own pleaded with her for premonitory clues.

She couldn't tell Natalie that she felt something – no, she saw something…a large stain of blood on the floor, soaking one of the white sheets that were candidly protecting Catherine's paintings from curious eyes. Her heart pounded in her chest and her head spun, as a merry-go-round of events quickly flashed in front of her eyes. She reached a hand down to feel the book of prayers through the thin fabric of her large purse, closed her eyes to shut away the vision, and focused on regaining control of herself before Natalie would notice something was wrong. Unfortunately it would not be long before she found out on her own.

"Could you give us some sightseeing suggestions? This is my uncle's last day here, and I really wanted to make today sort of special." Melody told the clerk at the reception desk of her hotel.

"Have you been to the popular sites, Trafalgar square, Piccadilly Circus, and Buckingham Palace, already?"

"Yep, we've seen all that. I was looking for something a bit more unusual."

"What about the London Eye? Have you been on a flight?"

Melody's throat tied into a knot the moment she heard the clerk mention the London Eye – that was one of the things she had hoped to do with Mario after Paul left to go back to the States.

I just wanted to bring back something that shows you how I feel...

She couldn't erase the sound of those words from her memory, and each syllable was a knife wound to her heart. Afraid to burst into tears in front of the clerk, she thanked him quickly and left the hotel. She gulped air and tried steadying her breathing before going back inside. She didn't know how to face Mario today. When she left the room, a half hour earlier, he was still sleeping but it wouldn't be long before he woke up. Even if she kept to herself during the stay in London, they had to leave together to get back home, and most importantly, she didn't want to worry Paul on his last day here. Love for her uncle pumped steel into her spine, and she decided to keep quiet about the necklace.

She went upstairs, and the moment she opened the door Mario called out to her. "Is it you, Honey?"

Her determination to check her mouth vanished the moment she heard his syrupy tone. "Yeah, it's only me, unfortunately."

"Melody? Is something wrong?"

She exploded. "Is something wrong? Why don't you tell me, Mario? Or maybe you will tell her first, since there is so much you would like to say, if you weren't afraid to rush her."

"Melody?" Mario looked at his wife, confusion written on his face, "Who's "her"? I don't have a clue what's going on."

"Let me refresh your memory then!" she yelled as she flew across the room, took the suitcase out of the closet and spilled out the contents on the floor until the rectangular velvet box came into sight. "What the hell is this? I heard you, Mario; I heard you telling her that you wanted to bring back something that showed her how you feel."

"Haven't we already had this conversation last night? I was talking to Branson, Melody."

"Oh yeah? And where is the book about fox hunting then? Or are you bringing Branson a nice necklace instead?'

Mario stood up, his smile increasing in size as he walked across the floor to the desk. He opened his carry-on bag and pulled out a book; a pretty red fox on the cover stared Melody in the face.

"But...but...the necklace..." She stammered, now totally confused.

"The necklace is for you, Melody. It's a gift for our upcoming anniversary."

Melody's legs shook violently, her head spun, she thought she was going to faint. "Oh my God…I'm such a loser…I thought you were seeing someone, Mario."

'I thought we settled that doubt last night, Melody."

"We did…you did…I thought…I am so sorry…"

"Maybe I should remind you right now."

"Maybe you should. I think I'm a bit hard of hearing."

Mario laughed as he picked her up and carried her to the bed, "I would like to argue my case again, Your Honor."

She laughed and cried at the same time. Tears had never been so sweet.

Ryan looked out of the window while his cab sped through the streets of London toward his hotel. He had a lot of time to think on the plane. He loved Ashton, but felt he rushed into things when he suggested to her they should continue to be together. His mother wouldn't exactly be thrilled if she knew her son was fixing to shack up with a waitress, even only as a mistress.

He shook his head, as if that could help clear his mind. Back in Wilmington, just the day before, he had no doubt that he wanted to be with Ashton – if only discreetly -- but now he wasn't too sure any more. Maybe he just didn't want to screw up, knowing what was at stake. For once, he wanted to think with his big head instead than the smaller, more convincing one. He could have everything he wanted if he married Natalie – a beautiful, talented wife, the money to save the good name of his family, and the respect of his parents. He didn't love her, that much was true, but didn't people say that love comes with time if you share enough common interests?

While his cab struggled to get through the traffic, he noticed a large crowd gathered on the street, some people wearing name tags, but before he could figure out what was happening, the cab gained speed, and the crowd was left behind. They pulled in front of the hotel a few minutes later and the driver quickly came around to open the trunk and pull his travel bag out. He crossed the lobby and almost ran into a gigantic man with gray hair and a fishing hat with a hook threaded through the visor. He apologized, and realized from the man's accent that he was an American.

"Hey, where are you from?"

"Louisiana, what about you?"

"North Carolina. My fiancée is having a show here, and I came to support her. She doesn't know I'm here yet, I'm hoping to surprise her."

"That's great. My niece is from North Carolina; she's here too."

"Yeah? Where in North Carolina?"

"Clayton, I think; it's a small town near Raleigh."

"Oh yes, I'm from Wilmington, on the coast."

"It's nice to meet you," Paul said, "well, I'd better be going. My niece and her husband are waiting for me to go sightseeing a bit before I fly back tomorrow."

"Nice to meet you, too. Maybe I'll get to meet your folks before they leave."

Paul nodded, and the stranger went to the reception desk after nodding himself.

Euphoria was growing by the minute; he felt in his heart that he was finally closing in and the rosary would be his in a matter of hours. He had it all planned out – he would get into the gallery and hide, then wait for the right moment to approach Natalie alone. The housekeeper presented a problem. He thought he had killed her at Catherine Bouvier's house, but she survived. He couldn't keep making mistakes of this kind, and he wondered if he should get rid of her even before approaching Natalie. He wasn't sure if she had seen him that night in the closet when he struck at her with his gun, but if she had she might be able to recognize him, and that wouldn't do.

He stood across the street, watching the crowd increase in size, and keeping out of sight behind a newspaper and dark glasses – didn't he hear somewhere that British people often read the newspaper on the street? He saw the door of the gallery open, and his heart skipped a beat. A woman walked outside – the housekeeper! She was alone, and got ready to go down the steps when Natalie came out after her and the two exchanged a few words.

He was too far to be sure, but he thought that what he saw around Natalie's neck was the rosary. His heart thumped wildly in his chest and his legs shook from the emotion of being so close to it. The rosary's red and black stones seemed to hum a silent melody only he could hear – a siren song that had him under its spell. The two women walked back inside together, and he cursed out loud as he saw his chance of getting rid of the housekeeper dissipate like fog in bright sunshine.

His best bet was to walk in once the doors opened and mix with the rest of the crowd, steering away from the housekeeper. The exhibit would open soon, but he couldn't go in yet. First, he had something else to take care of.

Phillip stood in front of the mirror and checked the knot on his silk tie.

"Phillip, are you ready yet? I think Natalie mentioned that the doors would open at five, and it is already almost five. I wish you didn't leave earlier, this was hardly a day to indulge sightseeing."

"I'm sorry, Angie. My idea was to stay away long enough to let you have a nap and then I lost track of time."

"It's okay, Darling. I believe the gallery is fairly close to here."

"Yes, I think it is. Do you have the piece of paper on which I wrote the address this morning?"

"It's right there, on the desk, near the magazines."

"Oh, good. I really think we need to do our best to be supportive of Natalie, tonight. It's a huge thing for her."

"I guess so, Phillip. Yet, I can't believe we came all the way here for this."

"Well, we didn't just come for the art show. We have other reasons too, don't we?" He drew her to him and kissed her lightly on the lips.

In part, he was being honest.

Chapter Nineteen

"Are you ready, Natalie?"

"As ready as I will ever be, I guess." Natalie answered nervously as Tom walked across the hall to open the main door.

"There's quite a crowd out there" Tom said, "Marcie Walker's work is highly sought. Her fans will be saddened by the fact that she is dead, but thrilled knowing that her niece has similar talent. A new star is about to be born."

"I hope so. God, I've never been so scared in my life."

Someone knocked lightly on the door. Natalie took a big breath and waited anxiously to see who it was. The faces of her parents and Ryan beamed from the doorway.

"Ryan? What are you doing here?" She asked, shocked to see him there.

"Look who we found outside, Sweetheart. Such a wonderful surprise!" Her father said.

"The nice surprise was mine, Mr. Sanders. It's always a pleasure to see you and your lovely lady." Ryan's voice was dripping sugar.

Natalie couldn't decide if it was nauseating or funny, but it was the distraction she needed to defuse some of the anxiety she felt. "I didn't even know you were in town, Ryan, why didn't you call me?"

"I didn't want to get in your way while you got ready for your big day, Sweetie, but I wanted to be here for you. I just arrived this morning."

"I'm sorry I got so busy before I left. I didn't even call to say good-bye." She said, unsure if she should believe him or not, after what she heard from Mr. Dillard.

Ryan rushed to her and drew her into a warm embrace, "It's okay, Sweetie. I knew you were excited." He answered as his muscular arms folded gently around her.

Other voices filled the room, as a crowd of art enthusiasts began to spill in from the street. Natalie's stomach tied into a knot, and she felt her legs tremble as she stared at the many unknown faces eager to see Marcie Walker's unreleased works. Tom had withheld the news of Catherine's death, and since no one knew her true identity, he was sure that once it became public knowledge, the value of her paintings would instantly skyrocket. Lakeisha walked her way to Natalie through the thick crowd.

"Here you are, Lakeisha. You've already met my parents and Ryan, I believe."

"Yes." Lakeisha extended her hand and quickly dropped it when she realized that her gesture was not going to be returned. "How are you?"

"Very well, thank you. Lakeisha, right?" Ryan said with a charming smile.

"Right." She said with no further ceremony, "Natalie, I'm going to look around and see if I can hear interesting comments. I will be the reporter in disguise." She winked at Natalie and disappeared in the midst of the crowd.

"Ladies and Gentlemen," Tom's voice thundered above the buzz, "as you know, I have announced that we will be unveiling some of Marcie Walker's unreleased paintings. It is with great sorrow that I have to inform you of something else..." his voice dropped lower and embodied a more somber tone, "...our beloved Marcie Walker passed away a few weeks ago."

Shock registered in the crowd, and whispers filled the silence left in the aftermath of Tom's explosive announcement.

"But I have yet another important bit of breaking news for you, Ladies and Gentleman."

The buzz came to a stop.

"We have here with us, just for today, Natalie Sanders, Ms. Walker's niece, and I can assure you that her work is just as stunning as her aunt's."

Natalie felt her cheeks burn as all eyes in the room focused on her, and she glanced nervously at the confused expression on her mother's perfectly made-up face. She saw her mother turning to her husband for answers, but he simply made a gesture to indicate she should listen.

"Ms. Walker has chosen to grace our world with her impressive art, but never opted for her real name to be known. The paintings I will present you today are signed with her real name, Catherine Bouvier."

Natalie heard her mother gasp and even without looking, she was certain Angela Sanders was probably as white as a ghost. The crowd went mad. Voices were overlapping and spectators stared at Natalie as the new incarnation of their favorite artist. Tom allowed the excitement to settle naturally, before he spoke again.

"Most of the paintings you see in this room are being released for the first time, and they are managed by Ms. Sanders through the Marcie Walker Foundation. You will find Ms.

Sanders's collection in the adjacent room." He extended his arm to indicate the room to the right. "Please do take your time to view all the paintings, since this is your chance in a lifetime to see two debuts in one day – Ms Bouvier's only collection under her real name, and Ms. Sanders's first exhibit. Thank you for coming, and enjoy your evening."

When Tom replaced the microphone, the crowd scattered around. Some people remained in the room to admire Catherine's previously undiscovered paintings, while some others filed next door to compare Natalie's skills to those of her famous aunt. The moment she had the opportunity, Natalie turned back to look at her mother. Angela's face was ashen, and her eyes glued to the portrait of the young child flying a balloon. Phillip was standing next to his wife, silently scrutinizing her for signs of distress.

"If you and Paul want to go ahead, I should be back in shape shortly. This new migraine medication really works fast," Melody said apologetically.

A shadow of concern darkened Mario's handsome face. "We can wait for you to feel better, Melody. It's not that we have specific plans to be anywhere at any particular time. In fact, I was thinking of just going for a walk and do a little more sightseeing on my own while you rest."

"This is Paul's last day here, and I really don't want him to remain stuck into a hotel room catering to my headache. I worry about him sitting around too long, especially since he will need to sit on a plane for many hours tomorrow."

"I still think we should wait for you."

"Nonsense, Mario," she told him as he leafed through some fliers, "why don't you just ask him to for a walk? I will meet you all in a little while."

"Okay then, you rest, and we will be right down the street. There is an interesting exhibit at a gallery near here. Maybe I will ask Paul if he wants to go, and then we will come back to the hotel to pick you up later."

"That sounds like a perfect plan. But do you think Paul is interested in attending an art show?"

Mario shook his head. "I'm not sure if he is or not, but I think I remember him mentioning something to that effect before. It doesn't hurt to ask, unless he is too tired to go out right now. I'll tell you what – I will go take a look on my own first, to make sure it is not abstract art, and then I will come back to ask Paul if he wants to go. If he doesn't, then we will find some other way to spend the afternoon." Mario walked up to the bed and gently kissed Melody's forehead. "Feel better soon, sweetheart. I'll miss you."

"I'll miss you too. Our honeymoon starts tomorrow."

After Mario left, Melody laid her head carefully against the pillows and tried to go to sleep. Rest was the only effective medicine, she knew, that would cure a migraine.

Mario passed by Paul's door on his way out and stopped a moment to listen in. There were no sounds coming from the room, so he continued to walk toward the elevator. Within moments he was out of the hotel, and headed to the art gallery.

The old man mingled with the rest of the crowd, and adjusted the carnation in the lapel of his jacket. He leaned on his cane and stood smiling, watching as all other spectators talked excitedly among one another. Everything was happening on perfect schedule, if he could say so himself.

He looked at his manicured nails and then raised his head to take a second look at a lady who just walked by, the sweetheart neckline of her dress barely covering her soft gifts. He laughed and bowed to her, as she joined a friend who stood in the middle of the room holding a program in her chubby hand. Oh, he so wished he could be a few centuries younger sometimes...

Paul was stretched out on his bed watching mindless TV, when someone knocked on the door. Assuming it would be Melody or Mario, he opened without a second thought, and was surprised to see a young lady standing by the doorway. She was petite and had light blond hair, cut at the shoulders; her face was extremely pale and her skin had a strange translucent tone which Paul blamed on the dim light of the hallway. She had huge blue eyes and wore a uniform that he hadn't seen on anyone else at that hotel – wrong color and wrong style. Paul was an old man, and not always too keen on noticing details, but this one really stuck out, as if she was a figurine cut out from a twenty-year-old magazine and pasted on a new digital photo.

"May I help you?"

"You are Paul, right?"

Paul raised his eyebrow, confusion glazing his eyes.

"I am, but who are you?"

"There is no time to explain that. Go take care of Melody, she will need you soon. Tell her to wear the rosary. That's all you need to know for now."

Paul felt a shiver curse through his massive body. The time had come.

"Hurry Paul, don't leave her alone."

Paul ran his hand over his face, his heart racing wildly. His eyes were probably only closed for a second; when he opened them again, she was gone. He rushed to Melody's room without even bothering to close his own and knocked frantically on her door.

A weary Melody came to open after a moment, her eyes heavy with medicated sleep and her movements slow. "Paul, what's wrong? Did something happen to Mario? You didn't go?' The mere thought that something could have happened to her husband shot adrenaline through Melody's blood stream, and in seconds she was awake.

"I don't know where Mario is, but I think something is ready to happen. I don't really know how to explain it to you, but can I come in?"

"Of course...but didn't Mario come to get you? He was going to take you to an exhibit near here. He said you might enjoy it."

Paul looked at Melody, puzzled. "He said that? Melody, honestly, I'm a fisherman; I don't know the first thing about art."

Melody went to the table to pick up the flier. "Here it is. This is the exhibit he was talking about. He said you mentioned something about being interested in art shows."

"I don't know what's going on here, Melody, but I'm sure going to find out."

"We'll find out together, Paul." She grabbed the first outfit she could get her hands on, and went to the bathroom to change.

"Take the rosary with you, Melody. Don't ask me why -- just do it."

Too shaken to think or even formulate questions, Melody took the rosary out of her travel jewelry case and placed it around her neck. They were out of the hotel in minutes, and, map in hand, they walked briskly toward the art gallery. By the time they arrived, a crowd was filing out of the building. An older gentleman was standing by the door, saying good-bye to some of the visitors, and shaking hands with others. When he saw Melody and Paul approaching, he turned his attention to them. "I'm sorry, but the exhibit is getting ready to close."

Paul thought quickly, his mind pushing words out of his mouth. "My niece is a huge fan of Marcie Walker," he said after he glanced at a poster hung outside the main door of the gallery, "Is there any way we can get a tiny glimpse, even for just a few minutes? We'd be happy to pay full admission."

The man stood transfixed, his eyes glued on Melody. "Oh my God, you look exactly like Natalie Sanders, one of the artists featured in the exhibit."

"Really?" asked Paul, "is Ms. Sanders inside?"

Tom nodded, still unable to peel his eyes away from Melody's face. "Yes, please come in. I think the two of you should meet."

Paul's hair stood up behind his neck…too many coincidences. He was glad he had gone back to his room to take his gun before leaving the hotel. God knew he had enough trouble getting the airport people to pass it through – he finally had to put it, broken down, inside his checked-in suitcase. They walked in through the main door but the door to the room with Catherine's paintings was locked.

"That's odd…it was open a minute ago before I walked outside." Tom said, looking for his keys in his pocket but unable to locate them.

"Is there another way in?" Paul asked calmly, hoping to not betray the sense of foreboding he felt.

"Of course…this way." Tom led the way and Paul and Melody followed him. They came upon another door. Tom opened the small drawer of a table standing nearby and took out a key. He unlocked the front door and led Melody and Paul to the exhibit room.

When they got there, Melody's breath caught in her throat, and she wondered if her lingering migraine was playing tricks with her mind and she was seeing things. Mario stood by a chair holding a knife to the throat of a black woman who just sat with her eyes closed. The blade was resting against her sweaty deep caramel skin, and another woman stood a few steps away, obviously terrified. They all turned when Melody and Paul walked into the room, and the young woman standing on the side gasped. Melody honed in on her face and sucked in her breath, as a feeling of familiarity spread through her entire being. The woman standing in front of Mario looked exactly like herself with short, lighter hair. Her gaze shifted back to the black woman tied to the chair, and her mind was suddenly grasping for straws. Alex! The woman in the chair was Alex, Maurice Abudah's granddaughter, whom Melody had the misfortune to meet back in Louisiana on the fateful night when she lost the Book of Obeah! Why was Alex here?? And why was she tied to a chair?

Paul wrapped his hand around the gun in his pocket, moving slowly enough that Mario wouldn't notice. Mario looked at Melody and smiled, just as a sinister look danced in his eyes. "Why, hello Melody, thank you for coming. You too, Paul." Then, he saw the rosary around her neck and he stared directly into her eyes. Melody shook her head in disbelief, too shocked to say anything.

"You see, I was a little surprised when I found out there were two rosaries out there, and even more surprised when I found out that Alex, here, decided she was no longer going to live a life of sin, entered that order of nuns and changed her name. A small world, don't you agree? I didn't even recognize her the night I saw her at the Bouvier home. It wasn't until I got to London that I realized Alex and Natalie's friend are one and the same."

"What do you know about all this?" Melody asked in a voice she barely recognized as being her own.

Mario laughed, insanity dripping from of his words. "I know enough. My own family knew some of the details, though not all. Then I met Celeste, a drug addict who happened to be related to another nun in Alex's order, so I found out the rest. Celeste knew that one rosary alone is useless. The rosaries are twin jewels that have power only if they are used together. When separated their power is dormant, but until a few minutes ago when you walked in and I saw it around your neck, I didn't know you had the other one. All along I thought I would have to search for the missing rosary, and instead it found me. I'm a little hurt that you never trusted me enough to tell me, Melody." He pouted, and then his lips twisted into a sinister grin.

Paul had a good grip on his gun, but the man's knife was so close to Alex's throat that he preferred not to take any chances.

"You can't do this!" The words shot out of Lakeisha's mouth before she could stop them. Mario pushed the edge of the blade deeper into her skin, madness dancing into his eyes. "You're wrong, Alex...you see, I can. You have really come a long way since that night in the swamp, when all you could think of was to claim the power as your own. Listen to you now...I'm glad Celeste told me she sold the rosary to someone in Wilmington. I just feel bad for the lady at the shop...I wish I didn't have to kill her."

Natalie looked at the man with a terrified look on her face. "Oh my God...you killed Mrs. Allen?"

"Yes Natalie, I did, and I really hated to do it; she really was a fine lady, but unfortunately she saw me. I thought I killed your friend here, too, but she got lucky. Until now, that is." The blade moved slightly, and in that moment something strange happened.

Lakeisha closed her eyes and prayed in an unknown language. The moment she opened them again, her eyes were glazed, and a rivulet of saliva dripped from her parted lips and hit the blade of the knife.

"The dead come back to protect the innocent." With those words, she locked her gaze with the man standing by her, just as a large spider crawled up on his hand, seemingly coming out of nowhere. He screamed and jerked his hand back, the knife quickly slicing through Lakeisha's throat. Blood shot out of the wound at Natalie who screamed and jumped back.

Mario reached into his jacket and pulled out a gun, ready to shoot Natalie, but Melody had already seen him. Her anger and fear came together in a powerful cocktail, and drunken with the intensity of her emotions, she sprung toward him, a tigress in distress pulled into action by a primal instinct she could not deny.

Surprised by her reaction, Mario turned and aimed the gun at Melody. Natalie, no longer in the line of fire, leaped to push Melody down and fell on top of her. The impact felt strange, almost as if a pillow was placed between the two of them, at waist height, to soften the impact. Suddenly everything became still, and the instant she and Melody touched, Natalie felt heat coming out of the rosary she was wearing. She thought she saw an old man standing by the old Grandfather clock, and recognized him as someone she had seen earlier in the crowd; clad as he was, in his flashy suit and Fedora hat, he was not an easy one to miss. It occurred to her only now that she had seen him before, smiling from one of Aunt Catherine's paintings.

The sound of a gunshot ripped through the air and the bullet hit Mario square in the chest. Paul stood there, the gun still hot in his hand. He looked at it, dropped it on the ground and glanced at Melody still lying on the floor. Blood flowed freely from the wound on Mario's chest and quickly soaked into one of the white sheets used earlier to cover the paintings. As the stain continued to spread, Melody felt her anger flow away with Mario's blood, replaced by intense agony. "Mario…why?" she cried out as she stood up and went to kneel beside him.

"I'm sorry Melody. I never meant to hurt you. I didn't even know you had the other rosary. I loved you but I wasn't in love with you. I couldn't divorce you, but my heart truly belonged to someone else, so I thought that getting my hands on the rosary would give me the power to fix the mistakes I made, among all other things. I'm not too different than my brother, Melody. I, too, wanted the power of Obeah for myself."

He struggled to talk, his breathing becoming labored as his skin began to get cooler and beads of sweat formed on his brow.

Melody was crying openly by now. "Why couldn't you divorce me, Mario? How could the rosary help you?"

"I am in love with Tess, Melody – Teresa Booker, a lady I work with. She is a woman of strong faith, and she would never agree to be with a married man, even a divorced one. The rosary has the power to change time, and maybe it could have taken me back to the day I proposed to you. I never meant to hurt you, you have to believe that. I was going to leave tonight, after taking Natalie's rosary, and I would have created a new life here in London while I searched for the other rosary. In time, and with the help of both rosaries, I would have found a way to bring Tess here. I even changed my name to Chris. Do you like it?" He grinned, and his eyes flashed a light of madness. Within seconds, Mario's body began to seize, and he was gone right before the police arrived.

"Natalie is not answering her phone. I wonder if she is still at the gallery" Phillip told his wife after they decided to treat Natalie and Ryan to dinner at a new famous Indian restaurant he had read about on one of the magazine on the plane.

"Where is Ryan, by the way?" His wife asked.

"He said he wanted to surprise Natalie with something tonight, so I believe he went back to his hotel right after the exhibit closed. I saw Natalie hugging him before he left."

"Well, I guess it wouldn't hurt if I go back to the gallery before she makes other plans for the evening."

"That's fine. I will stay here. I think I need a little rest after today's revelation."

"I'm sorry, Angela. I found out right before we left, but I didn't say anything because I was worried that you wouldn't come if you knew. I really want us to have a fresh start, and London is the perfect place to begin our new life together."

Angela smiled warmly, "It's all past, Phillip. I do love you, and I want to spend the rest of my life with you. I don't think I even knew how deeply I care about you until we were apart for a while."

The relief Phillip felt was overwhelming, and he fought tears pushing against his eyelids as he held Angela close to his racing heart. He kissed her lips and smiled before rushing out of the room to fetch a taxi.

Lakeisha was still breathing when the paramedics arrived, but she was already unconscious. Paul, Melody and Natalie stood in a corner, unable to talk to one another, their eyes transfixed on the surreal scene still unfolding in front of them.

Natalie told the paramedics she was going to the hospital with Lakeisha, but one of the police officers – a detective, she assumed - stopped her. "I'm sorry Miss, but I do have a few questions for you before you go. I will be happy to give you a lift to the hospital afterwards."

Natalie nodded, too exhausted and shocked to argue. She sat on a chair, took a sip of the water the constable handed her. She saw Melody and Paul walk into a different room with another officer, but her mind registered the last events in slow motion. When her father entered the room, making way among the crowd of uniformed officers and medical personnel, he found her like that, sitting down, her eyes glazed by a deep state of shock. The interrogation had gone on for a while, but the constable was still asking questions.

"I believe my daughter needs a few moments, sir."

The constable nodded. "It should be enough anyway. I told Ms. Sanders I would give her a lift to the hospital."

"I will take care of that. My taxi is still waiting outside."

The constable agreed and closed his notebook, before handing Phillip a business card. "Please tell Ms. Sanders to call me if she remembers any other details."

"I will do that. Thank you for understanding."

The constable left, and Natalie looked up at her father. A little nervous smile crept up on her lips. "I don't know what happened, Dad."

"Don't worry Natalie. It's over now, sweetheart. Let's go."

Natalie looked around. "Where is the woman that was here, Dad?"

"I believe she is still in the other room with the older gentleman."

"I know it sounds crazy, Dad, but I've seen her before…in a dream." She thought Phillip would laugh now, and would believe that his adoptive daughter wasn't just a disappointment, but also crazy. But Phillip didn't laugh, in fact, he looked at Natalie with tears in his eyes. "I believe that young woman there is your sister, Natalie."

Natalie's mind had already reached capacity, but this was too big to flush out. "What? How can that be possible?'

"When your mother became very depressed over our inability to conceive a child, I looked for a baby to adopt. Well, my original hopes of finding a little one were quickly dashed, as I discovered that it would take months, maybe years, to find an infant and finalize all paperwork. We could easily take in an older child, sure, but your mother's screaming instincts needed a baby to love and claim as her own. Her mental state was so fragile that I was terrified she would do something crazy if I told her of the challenges ahead. Instead of talking to her, I spoke about it with a man I was still in touch with from law school. He knew a doctor that facilitated adoptions, and I was put in contact with him. He told me he had a lady who was ready to have a baby she didn't want, so I jumped at the chance.

I flew out to meet him in Raleigh, at the hospital where he worked. You were premature, so you had to remain hospitalized for a while. I asked to meet the mother, but he told me that she was not willing to meet the adoptive parents. I stayed at a hotel, while all the papers were drawn. Being an attorney, I knew the channels to speed up the paperwork. The doctor asked me to keep things between us, since he didn't want social services to get involved. The young woman, he said, was the daughter of close friends of his, and he had promised them he would keep the adoption extremely private.

When I took you home and saw the look on your mother's face I knew it was all worth the effort. Angela was happy and her depression lifted like fog on a summer morning."

Natalie felt speechless, but managed to whisper a few words. "Is my real mother still alive?"

"She is, Natalie. A few years after the adoption was finalized, I heard that this doctor was being investigated for other adoptions he arranged. I discovered that he targeted mothers of twins, triggered an early labor by scraping their membranes during routine check-ups, and then told them they had given birth to only one live twin."

"But, didn't anyone witness that? Where was my real father?"

"The staff was investigated too – they were all in it with him - and fathers did not attend births back then. When the whole thing blew over and I discovered the truth, your mother was happy, and I just couldn't let her slip back into her depressive state. I shuffled things around a bit and paid a few people to keep quiet. Your birth records were never found."

Natalie stood up and looked at her father, her expression a mask of anger and pain. "So my mother never gave me away…I was stolen and sold to the highest bidder."

Phillip hung his head low, unable to look at his daughter. "That's right, Natalie, but I didn't know about it until it was too late, sweetheart. I should have told you when I found out, but I never found the courage."

"And now what, Dad? Where do we go from here?"

"I believe in destiny, Natalie. If you and your sister were reunited under such odd circumstances, then who am I to stand between you? Just give me a few days to tell your mother…please."

Natalie nodded. Years of self-doubt, endless nights of pain and rejection lifted off Natalie as the realization of what her father said sank in. She ran to the other room and looked silently at the woman standing in front of her; her feelings at that moment she just couldn't describe. Melody stood without speaking, afraid to break the spell between them. Natalie's tears flooded her face as she ran toward Melody and hugged her, her chest violently shaking with deep sobs. Paul sat on a chair by the window, unable to make sense of what was happening but fully aware that he was witnessing a miracle.

Chapter Twenty

Lakeisha was still unconscious when Natalie and her father arrived at the hospital. Her throat was covered in bandages, and she was hooked up to what looked like at least half a dozen tubes. A nurse approached them as soon as they walked up.

"I'm afraid you can't go in, Miss. Doctor's orders."

"Is she okay? May I speak to the doctor on duty?"

"He has already done his rounds for tonight. I don't think you will be able to see him until the morning, but you can speak to the head nurse if you wish."

"That would be great, thank you."

The nurse left to go find her supervisor and Natalie looked up at her father. "She is going to be okay, won't she?"

Phillip wrapped his arms around her and inhaled the scent of his daughter's hair. For the first time in many years he felt she was his little girl again, and fought to keep his voice steady. "I hope so, Honey. I am so sorry about Lakeisha, too. I really wasn't too nice to her; there was something about her that always intimidated me."

"It does feel like she can read through you sometimes" Natalie said smiling at her father, "she really is a special lady. There is a reason why she came with me, dad."

"I figured that much, although I still can't figure out what's happening."

"It's a long story, dad. Someday we will sit down and I will explain everything. You might not believe some of it, though."

"I can believe more than what you give me credit for, Natalie, and it is my fault that you don't know me too well. I guess I've always alienated myself, but that's going to change starting from today. I am planning on starting things anew with your mother and with you."

"Dad, Aunt Catherine's daughter, Suzanne…she's dead."

Phillip drew a deep breath. "I'm glad Catherine will never have to go through the pain of knowing that her child was dead. She always imagined her happy and well adjusted like the little girl in the painting."

"I know…hopefully they are reunited now."

"Miss? I am Lorna Stewart, the head nurse." Natalie and Phillip turned to look at a pleasant looking woman with kind blue eyes and a sprinkle of freckles on her cheeks. Her mid-length blond hair was pinned away from her face and kept tidy under a white nurse's cap. Give or take an inch, she was about as tall as Natalie and quite petite otherwise.

"It's nice to meet you, Ms. Stewart. Thank you so much for coming to talk to us."

Lorna smiled and nodded once, "No problem at all. Unfortunately I don't have good news for you…Ms. Jackson has lost a lot of blood and is very weak. She had a cranial trauma that hadn't properly healed yet, and this new blow to her system is compounding the problems she was probably already having."

Natalie nodded, "Yes, she was attacked once before, by the same man."

"Unfortunately, this new trauma has created a very intense shock, and her heart is giving signs of severe distress."

"Will she be okay, though?"

"It's too soon to tell, but if she can make it through the night our hopes will certainly increase."

"May I stay here with her tonight?"

"We don't usually allow anyone in intensive care, but I think I can make an exception. If you'd like to stay you are welcome to."

"Thank you, I would really like to stay. Is it okay with you, dad?"

"Sure, Honey, do you need anything? Oh yes, by the way" Phillip said as he pulled a silver cell phone from his pocket, "the police have recovered this phone at Catherine's house. Since Catherine never owned one, I wondered if it is Lakeisha's, so I brought it along to give it to you at the exhibit."

"Thank you, Dad. I'll give it to her when she wakes up. And no, I don't need anything. Please let Ryan know that I appreciate him coming here."

"I think he had something in store for you, a surprise I believe."

"Dad, I think Ryan wants to marry me to save his family from a financial catastrophe."

"Ryan Wheeler? His is one of the most solid families in the southeast."

"Only on the surface, Dad. They are experiencing some very hard times."

"I think he is planning on meeting us for dinner." Phillip said looking at his watch, "Or was planning to, anyway. I've been missing in action, your mother is probably furious…I only left to come back to the gallery and tell you to join us for dinner, since you weren't answering your phone. She is probably worried out of her mind. I will call her on my way back and explain. I really should run."

"Bye Dad, I will call you in the morning." She kissed her father and watched him until he turned the corner, before she said: "Please, give Mom my love."

Phillip beamed at her, "I will, Honey. I will."

After her father left, Natalie walked back to Lakeisha's room and sat on the faux leather chair in the corner. She was so tired that within minutes she fell asleep.

After taking Melody back to her room, Paul wearily dragged his feet until he reached his own. He was exhausted. In the course of a few days he had gone through an assortment of emotions, from the bittersweet feeling of giving his daughter away in marriage, to being the one who killed his great-niece's husband in order to protect her. He needed a hot shower and a cold beer, both of them good means to warm the cold right out of his old bones.

He intended to extend his stay. He certainly couldn't leave Melody to deal with the hassle of going back alone and arrange to have her husband's remains flown back for the funeral. He also needed to call Olivia. Even if she was on her honeymoon in Scotland, and probably having the time of her life, Paul knew that Olivia wouldn't forgive him if he didn't call her to update her on all that had happened. After he got out of the shower, he wrapped a towel around his waist, and picked up the phone.

"Hello" Olivia's voice sounded happy and vibrant.

"Olivia, it's Dad. How are you, Sugar?'

"I'm wonderful, Dad; what about you? Are you ready to fly back tomorrow? Did you confirm your reservations with the airline, or do you want me to do that for you?"

"Olivia, I'm not leaving tomorrow. There has been an accident."

"What kind of accident?" Laughter left Olivia's voice the moment the magic word was uttered.

"It's Mario, Olivia…he died today."

"What?! You are joking, right?"

"I wouldn't joke about something so tragic, Honey."

"But…what happened? Is Melody okay?"

"Melody is fine; well, I guess she isn't fine, but she is safe and sound."

"Dad, I'm calling the airport right now to see if Graham and I can fly back into London tonight."

"No, Olivia, please don't do that."

"Dad, I'm coming back." There was steel in her voice; Paul knew better than continue the argument. "Okay, Sweetheart. Call me when you get in."

"I will. Let me run now, so I can call and make arrangements…Dad, are you okay?"

Paul smiled; never once did he talk to Olivia without her asking how he was, no matter how good or bad anything else was. "I'm fine, Olivia. I miss you."

"I miss you too, Dad. I will see you tonight or at the latest tomorrow. We'll keep in touch."

"Okay, Honey. Goodnight. I love you."

"I love you too, Dad."

He hung up the phone and got dressed, ready to leave the room in minutes.

When he knocked on Melody's door, she didn't answer at first, then he heard her get up and coming to open. Her eyes were swollen and her face was blotched from crying. Paul said nothing and just took her into his massive arms. Melody cried openly against his chest, deep sobs rattling her whole body. Paul let her cry, then lifted her chin gently and kissed her forehead. "Would you like a little company?"

Melody nodded, and stepped back to let him inside the room. She plopped back on her bed, a rag doll that had been pushed around once too many times. Paul sat on the chair at the small desk, picked up a pen with the hotel logo, and started fiddling with the top.

"He's gone, Paul. He's really gone. Deep down I knew something was wrong, but I couldn't put my finger on what it was. What am I going to do now?"

"I don't know, Child. I just don't know. Mario had us all fooled. Or maybe, he was the one who was fooled into believing that power and ego are more important than the people who cared about him."

Melody nodded, and Paul saw that tears were welling up in her eyes again, so he decided to change the subject. "Say, I was about to go down and look for a place to have a beer. Wanna go with me and keep this old man some company?'

Melody smiled, "No, Paul; I really appreciate the invite, but I think I will stay in. I'm really not up to seeing people right now."

Something in her voice told Paul to not push her any further, so he stood up and kissed her forehead again before he left. "You take care, Sweetheart. I have my cell phone with me, if you need me. Olivia would beam if she knew I said that. I've always told her I don't need those modern contraptions – I'm old school all the way, baby."

Melody laughed in spite of it all. Paul always had a way to bring out the best of her.

He left Melody's room and took the elevator down to the lobby. Aside from the front desk clerk, there were only two other people in the hall, a middle aged lady with hair the color of carrots checking in, and a man with no hair reading the newspaper in one of the oversized chairs near the sliding entrance doors. Paul walked outside and enjoyed the cooler breeze. Even in the summer, London was not warm – compared to his hometown in hot and sticky Louisiana, London felt downright cold to him, but it was pleasant for a mind-clearing walk and he inhaled deeply as he strode down the street.

He saw a bar nearby; from the outside he could hear music being played by a live band, so he walked in. The band played mostly alternative rock – definitely not Paul's cup of tea, but it was good enough to take his mind away from the overwhelming chain of events that had taken place in the afternoon.

He sat at the bar counter and ordered a pint of Guinness, which he sipped with pleasure until he heard the stool beside him being moved. Unwilling to make conversation, he moved slightly to turn away from the other patron, but he froze the moment he laid eyes on the man sitting next to him. This time he was dressed more casually – a red shirt opened on his chest to reveal a unique gold pendant, black slacks, a red shiny belt, and black leather shoes that looked like they had just been polished. He gestured to the bartender to bring him a Guinness too, and then he turned his attention to Paul. "We meet again, Paul."

Paul nodded and smiled "I reckon we are."

"You've done well, my friend. Everything is as it should be."

"Is it, though? Did you know about my niece's husband?"

The stranger nodded his head and took a sip of the beer in front of him. "I did. As I told you back at the store in Louisiana, people aren't always who they appear to be."

"I see. My niece could have been killed, or her sister."

"Neither of them was supposed to leave, Paul, it is written that way."

"What about the other lady? Will she be okay?"

"I can't tell you that, Paul, but know that both of you have fulfilled your tasks."

Paul smiled uneasy, "Oh yes, you told me that being there for Melody was my final task. Does that mean that I am going to kick the bucket now, too?"

The stranger laughed heartily, "Maybe you will, or maybe you won't, Paul. Do you really want to know?"

"Well, that would give me the chance to straighten out some things…"

"Then go do it, Paul, no matter what happens. Life is on borrowed time, every minute of it, and every one of those moments you should always feel as if it's going to be your last. Don't wait until tomorrow to tell your daughter you love her –

do it now; don't wait to fix all of your earthly problems when it's too late… there are enough lost souls who remain anchored on earth because they feel they didn't complete one thing or another. Do your best to always be ready to go, and while you're here, make sure you have a hell of a fun ride."

Paul smiled, amused by the stranger, and renewed in his propositions. "I suppose you're right. I will call my daughter back tonight, to see if she found a flight, and I will tell her how much I care. Who knows? The last time I met you, you preceded a small war; I don't even want to think of what might happen when I leave here."

The stranger stood up and announced that he would be right back; Paul knew better than that. Elegba had made his stop and things were now in place – it was time for him to move on and go assist other souls. Paul finished his beer, and then left the bar, breathing in the cool air with fully open lungs. He stopped a moment and reached his hand into his pocket to take out his cell phone. He dialed Olivia's number, and the moment she answered his heart leaped with joy. "Olivia? It's Dad…I just wanted to tell you how much I love you."

Natalie woke up with a strange feeling. When she opened her eyes, she thought she saw a shadow by the foot of Lakeisha's bed. She touched the rosary still around her neck and tried to focus on the figure, but couldn't see it anymore. She heard a soft moan, and her heart skipped. She looked at Lakeisha and saw that her friend was moving her head slowly, trying to open her eyes. She called the nurse and ran out into the hallway when nobody came. She almost ran into the head nurse,

Lorna, who was standing in the hallway right outside the door updating charts. "She's waking up! Please, hurry!"

Ms. Stewart went in and confirmed that Lakeisha was waking up. She checked her vital signs and pushed a button to alert the doctor on duty. She was ready to send Natalie out, when Lakeisha grabbed her arm, and gestured for Natalie to stay. She pointed at the tube in her mouth, silently asking for it to be removed. Nurse Stewart thought about it for a moment, unsure what to do until the doctor arrived, but Lakeisha continued to make grunting sounds and pointing at her tube, so the nurse disconnected it, and gently pulled it out of her mouth. Lakeisha's voice was barely perceptible and scratchy, so Natalie came closer and leaned over to hear what her friend had to say.

"It's happening, Natalie..." she whispered in a raspy voice, her severed vocal cords too injured to create pleasant sounds, "The rosary is yours to keep now. Make sure you always protect it. You and your sister have a prime role in changing the consciousness of all."

Natalie's tears were flowing freely. "You will be here with me, telling me what to do to keep it safe, Lakeisha."

Lakeisha painfully moved her head, "No, I won't, Natalie. She's waiting for me, do you see her there?"

Natalie turned to see who Lakeisha was talking about, but all she could see was the white wall of the hospital room. "I don't see anybody, Lakeisha...who's there?"

"She's not for you to see, Natalie...she's waiting for me. Catherine said to tell you thank you for bringing her and her little girl together. Her final task, before she crosses over, is to see me home."

276

Natalie jerked her head toward the wall, but again she saw nobody. "Is that who's there? Aunt Catherine?"

Lakeisha moved her lips to form a yes, but no sound came out. Nurse Stewart touched Natalie's arm gently. "She shouldn't talk. Maybe it is best if you go out right now."

Natalie nodded, her face streaked by tears, and headed toward the door.

"Natalie..."Lakeisha's voice was a tiny whisper, "...Good-bye."

And in that moment Natalie knew; Lakeisha was not coming back, she was leaving with Aunt Catherine; she had only briefly awakened to say goodbye. She turned around and blew her friend a kiss. "Good-bye, Lakeisha. Thank you..."

"What in hell...?" The voice of Nurse Stewart was filled with surprise when Lakeisha's vital signs dropped and she expired. Natalie wasn't surprised at all.

Ryan hung up the phone after receiving the craziest news he heard in a while from Mr. Sanders. He couldn't believe what happened after he left the gallery, and yet, he was sure Mr. Sanders was not joking. The whole episode brought home something Ryan rarely thought about: Life is short and fragile, and should be lived minute by minute.

As he lay back on his hotel bed and tried to process all the new information, his mind was flooded with thoughts of Ashton and his heart instantly ached. When he first arrived in London, he had come to the conclusion that breaking up with her to pursue his plans to marry Natalie was the right thing to do;

somehow, his determination to save the family's financial future had temporarily blinded him.

It wasn't Ashton's fault that she was born in a poor family, and she was no different than he or his family. Ashton was a nice girl and she was going to make a good wife; his parents were going to accept her in time, and if they couldn't, oh well…then she and Ryan would have to learn how to live without their approval. For the first time in his life, Ryan saw everything clearly, and he felt ashamed that up until now, he had chosen to look at the world through the perception of others.

He took the ring he bought for Natalie out of his shirt pocket, and looked at it in the light of the lamp on the night stand. It was a beauty, but he really could not afford it. He would love to give Ashton something that beautiful – God only knew she deserved it – but maybe he could do that later on in their marriage. For right now, he was going to take the ring back and buy a smaller one; then he would call Ashton before he boarded the plane and have her meet him at the airport to pick him up.

He didn't know what would happen to his family's finances, but he felt that deception wasn't going to be the way to fix something that was caused by the same cancer. He would come up with an idea; for right now, he needed to head off to the hospital and be a friend to Natalie. Suddenly, Ryan felt very, very relieved.

"What do you mean her sister is here, Phillip?"

Phillip felt an overwhelming urge to look at the ground, but he fought it and stared at Angela's face instead. "Natalie's adoption went a little differently than the way I disclosed to you, Angie; her mother had twins, and the doctor sold one of them, unbeknownst to her; the staff gave her a different baby to bury, one the parents had signed over to the hospital for medical research when they found out she was stillborn."

Angela exhaled and looked deflated for a moment. "Oh my God, Phillip, what have we done?"

"We didn't know, Angie; we didn't know."

"So, Natalie's real mother is still around."

"Yes" Phillip replied, his eyes still locked with Angela's, "She is, and I am sure that Natalie will want to meet her at some point. I have the phone number of the uncle right here. I believe we should all get together and discuss what will happen."

Angela agreed, "We must. Natalie needs to meet her real parents, and know that we will support her through it all."

Phillip felt a knot forming in his throat. "I knew you would understand, Angie. And by the way, when I left the hospital, Natalie asked me to give you her love."

The phone rang; it was Natalie. Phillip listened for a while without interrupting, then said, "I will be right there, Natalie. I am sorry, Honey."

"What happened?" his wife asked after he hung up, although in her heart she already knew the truth.

"Lakeisha passed away. I'm going there to pick up Natalie, and make arrangements to have the remains flown back to the US."

"No, Phillip, *we* are going. I'm coming with you. Let's go and show our daughter she can count on us."

Natalie was sitting alone in the waiting room when Ryan arrived. Her head was leaning against the wall and her eyes were closed. Thinking she was asleep, he sat beside her and crossed his hands over his abdomen without disturbing her, but she immediately opened her eyes, and the sadness he saw in them pierced his heart. All he wanted to do was to take her in his arms and comfort her, as a friend should.

"Thank you for coming, Ryan. She's gone. She passed away thirty minutes ago."

Ryan touched her hand lightly. "I'm sorry, Natalie. I don't know what to say."

Natalie shook her head, "there's not much to say, Ryan. She was a friend, and now she has moved on."

Ryan reached out to hug her, thinking that she would push him away, but she didn't. She laid her head on his shoulder and cried quietly.

Chapter Twenty-One

Olivia's flight landed at London Gatwick at 8:35AM. She had hardly slept the night before, and had almost lost all hope of finding a flight that would get her into London early in the day.

By the time she arrived at the hotel, she was so worked up that it took Graham ten minutes, before they went up to see her father, to calm her down. In Olivia's world, efficiency and self-discipline were the names of the game, but right now she felt as if she could burst into tears. Maybe it was because she had just gotten married, and knew how important her husband was to her, that her heart broke for Melody.

She went to check on her father first, then went straight to Melody's room even before she checked into her own. Melody looked like the ghost of the woman Olivia knew – gaunt and pale, a look of despair haunted her usually bright eyes. Olivia said nothing when her cousin opened the door; she simply hugged her, and Melody melted in her arms, clinging tightly to her neck and bursting into bitter tears.

"Melody…I just don't know what to say…Dad didn't really explain a lot; he just said something awful happened to Mario."

"Your father told the truth, Olivia. I always thought Mario was my knight in shining armor, and my love for him blinded me from seeing that even a white knight has some dark shadows. I didn't know, Olivia…I didn't know that his heart belonged to someone else, but I felt that something was wrong.

281

I should have trusted my intuition, and maybe this mess would not have happened."

Olivia marched into the room and sat on the bed beside Melody. "Listen to me, Melody Bennet," she said staring directly into Melody's eyes, "You can't prevent everything. Look at me, I'm a control freak, and weird stuff still happens in my life. What I am getting at is that you can't always know how something will unfold. You can only hope for the best."

Melody laughed bitterly but didn't say anything. Right now, she certainly didn't feel in control of anything, and sadly, she had no hope left.

"What are you going to do now, Melody?"

"Well, I suppose that I will need to go through the motions for the time being. I will go back to North Carolina and stay at the farm; I will take care of Mario's burial and make sure his remaining family is notified of his death; and, most importantly, I will work on establishing a relationship with my sister."

"Sister?"

"Oh, Paul didn't tell you?"

Olivia arched her eyebrows, silently letting Melody know her father said nothing about a sister.

"I am a twin, Olivia. I didn't even learn that until I was an adult and my grandmother left me a letter informing me of it. I was told that my twin was stillborn, but it appears that she was in fact stolen by the doctor who delivered her; he made it a little side business of his to sell babies to affluent childless couples, letting them believe that the mothers didn't want their offspring. He told the mothers the children were stillborn."

"Oh my God! That's terrible, Melody! But how did you come to meet her?"

Melody laughed, "You know crazy things always happen to me, right?"

Olivia grinned, "Yeah...you're the poster child for someone who's a magnet for calamities."

"My grandmother left me a rosary, which is supposed to be a key element, along with other items, to trigger an ancient prophecy. Grandmama told me in her letter that the rosary was associated with the cult of the twins. What she didn't explain was that there are two rosaries, and twins are supposed to be their keepers. When my sister – her name is Natalie – and I came together into the same room, and we accidentally touched, I felt heat coming out of the rosary I was wearing around my neck. I can't help but think that maybe the rosaries came out of their dormant state to save us both from sure death."

Olivia whistled. "That's pure sci-fi, Melody. You know I am kind of new at this stuff."

That made Melody laugh, and God, it felt so good!

"Yeah, I know; I don't think many would even believe what happened. Paul was there, but he is a veteran when it comes to weird things by now, and Tom, the gallery owner, is probably still in a deep state of shock."

"So, tell me...what does your sister look like?" Olivia enquired, curiosity eating at her beneath the skin.

"Oh, Olivia, you are not going to believe it when you see her; she is me with a wig."

Olivia laughed. "For real? I can't wait to meet her."

"I have her phone number here; I was just thinking of calling her right before you arrived. Maybe we can all have dinner together; after all, she is your cousin too."

That one last sentence hit Olivia directly in the stomach. "Oh dear God, I hadn't even thought of it that way! That's so awesome!"

"That's settled then. I will call her in a minute and we'll see about getting together tonight or tomorrow. Hey, you want to know another freaky thing? All our lives, my sister and I have lived only a hundred and fifty miles apart from each other; that little tidbit still blows my mind. If we didn't come here for your wedding I would still be married to a player and I would never have met her – I lost a cheating husband and gained a sister; God always fills a void."

"I have a few things to explain, Natalie." Ryan told her as he took her hands into his while they sat at a booth in the hospital cafeteria.

"If you are talking about relationships, I'm not really up to having that conversation, Ryan. I thought about what you said, and I really don't think I am ready for a serious relationship. I need to learn how to love myself, first, before I can make someone else happy."

Ryan exhaled loudly. "I could kiss you right now, Natalie. You just made life much easier for me without knowing it." He said, a wide smile quickly spreading on his handsome face.

"What are you talking about, Ryan?"

284

Ryan shifted uneasily, his cheerful attitude instantly gone. "I have lied to you, Natalie." He said and pulled his hands up in a defensive gesture.

"I know you have, Ryan."

He looked at Natalie raising his eyebrow. "Pardon me?"

"I know you are in deep financial trouble, due to your father's gambling habit."

Ryan's face flushed to a deep crimson, the vein in his neck beating furiously. "How long have you known?"

Natalie smiled, "Since Lakeisha told me you were deceiving me. I thought it was an insane idea at first, but I dug around a bit, and found out about your family's hardship."

Ryan exhaled loudly. "Oh my God, I am so embarrassed right now..." he said slightly stuttering, his face blood red. "It wasn't all about that, Natalie; I really liked you."

Natalie smiled. "And I really liked you, too, Ryan, but I don't love you; I never have. I only tried to convince myself I did because I was lonely."

He wanted to tell her about Ashton, but quickly changed his mind – no reason to add insult to injury. "Are you really mad at me, Natalie?"

Natalie thought for a moment..."No, Ryan, I'm not mad. I guess I respect you in my own strange way, for willing to sacrifice yourself for your family."

Ryan looked down at his hands, clamped over the table. "Wow, now I feel even worse. You are a wonderful girl, Natalie, and you deserve to meet someone who can truly love you and cherish the amazing person that you are."

Natalie smiled, "He will come. For right now, how much money do you need to get out of debt?"

Ryan looked up from his hands, a confused look steadily settling on his face. "Why do you need to know?"

"Because if I have a number, I can call Mr. Dillard and arrange to have him write you a check; I still don't have all those details worked out yet."

"What…? What check are you talking about?"

"Get with the program, Ryan; I'm loaning you the money you need to get your company back on its feet…wait, companies don't have feet…"

Ryan laughed and tears of relief ran down his cheeks. "You don't have to do that…why would you do that?"

"Because you are my friend, Ryan; because your family and mine have been close for generations; and because I really appreciate you being here right now. I really want to do something to help, if you will allow me."

"I don't know what to say, Natalie; I doubt there are words that can express how I feel right now. I promise you that I will pay you back every red cent with interest as soon as things turn around."

"Shhhh…." Natalie put a finger in front of her nose, "don't make promises, Ryan. Just accept what I am offering you."

"I do accept, Natalie, and I am deeply humbled not only by your generosity, but mostly by the kindness you are showing toward someone who attempted to deceive you."

"You weren't doing this to hurt me, Ryan; one can't fault a drowning man for trying to reach a life preserver."

Sister Justine paced back and forth like a caged animal. She hadn't heard anything for two days now, and Lakeisha didn't send the daily report Justine had come to expect every night. Although she had no way of confirming anything was wrong until Lakeisha called or wrote, she couldn't ignore the feeling of unease that had taken a hold of her. When her phone rang she almost leaped across the desk to get to it – she was amazed at how frayed her nerves were. The voice on the other side of the line was not the one she had hoped to hear.

"Sister Justine? My name is Natalie Sanders; I am a friend of Lakeisha Jackson."

An icy grip squeezed Justine's stomach; now she definitely knew something happened. "Yes, This is Sister Justine; how can I be of help, Ms. Sanders?"

"Your number was the only one listed in the address book of Lakeisha's cell phone. I am glad the police retrieved it at my aunt's house just before we left, or I wouldn't have been able to call you…"

"Yes?"

"Ma'am, I don't really know how to say this, but something happened to Lakeisha."

"Please continue Ms. Sanders."

"There was an accident…Lakeisha is gone."

Sister Justine closed her eyes and silently said a prayer, a stray tear descending down her cheek. Natalie waited a moment to let her absorb the shock, and then said, "I will make arrangements to have her remains flown back to the US within the next day or two; I was wondering if she has any family, or if you are aware of any burial wishes she might have shared with you in the past."

"Sister Lakeisha must be buried here in New Orleans, Ms. Sanders. We have a small section of tombs in St. Louis One that are reserved for our order. If you can arrange to fly her remains here, we will be happy to take care of all expenses."

"That's not necessary, Sister, I can take care of the expenses. Would it be possible for me to fly down as well? I would like to be there for the funeral."

"Lakeisha thought highly of you, Ms. Sanders. She would be honored to see you at her funeral, I'm quite certain. There are some things you and I must discuss anyway, so it is just as well that you come here."

"Thank you, Sister. I will be in touch within the next couple of days."

Justine hung up the phone and went to the secret ritual chamber. The rosary made it to its semi-final destination – it was time to alert the elders.

Melody was preparing for dinner, when she sensed a presence in her room. Thinking that maybe Olivia had forgotten something and had come back in unannounced, she stepped out of the bathroom and nearly screamed when she saw a young girl sitting at the edge of her bed. "Who are you? What are you doing here?" Melody asked unnerved. The girl lifted her eyes to look at her, and smiled gently while rubbing her slightly swollen abdomen. "I've been waiting for all of this to be over, so I could give you some news, Melody."

"News? What kind of news?" God only knew Melody didn't need any more surprises.

"You lost a lot, Melody, but you gained even more."

"Yes," Melody said sweetly, fully aware now that the girl was not of this world, and yet not feeling at all scared. "I found my sister. Too bad I had to lose my husband."

"You didn't lose your husband, Melody, only his body and his ego. The best part of him, the innocent side of his being, is living and thriving inside of you."

Melody was confused, but suddenly remembered the feeling of warmth she felt when the man at the gallery was ready to shoot her. It felt exactly as a hand closing in over her stomach, trying to protect it. "What do you mean by the innocent part of him?"

"I lost my baby, Melody, no matter how badly I wanted to keep her safe. My final task was to protect yours."

Melody stood in stunned silence, the towel she wrapped around her wet hair slowly slipped off, as she instinctively touched her abdomen. "You can't possibly mean...no, this is not happening..."

Suzanne smiled. "It is, Melody. You are expecting a child - Mario's baby. I made sure it remained safe."

Melody felt her legs shaking violently, and quickly went to sit on the edge of the bed and closed her eyes. When she opened them again, the young girl was gone.

Melody, Olivia, Paul and Graham sat at a table in the far corner of Royal India and attempted to make small talk until

Natalie arrived. Although all four tried to appear nonchalant, their heads automatically turned toward the entrance anytime someone walked in.

"Are you okay, Melody?" Paul said reaching across the table to cover one of her small hands with his own massive one.

"I'm nervous, Paul. I don't even see why we met in a restaurant. My stomach is in pieces, I doubt I will be able to eat anything." She said with a small nervous laugh.

"Same here" Olivia said, "I'm getting ready to meet one more member of my family."

"I must say, Olivia", Graham threw in to lighten the mood; "one never gets bored around your family."

"Ha! So you say, Graham, but believe me, you haven't seen the half of it."

"Olivia told me about some of the other adventures today, Paul. They are nothing short of unbelievable."

"But true." Paul exclaimed. Before he could add anything else, Natalie and Ryan walked in and strolled to the table.

Olivia and Graham stared at Natalie from the moment she came around the corner until she sat down. "Oh my God! You and Melody look exactly alike. It's crazy…" Olivia said, her eyes open wide and filled with surprise. She extended her hand in Natalie's direction. "Well, we might just want to cut through formalities, since we are family. I'm Olivia, your cousin."

Natalie smiled and shook Olivia's hand; she repeated the routine with all of them except Melody whom she hugged instead.

"This is my friend Ryan. He figured he should come along to support me. I am still a little shaken about this." Natalie admitted smiling.

"It's nice to see you again, Ryan" Paul said as he shook his hand, "I believe we met the day you arrived. We are staying at the same hotel."

"That's right! You told me your niece is from North Carolina."

"Yep, here she is. As it turns out she is your friend's sister."

"It really is a small world, and a strange one at that," Ryan said and sat down beside Natalie.

"We have lived a hundred miles apart our whole lives, and had to travel four thousand miles away from home to meet," Natalie said softly, unable to stop grinning.

"Isn't that the truth?" Melody said, a smile also spreading on her face. "Natalie, I know it is early days, but we will need to arrange for you to meet our mother at some point."

Natalie's stomach did a somersault. "Oh God, I hadn't even thought of that…how will she react?"

"She will be shocked, Natalie, as we all are, but I think she will be thrilled."

"Yeah, she will." Paul said looking lovingly at his daughter. "Olivia and I didn't meet until she was a grown woman, but I couldn't imagine my life without her now."

Olivia reached across the table to touch her dad's hand, "I couldn't either, Dad."

"So, where do we go from here, Melody? With the rosaries, I mean. Lakeisha told me of an ancient prophecy but I am still very confused about all of this."

"I'm not sure, Natalie. I suppose Spirit will lead us through the rest of the journey."

Melody thought a few times about sharing the young girl's revelation with her family, but decided to keep the secret for herself a little longer, at least until after they got back home.

Everyone was so engrossed in the conversation, eager to get to know each other, that none of them noticed the man sitting in the dark corner of the bar. He pulled out a map from his pocket and laid it out on the bar counter; an "x" was already traced over New Orleans, and now he drew one over London. Only when all four signs had manifested, and all four of the keepers were led by fate to bring the items to the sacred point of meeting, would the Elders know it is time to trigger the shift. Two more cities to go, two more signs to manifest, many more lives destined to change.

Epilogue

Less than a week had passed since she returned from London, but to Natalie those days felt like a lifetime ago. Everything had been so surreal that by the time she returned to a more familiar environment, all that happened felt like a dream. Her parents and Ryan changed their flights so that they could all travel together, and Lakeisha's remains were flown directly to New Orleans. Natalie was now on route again, this time to attend the funeral of her friend.

It was already arranged that upon her return she would go to Raleigh to meet Annie, her real mother. Her parents were a bit apprehensive, but they had nothing to worry about. Regardless of their struggles in the past, everybody was working hard to overcome their differences, and Natalie felt that even Angie, her adoptive mother, was now trying her best to reach out to her.

When her plane landed at New Orleans International Airport, she took a cab to the French Quarter. They drove by a cemetery, and Natalie wondered if it was the one where Lakeisha would be laid to rest. She was almost tempted to ask the driver the name of the cemetery they just passed, but he didn't seem to speak much English, so she killed that idea in its infancy. It took about twenty minutes to arrive at their destination. The driver pulled up in front of a dated two-story brick building near the intersection of Royal and Dumaine. Natalie stepped out of the cab, paid the driver and looked up at the wrought iron balcony. As she did, she noticed a curtain

293

move behind one of the windows, and within seconds, a woman dressed in nun garb opened a door and stepped outside to meet her. "Ms. Sanders?"

"Yes, how are you? Are you Sister Justine?"

The woman nodded, as her blue, loose gown gently waved in the breeze coming from the Mississippi river nearby. "Please come, my child. We are almost ready to go. I will show you to your room to drop off your things and then we can leave for the cemetery. Sister Lakeisha has already been prepared for burial."

She led Natalie down a straight and narrow hallway, kept purposefully dark to shield away from the scorching heat of the day. Natalie's room was simply decorated, with a twin bed placed near the window and a heavy, antique dresser pushed against the wall in the opposite corner. The wall were stark white, and the only other amenities Natalie saw were a small lamp on a matching bedside table, a mirror near the dresser, and a small desk in front of the window. Although very humble, the room was immaculately clean. Worried at the thought of delaying plans, Natalie dropped her bag at the foot of the bed and told Sister Justine she was ready to go. Within moments, another nun came into the sitting room to announce that the van was ready and they would leave in minutes.

When they arrived in front of the cemetery, Natalie's artistic eye was immediately enthralled by the view: The whole yard was surrounded by a high wall, and access to the cemetery was granted through small iron gates which looked old and unassuming. Many of the graves – all above ground mural structures since the cemetery was built below sea level – were in a state of disrepair, and Natalie wondered why they were not restored. One of the things that drew her attention was the fact that each grave had multiple names inscribed on the front, and she asked Sister Justine about it.

"We bury our dead differently here, Ms. Sanders; after a year and a day, the coffins, which are manufactured of simple wood and not sealed to assist in a quicker decomposition of the body, are opened and the bones are taken out and placed in a smaller box. The box is placed in the back of the tomb, to make room for the next member of the family."

They came up to an open tomb, surrounded by a small group of nuns; a wooden coffin was already placed inside the tomb, and fresh flowers were arranged on the ground. Natalie swallowed hard. Her friend was in that coffin, and looking at it now brought home the reality that she would never see Lakeisha again.

Sister Justine opened a small book of prayers, and led the sisters into a chant that quickly flooded the empty pockets of silence. The sun shone bright, and the sticky hot air felt as an invisible embrace from all the souls that stood there as witnesses of this solemn moment. Natalie stood on one side, her eyes fixed on the open mouth of the tomb. She silently said her good-byes, and prayed that her friend would watch over her in the days to come.

Melody returned to the farm alone. She was numb throughout Mario's funeral, and barely heard Father Rudino's words during the service. She still didn't have the nerve to tell her mother about Natalie. Although she was sure Annie would be thrilled, she was too exhausted to deal with the drama that would surely ensue from the revelation.

She went inside the farmhouse and went directly upstairs to her bedroom, the same one that had belonged to Grandmama and Grandpapa Henry, and nearly collapsed on the large bed. She lay there until the light of the day switched shift with the first shadows of the evening. Suddenly, something caught her eye, a picture of Grandmama, happily smiling from a small portrait on the dresser, and in that same moment she felt her child flutter inside of her the first time. She protectively touched her abdomen, feeling an overwhelming sense of love toward the tiny being, and she was taken by a deep sense of peace. She had, so far, only shared the news of her pregnancy with Paul and Olivia, but she knew now that it was time to tell Annie.

"Grandmama" she thought out loud, "did you know all this was going to happen? Did you know that my life was going to turn upside down when you first sent me to Louisiana to bring your ashes? So much has happened these past two years that I don't know what I need to do next. I have a baby I am responsible for now. Please give me a sign of what I must do next."

She listened to the silence of the room, waiting to hear something, but nothing came. She sat up on the edge of the bed and her eyes focused on the small key charm she normally wore around her neck, which was now resting on the dresser beside Grandmama's photo. She walked up to the dresser, picked it up, and held it tight in her hand. Strangely, it felt warm to the touch, although it had been sitting there since before the funeral when she took it off to wear a different necklace. "Please, Elegba,

296

don't abandon me now," She said to the long shadows dancing in the orange light of a glorious sunset, "Stand by me until my purpose is fulfilled."

Ryan Wheeler took Ashton's hand into his own as they walked together toward his parents' house. As they neared the door, Ashton stopped and locked eyes with Ryan.

"You can still change your mind, Ryan. You already know that your parents will not accept me with open arms."

"It doesn't matter, Ashton. I love you and if they love me they will need to accept you, because you are going to be a part of my life. It's time the Wheelers catch up with the current century. Besides, I have no doubt they will fall in love with you in no time; just bear with my mother trying to teach you how to play Bridge."

"Your mother is an amazing woman, Ryan. I have always admired her, although I doubt she even knows I exist."

"She's a good lady, Ashton, just a little too attached to status, but she will come around; I'm sure of that."

They rang the doorbell and Mr. Wheeler opened the door. "Why, hello Son; what good wind blew you around?"

"I came by to say hi, of course, and I also would like to introduce you two to a very special lady."

"Well, come on in then. It is very nice to meet you...I'm sorry, what is your name, young lady?"

"Ashton Logan. Ashton, this is my father." Ryan interjected.

"It's very nice to meet you, Sir." Ashton said, shaking Mr. Wheeler's hand.

"Likewise, Ashton. Please come in."

Mr. Wheeler led them in the living room, where his wife was sitting and reading a magazine. She raised her head and smiled as soon as she saw Ryan walking in. "Hello sweetheart! What brings you over?"

Ryan was tempted to lie, then decided to take the bull by the horns. "I came by to introduce you to my girlfriend, Mom and Dad. In fact, I should say my fiancée since I asked Ashton to marry me."

Mr. and Mrs. Wheeler exchanged looks, and Mrs. Wheeler spoke first. "My dear child, as parents we are -- rightfully so -- the last ones to find out happy news, but I do need to share something with you…I have known for a while that you and Ashton were an item."

Ryan looked at his mother without speaking, already bracing for the harsh words he knew were ready to come. Sensing Ryan's uneasiness, Ashton ran to his rescue. "Mr. and Mrs. Wheeler, I know I was not raised in a privileged life, and it might take me a while to catch up with all the rules of etiquette, but I can promise that I will do my best to learn quickly. I love Ryan, and I will live to be a good wife."

Mrs. Wheeler laid her reading glasses on the marble-topped coffee table, and settled back on the black leather couch. Her husband, afraid to say the wrong thing that would set his wife off, chose to keep silent. For a moment, the air in the room felt thick with judgment.

"Well, how do you plan on catching up, Ms. Logan?"

"I…I am not sure yet, but I will do everything in my power to not be an embarrassment to your family, Ma'am."

"The thing that would embarrass me most, Ashton, would be to have a daughter-in-law who can't play Bridge. I will expect you here at five when you get off work, tomorrow, to start your training."

It took Ryan a moment to process what was happening, before his face lit up. He hugged Ashton and shook his dad's hand, then he leaned over his mother and softly kissed her cheek. "Don't worry, Mom, you'll make a champion out of her in no time at all."

Paul had already closed his store and was stocking up some items, when the sun began to set. Lately, he stayed at work past closing time more often. He missed Olivia, and although he was comfortable knowing she was happy, he loathed being home alone. Even if Olivia never formally moved to the bayou and preferred to keep her address in New Orleans, she spent more time at his house than at her apartment in the city, and Paul was always happy to rush home and cook a good country meal for her. Now there was no one to cook for, and he found it easier to stay at the store until bedtime.

He finished stocking up for the next business day when he felt a sharp pain shoot through his chest; it only lasted a few seconds, but it left him breathless. Thinking he had maybe pulled a muscle while lifting the heavy bags, he tried to stretch out his arms. He decided to move on to something lighter, and went to the back to get a case of soft drinks, but as soon as he lifted the box he felt the shooting pain again. This time it lasted longer, and his arm went slightly numb. His forehead was beaded with sweat but he felt chilled at the same time; his stomach started hurting as if he had swallowed a rock.

"That stew I ate for lunch didn't agree with me," he thought out loud as he walked toward the bottle of Rum he kept behind the counter. He opened the bottle and took a long swig – the spiced liquor traced a fiery path to his stomach, and he figured he would feel better within minutes.

The air in the store felt stuffy and hot, so he went outside to take a breath of the cooler evening air; he listened to the door chime when he opened the door – funny, it rang three times, as it had the night Elegba came to visit. He sat on the bench outside the front door, instantly welcomed by the mating song of cicadas. There was no place like the swamp at night; when the sun went down life literally pulsated through the thick forest.

He felt the sharp pain again, stronger this time, and his breathing became labored. He gulped air in, hoping to slow down his racing heart. What was happening? Then a memory flashed through his mind... *That's your final task, Paul; then you will be free.* The old man's words echoed into Paul's mind as the song of the bayou sped its tempo and became louder.

Saving Melody was his final task, and he was now free to go. But he didn't want to go...what would be of Olivia, and of Melody even, now that Mario was gone? Who would be there to take care of them?

As quickly as that thought came on, so did the answer to the question – Olivia was married now, and Graham was a good and decent man; Melody was going to be fine, too. What had Elegba said? Oh yes, *Be careful, because who you think is, is instead who is not,* but Melody had nothing to worry about any more; he was just as surprised as Melody when he saw Mario and Alex at the gallery, and at first he wondered if Alex was whom he should protect Melody from once again. As it turned out, Alex had changed and was no longer a threat to anyone – especially Melody, the keeper of one of the sacred rosaries. Two new chapters of Melody's life had just begun – she had found a long lost sister and she was going to be a mother. Yes, Melody was going to be alright.

When a new surge of pain hit, Paul closed his eyes and took a deep breath; he needed to feel the sweet air of the bayou enter his lungs for one last time. He focused on the darkness ahead, and saw shadows dancing among the trees, before his attention was stolen by the sound of the chimes on the door ringing three times. With one final breath, Paul was gone.

The cleaning crew was rushing around in the gallery.

One of the workers, a large Jamaican woman in her early fifties looked at the hands of the Grandfather clock, and wished they could move faster. Her granddaughter was coming over tonight, and she was determined to get home on time. She normally didn't mind to work a few hours past her regular schedule; the money was good and Mr. Hadley usually threw in a nice tip for her when she did extra work, but tonight she was eager to be done. She vacuumed the floor and dusted the window sills, and was ready to close up when a large spider came out from behind one of the baseboards and scurried across the tiled floor. The cleaning lady screamed. She didn't like spiders to start with, and this one was so big! She stepped on it only seconds before it disappeared behind the clock, and took a deep breath of relief knowing the ugly beast would not be there to surprise her again the next day. She turned off the lights and double checked that all doors were locked; then, with sugarplum visions of her little angel clinging tight to her neck she went home for the night.

When the door closed, the spider, still alive, dragged its mangled body a few steps on the polished floor. Its legs were broken, and its head was almost completely crushed. It felt life slowly seeping out and curled up waiting to die. A few seconds later, Belinda Allen was finally free to join her husband Jim, and looked gratefully upon the discarded shell of the spider she had been allowed to inhabit, briefly, to make things right; her mother told the truth – spiders guard the dead and restore justice. Jim was waiting by the door. Belinda smiled as she walked toward him and into the light.

THE END

About the author...

Sandra Carrington-Smith is an Italian-born author who relocated to the United States in the late 80's after marrying a US soldier who was serving overseas. Moving to a new country provided several challenges, the biggest one being the language barrier she encountered when she first arrived. In order to become fully integrated, Sandra tapped into her love for reading, and over time her vocabulary grew extensively. Her first novel, *The Book of Obeah, was followed by* a self-improvement book, *Housekeeping for the Soul: A Practical Guide to Restoring Your Inner Sanctuary.* Currently, Sandra is working on a new novel, *Shadows of a Tuscan Moon. Killer in Sight (A Tom Lackey Mystery)* was released in May 2012. Sandra Carrington-Smith lives in Raleigh, NC, with her husband, children and three cats. (Photo by Wall2Wall Photography.)

www.ingramcontent.com/pod-product-compliance
Lightning Source LLC
Chambersburg PA
CBHW031249170626
46807CB00001B/52